ZANE PRESENTS

Dare
TO BE
WILD

AN EDEN DAVIS SERIES

Dear Reader:

When Eden Davis created her three-part series, she was on a mission to fill a void by introducing readers to erotica for "grown and sexy women."

In *Dare to Wild*, her third book in the series, Livia Charles sheds her conservative image and attempts to emulate the more daring lives of her adventurous friends. So she designs a bucket list of sexual activities, and this list grows and grows as she crosses over to the wild side.

Eden Davis, the pen name of a critically acclaimed author, takes sensuality to the next level. Make sure that you pick up a copy of her other titles, *Dare to be Seduced* and *Dare to Be Tempted*. She continues her daring tales with three friends who participate in an auction for an up-and-coming heartthrob in her ebook, *Going, Going, Gone!*

Thank you for supporting Eden Davis' efforts and thank you for supporting one of the authors published under my imprint, Strebor Books. I try my best to bring you cutting-edge works of literature that will keep your attention and make you think long after you turn the last page.

Now sit back in your favorite chair or, better yet, chill in the bed, and be prepared to be tantalized by yet another great read.

Peace and Many Blessings,

Zane

Publisher
Strebor Books
www.simonandschuster.com

Z ANE PRESENTS

Dare
TO BE
WILD

AN EDEN DAVIS SERIES

EDEN DAVIS

STREBOR BOOKS

NEW YORK LONDON TORONTO SYDNEY

Strebor Books
P.O. Box 6505
Largo, MD 20792
http://www.streborbooks.com

ISBN 978-1-59309-343-3
ISBN 978-1-4516-0916-5 (ebook)
LCCN 2013933673

First Strebor Books trade paperback edition January 2014

Cover design: www.mariondesigns.com
Cover photograph: © Keith Saunders/Marion Designs

10 9 8 7 6 5 4 3 2 1

Manufactured in the United States of America

For information regarding special discounts for bulk purchases, please contact Simon & Schuster Special Sales at 1-866-506-1949 or business@simonandschuster.com

The Simon & Schuster Speakers Bureau can bring authors to your live event. For more information or to book an event, contact the Simon & Schuster Speakers Bureau at 1-866-248-3049 or visit our website at www.simonspeakers.com.

This book is dedicated to my mother-in-law, a breast cancer survivor, whose sexy verve and vigor continue to conquer all.

Acknowledgments

Welcome to the *Eden Davis Series*, hot and beautifully erotic stories written for grown and sexy women. In *Dare to be Tempted*, you met Aleesa Davis, a happily married woman who finds the line between fantasy and fidelity become a tempting blur when she finds herself dealing with a rough patch in her marriage. This time, in *Dare to be Wild*, it's Livia Charles's turn to shine.

Divorced, romantically bored and sexually uninterested, Livia has poured all her passions into establishing and growing her booming cake business. But breast cancer has changed all that. With her fuck-it list in hand, Livia sets out to find the lost side of herself, and in the process learns that one woman's "wild" can be another woman's wonder.

What about you? Do you have some hot fantasies you'd like to actualize secretly lurking in the recesses of your sexy mind? Maybe you'll find yourself inspired by Livia's journey and set out on a sexually adventurous and empowering one of your own. Check out my *Ticket to Paradise* at the end of this book. It will give you some tips on how to create a naughty and nice list of your own.

As always, I must thank my agent, Sara Camilli, for her sage guidance; Zane for her creative foresight, and Charmaine at Strebor Books for her gentle handling. And much gratitude to you for your continued love and support. Continue to reach out to me on Twitter @EdenStories and on Facebook at Eden's Stories. And please tell your friends about this book and invite them to experience a little paradise for themselves. Until then, enjoy Livia's story in good health and great sex!

Eden

P.S. You're going to meet Livia and Aleesa's friend, Lena Macy, within these pages. At work, Lena is bold, ambitious and always in control, but her private life is the victim of her professional ambitions. In *Dare to be Seduced*, the workaholic goes wantonly delinquent when she loses a bet to a hot stranger who turns her on, and out, in all the right ways.

Havin' Your Cake

"Have you tried giving him a professional?" the radio diva boldly asked her caller.

"They always work for me," chimed in her streetwise, male sidekick.

"A professional what?" Though Livia had not expected a response, sucking sounds, intermingled with soft grunts supplied by the special effects button, was the reply. So this is what relationship advice had come down to in the new millennium? Was oral sex now the modern day Band Aid to whatever ailed him?

"The real question is: Has he tried giving *her* a professional? Why does it always have to be the woman doing the giving? Thank God, I'm old and past the age of dealing with such mess," Livia decided and flipped over to 1010 WIN.

At 49, she wasn't actually ancient but certainly old enough and experienced enough to know that when it came to the game of love, sex was at best a short-term solution to any long-term issues. Particularly when the remedy was, as in most cases, one-sided and service-oriented. Besides, Livia and sex were on the outs these days. Her ex got most of her libido in the divorce. Hell, the truth be told, she'd actually lost that sucker somewhere around year ten. But then whatever smidgen she had left, radiation therapy had claimed as its own.

She didn't have time to concern herself with that now anyway. To stay on task, Livia started going through her mental "to do" list of every chore she needed to accomplish today. Livia Denise Charles, a list maker. With them, she stayed organized, and felt a sense of accomplishment with every completed job. Without them, she was lost and ineffective. In her life, lists were a good thing.

After this delivery, Livia still had a million things to do before the party tonight. She was the guest of honor. Well, actually, the twins were, and even though her friends were taking care of most of the arrangements, Livia had insisted on making the cake because, well, that's what she did. All it needed was a few finishing touches, but she had to tidy up both the house and herself before the guests arrived. And as with most things these days, both took a lot more time than they used to. No time to dilly dally.

"You have reached your destination," the navigation system interrupted her thoughts to inform her.

"Thanks, Minerva," Liv said, talking to yet another voice coming from speakers in her car. This little baby was well worth the extra dollars it cost her to install. Frankly, anybody who rode with Livia would have pitched in to pay double. Directionally challenged, she could get lost making a U-turn, so anything designed to save her time, frustration and gas money was a worthwhile investment.

Livia pulled her Lexus into the driveway and drove what seemed like another half block around to the back. Her client had left a voicemail, letting her know that nobody would be home and she'd leave the kitchen door unlocked. Since providing the winning cake for the *Today Show Throws a Wedding*, Livia no longer personally delivered her frosted works of art to private homes, but Naomi Maddox was a frequent and valued client. She was a well-connected part of a social circle whose elite members entertained often and had the money (and egos) required to afford couture cakes. When it comes to business, you gotta love the customers who buy into the ridiculous concept of keeping up with the Joneses, no matter what the economy. New clients, via Naomi's very lucrative word-of-mouth, had added over $10,000 to Livia's bank account in the last six months alone, helping to keep her bakery solidly in the black after only three years.

Havin' Your Cake was fast becoming one of the premier cake suppliers for the nation's cake aficionados. Thanks to the *Today Show* exposure, Livia had become the darling of wedding planners, bridal bloggers and brides-to-be across the country. Most thought that Livia was an overnight success, but her family and friends knew that this had been a long and tedious journey. Livia, who earned her MFA at New York University, had originally set out to be an artist. She quickly learned that talented, starving and poor didn't agree with her upper middle class sensibilities and settled for a job with a large non-profit organization. She spent years raising money for charitable causes before deciding to pursue her second love—baking. After graduating from the Culinary Institute of America with her Bachelors in Baking and Pastry Arts, Livia combined her love of art and baking, and Havin' Your Cake was born. And just in time to fill her days after her twenty-three-year marriage to Dale Charles ended in divorce.

Livia opened the hatchback of her RX450h, slowly pulled the tray with two large, square boxes toward her, got a good grasp on its edges and cautiously carried it to the kitchen door.

"Hello?" she called out gingerly as she twisted the knob and pushed the door open with her foot. "Anybody here?" Greeted with the silence she was expecting, Livia stepped inside and over to the center island that dominated the large kitchen.

You can tell a lot about a woman by her house. And if the kitchen is indeed the heart of the home, judging from this pristine room, Naomi Maddox was a direct descendant of the tin man. Nary a smudge, crumb or smear could be found in this stainless steel and granite space. With a floor clean enough to perform surgery on, Livia detected a sanitizing whiff of lavender and lemon. No lingering scents from last night's spicy beef stew or this morning's cinnamon buns, no unwashed dishes from a mid-morning snack or orphaned coffee cup. This was a show kitchen, a room designed to showcase wealth and good taste, neither of which had anything to do with food or family.

As per Mrs. Maddox's instructions, Livia found the cart designated for her latest creation—a three-dimensional pinup of Naomi's mother looking like she was kneeling on a floor of plump red pillows. The image was recreated from a photo taken when she was 22 with a young husband off fighting the Korean War. Liv found it to be an interesting choice, as the woman was turning 80 years old today. But hey, it was her job to fulfill the client's sugar and spice wishes, not determine them.

Remembering her pressing schedule, Livia quickly assembled the cake and wiped away any excess frosting. She cleaned up the remaining debris and with her ever-ready digital, took one last photo for her portfolio.

"Livia Charles, here's to another job well the hell done." She congratulated herself with her ritual shoulder brush. Livia turned to leave and that's when she heard them—the muffled sounds of low moans and groans, distinctly female, coming from down the hall. Fear turned her blood cold, causing her muscles to freeze as she pushed her face in the direction of the noise, straining to hear.

It sounded like someone was in trouble. God, was the birthday girl here? Had she fallen and couldn't get up? Livia's first impulse was to rush toward the sound and help the poor old lady out. However, the thought that kept her feet in place was the idea that the person who was in trouble might also be in the presence of the troublemaker. She'd already gone through her stint of staring death in the face. Did she really want to go through all that again?

Liv slowly edged her way over to the cordless phone and picked it up from the base. She'd just dialed the 9 and 1, when the thought crossed her mind that the last thing Naomi Maddox would want was a houseful of cops combing over her property when she was expecting an army of caterers.

There it was again, this time co-mingled with a deeper, more masculine timber. Muffled and unintelligible, Livia couldn't make out any words, but the tone sounded demanding. She had to do something. She took a quick look around the place and mapped out a plan. First, she went over and opened the kitchen door in preparation for a swift exit. She then picked a gleaming butcher knife from the block. Like the rest of the appliances, it looked as if it had never been used, so the blade had to be nice and sharp.

Yeah, sharp enough to fillet me if it got into the wrong hands.

She replaced the knife and looked around for another weapon, one that would maim instead of kill. Her eyes immediately were drawn to the set of keys hanging on a hook near the door. She pulled them off the wall and positioned the longest key between her second and third fingers.

Yeah, go for the eyes, she thought.

Armed with the key in one hand and the cordless phone in the other, Livia took a deep breath and went over her quickly concocted plan one more time—ninja down the hall, peek in, access the situation. If it's bad, dial 9-1-1, drop the phone for all to hear and burst into the room, weapon at the ready, sounding buck wild and acting crazy. Capitalize on the element of surprise and pray that God and some of her self-defense lessons kicked in.

That was the plan. She didn't know how good of a plan, but a plan nonetheless. Livia stepped out of her sandals and as stealthily as possible, tiptoed down the hall in the direction of the whimpers.

She didn't have to go far before the noise became louder and more intense. It was coming from a room that, through an open crack in the door, appeared to be an office/den of some kind. Slowly, she pushed the door further into the room, grateful that Naomi kept the hinges in her house well oiled. Liv leaned in slightly and what she witnessed stole her breath and caused her to jerk back into the hallway. She collapsed against the wall and slid down the partition, placing the phone and keys at her side. Weaponry was not going to be necessary.

Somebody was getting worked over all right, but it wasn't Naomi's mother. There was a man in the room watching porn and getting himself off. Livia's torso turned back toward the kitchen but her behind had other ideas. And without her brain's consent, it scooted across the floor, back to the door.

She couldn't see him. He was seated in a high back, yellow leather chair facing the opposite wall. All Livia could see was one golden-brown, muscular thigh flexed with sexual tension. His blue jeans were pooled around his ankles and his arm made peek-a-boo appearances as he stroked himself into bliss.

"Yeah, lick her good," a deep, buttery voice requested. "Make that pretty pussy wet. Take those panties in your teeth and pull them. Snap 'em. Yeah, that's it. Now play with your titties. Let her know how hot she's making you."

Livia watched, mesmerized as the women on the flat-screen followed his every instruction. It took a second or two to realize that he'd obviously seen this movie a time or two hundred. She could probably hit the back of the chair with the phone and he wouldn't even notice. Those two women—one chocolate, the other vanilla—had his full attention.

She was embarrassed to admit it, but they had Livia's as well. In fact, in her head, she even gave them names. Coco was lying back on a cream leather couch with her long, shapely legs spread, one over the back and up the wall. All she wore was a tiny g-string and high heels with strings that laced up her legs. She had a great set of breasts, real, Livia determined, with quarter-sized, yummy brown areolas and erect nipples begging to be sucked. Her lips, pouting with pleasure with each stroke of the blonde's tongue, allowed the frequent escape of a grateful whimper. Nilla was on her knees, her apple bottom ass high in the air with her head between Coco's pretty brown legs. Livia watched as Nilla licked her pussy through the whisper sheer panties, getting as hot as the two of them. Well, three, when you count the guy in the yellow leather chair.

She was sitting there, Vikki The Voyeur, a peeping Thomasina, getting turned on by watching other people have sex. Livia couldn't tell which version—the real man or the video vixens—was turning her on more. He was a stranger lost in his fantasy, pleasuring himself, and here she was intruding without his knowledge or consent. They were an erotic fantasy, soft and sexy beautiful women turning each other out. All of it made Livia feel freakishly naughty. And she liked it.

"Yeah, touch yourself, baby. Finger your pretty pussy while you eat hers."

The sound of his deep voice, alternately shouting out orders and getting wrapped up in his own physical pleasure added to the heat. Despite his crude language, his directives were forceful but stopped short of being demanding. More like requests that teetered on the line between a beg and bark. The kind that, from the right man, were impossible to deny.

Following his directions, and without conscious consent, Livia's hands joined the party. They slid down her skirt's waistband, separating her 100% cotton panties from her full pubic thatch. With his voice in Liv's ears, her eyes stayed on the screen, watching Nilla suck, lick and tug Coco's clit into crazed ecstasy. She parted the hair with her middle finger, reaching deep inside to find the creamy middle, lubricated her nib with her own juices, and furiously began to finger herself. As her legs began to tense with approaching orgasm, Livia bit her lower lip, forcing the sounds of carnal satisfaction back into her body to join the energy circling around her engorged clitoris. Judging from the sounds emanating from inside the room, the four of them participating in this secret and disjointed orgy were all about to explode. Liv couldn't speak for the others, but it had been so long since she'd been this hot, even longer since she'd actually had sex, that she couldn't have stopped herself if she'd wanted to. She came deliciously hard and silently, and then leaned back against the wall, gratefully gasping for breath, as her body attempted to recover.

A chorus of "YES," singing out in soprano and dominated by a baritone, first made her smile and then forced her out of her afterglow and back into reality. She was sitting in the hall of her best client's home, with her hand down her skirt, masturbating. Livia needed to get the hell out of there and fast. She picked up the phone and keys, got up, quietly power-walked back into the kitchen, and returned everything to its proper place. Quickly, she slipped on her shoes and went out the open door and into the safety of her car.

Livi glanced at the clock before backing out of the driveway. She'd spent nearly forty-five minutes on an errand that should have taken her twenty, tops. She conjured up her task list again and began checking off each completed job starting from number one. Anything to distract herself from dwelling on her most recent and inexplicable behavior.

Order more cake boxes. Check. Confirm the design for the Johnson cake. Check. Deliver Maddox cake. Check. Secretly give myself a mind-blowing orgasm in the company of strangers. Check. Check.

She drove about three blocks before pulling over to the curb and bursting out into crazy, what-the-hell-did-I-just-do laughter. Jasi, Aleesa and Lena were never going to believe this. Shit, she couldn't believe it herself. Then again, they'd never know, because Livia had no intention of telling.

My Cups Runneth Over

I
t was the Pavlovian equivalent of silverware kissing crystal that quieted the room and captured everyone's attention. When the din of female chatter subsided, Livia listened from upstairs as the smoky voice of one of her dearest friends, Jasi Westfield, took over the proceedings.

"Ladies, if you would all gather around, it's time to toast our guests of honor."

"This is her place, so technically she's the *host* of honor," Livia heard her sister-cousin, Aleesa Davis, interject, to which their mutual friend, Lena Macy added, "Guest or host, it really doesn't matter because it's the girls we came to see."

From on high, Livi tried to swallow her laughter. Her successful reconstructive surgery was the reason her friends had gathered downstairs for this ooglefest. The theme, *My Cups Runneth Over*, was smart-aleck Jasi's brainchild, and as Liv quickly pointed out, a bit of an exaggeration. Her cups did not run over because she'd chosen perfect, Goldilocks breasts. Not too big. Not too small. Just right 36 C's to be exact. Yes, it was a one-cup upgrade, but Liv figured since gravity was no longer an issue, why not go for the gusto.

It was actually Aleesa's idea to throw a party to properly introduce Livia's new breasts to the rest of the group. And even though she'd kept insisting that they didn't need a full-out debut, Livi was glad Aleesa hadn't listened, because the long and winding road leading up to this happy day had been paved with woe and tears.

They all deserved to celebrate because while they were all light-hearted and joking about it now, things were a lot scarier last year. During Livia's annual mammogram, her doctor had discovered that she had stage one breast cancer. This came as a complete shock because she had absolutely no symptoms, and nary a cold that year. But after two lumpectomies and accompanying rounds of radiation, the cancer still wasn't gone, so Livia elected to have a double mastectomy and be done with it. The physical discomfort associated with the surgery and treatment was real, but mentally was where cancer had really taken its toll. Both on Livi and the people who loved her.

But they were through the hard part now. Her prognosis was excellent and life was back to a new kind of normal—still full of ups and downs—but the ups seemed much more special and the downs much less significant.

Tonight, three months after she'd had reconstructive surgery, Livia was alive and well and standing at the top of the staircase dressed in a boob-busting outfit that put the want in wantonness. It was so not her, she being a woman whose daily uniform usually consisted of jeans and white knit tops of varying styles, but Jasi insisted the attire went with the theme. And tonight, after Liv's afternoon of unintentional, mind-blowing self-service, it definitely fit her mood. It also was the perfect accessory for her "what the hell" attitude that had been incubating these past months. Before her little "episode," as they all called it, Livia would have felt ri-diculous dressed like a man-eating, hoochie mama waiting to strut into a room full of women here to view her now bodacious tatas. But cancer had a funny way of changing a girl. First, it made you scared. But once you knew you had it licked, it made you

And then cancer made you bold. Because, damn, if you've survived the Big C, what can't you conquer?

"Ladies, raise your glasses to Livia Charles and the twins, Booba and Licious!" Jasi called out.

And apparently, having a friend with cancer made one crazy.

Livia heard her musical cue, the tacky beat of a stripper's snare drum (another of Jasi's bright ideas), sucked in her cheeks and stomach and donned her sorry interpretation of the supermodel walk—that awkward pony strut that Naomi Campbell made look so ridiculously sexy. With her counterfeit golden gait, Liv proudly sashayed her nubile young breasts, followed by a much less perky, almost fifty-year-old behind, into the room full of nine cheering friends and one Katie Mullane, who was too busy picking lint off her sleeve to watch. Livia wasn't sure why they'd invited Miss Her-Slice-of-Cake-is-Bigger-than-Mine to this happy soiree. She was undoubtedly the only one in the room who was actually envious that Livia had new breasts. Forget the fact that it took having cancer to get them.

"Just like Livia to make a grand entrance," Katie said, making sure her remark was loud enough for all to hear. Livia decided to ignore her sugarcoated snideness and reminded herself that any middle-aged woman who sported a mustache with braces is bound to be a bit testy.

"No, that's definitely not Livia's style," Aleesa defended me. "She's as background elevator music as they come."

Livia tried to eat her I-know-something-you-don't-know grin. Not just because her girls always had her back when the bitches cut up (though she wasn't quite sure if being compared to elevator music was an outright compliment), but because for once she actually felt like strutting her stuff. True, the foreground was never her favorite location. She was perfectly content letting others take center stage while she flitted around happily behind the scenes. Life was more entertaining that way, not to mention less embarrassing. But not tonight. For the first time in years, Livia was feeling hot and "look at me" sexy.

"Well, she's a show-boating fool today," Lena chimed in with a mouth full of laughter as Liv made her descent. "You're awfully frisky tonight, missy."

"Yes, she is. Did you get some today? Did you already break in the girls?" Jasi called out.

Through the catcalls, whistles and applause, Livia managed to get down the stairs and into the living room without tripping. She did a couple of runway turns and then fell to the couch with a burst of laughter. Immediately, the women pounced. Katie had the nerve to ask if she could touch her breasts to see if they "at least felt real" and once that ice was broken, Liv had more fingers and hands feeling her up than a stripper at a bachelor party. The consensus, by a margin of everyone else to one (guess who), was that the twins not only looked great but felt close enough to the genuine thing to be immensely proud of. And Livi did feel proud. Less of her new boobs and more that she'd not only survived this frightening ordeal but was flourishing.

"Time for gifts," Aleesa announced as she led Liv over to the appointed guest-of-honor chair and proceeded to further embarrass her cousin by tying a pink bra under her chin. The cups were decorated with streamers and ribbons and formed twin peaks on her head, making her look like some kind of sorry, medieval advertisement for Victoria's Secret. Livia left it on long enough for them to take blackmail pictures and then amid a chorus of boos, stuffed it under the chair.

"We felt the girls needed adornment," Jasi declared, before handing her a small, black gift bag.

Livia reached in, shaking her head in anticipation of the sick joke she knew awaited her. Crazy Jasi did not disappoint. To her delight and that of her other twisted friends, Liv pulled from the bag a pair of red tasseled pasties and a matching sheer red thong.

"If you're going to have stripper boobs, you need the right outfit!" Jasi screamed out, amid everyone's laughter.

Moving on.

Aleesa's gift was a racy demi cup concoction of sheer black lace adorned with pink bows. Katie Mullane skipped the brassiere giving and instead brought a travel lingerie bag. Barely appropriate for the theme, but still useful. The better gift was that her player-hating behind departed right after Livia opened her present.

For the next fifteen minutes, Livia opened boxes and gift bags containing beautiful bras (and most included matching panties), of varying styles, colors and fabrics, but with one recurring theme—the sexier the better and the extreme opposite of the sensible basics that currently occupied Livi's unmentionables drawer.

That was, until Lena's gift.

Inside a beautifully wrapped box, and in a complete departure from the colorful potpourri of satins and lace she'd been given, Livi's eyes were greeted with the familiar, though bland, color of oatmeal. With cups big enough to carry a set of bowling balls, was the ugliest, old lady bra she'd ever laid eyes on. Livi held it up by the straps and howled, "This belongs on a damn swing set!"

"I thought it was important to remind you what the rest of us will be wearing ten years from now. When you and your new bouncin' and behavin' hooters are sliding out of bed and still slipping into all of your pretty bras, we'll be lifting our 'swing low, sweet chariot' titties into this charming number," Lena replied with a crooked smile.

"Sorry, but don't blame me. They don't sell Grandma's saggy breasts at the boobie store."

"Game time," Jasi announced as Lena and Aleesa cleared away the gifts and brought out a fresh round of Livi's favorite cocktail— white wine spritzers.

Livia groaned as she accepted pen and paper with a wry smile. Jasi knew how much she hated the typical party and shower games, so Liv was sure there would be some kind of skewed twist on it. She took a deep breath. This was bound to be interesting, if not totally embarrassing.

"Okay, Livi, pick one from each pair. Lucy or Ethel. Polish or Italian. Leather or pearls. Battery or solar. Brangelina or Tomkat."

Livia wrote. The others drank and watched.

"Okay, now answer these," Jasi continued. "The room I hate to clean most is and why? My favorite place to shop is? And lastly, pick one: Beyoncé or Jay-Z?"

Liv quickly jotted down her answers with little consideration. Better to get this over with as fast as possible than dally over an answer that, in the long run, didn't really matter.

"Now let's see what we've learned about our lovely Livi," Lena said, taking Livia's answers. "I'll substitute a few words here and there to make things more interesting.

"Hello, my name is Livia. You've met the twins, Booba and Licious, and now I'd like to introduce, Ethel," she said while Jasi gave her crotch the game show girl, double hand point.

The female roar rivaled that of a Denzel sighting. Livia cringed. First of all, anyone who knew her would know she'd never name her body parts, especially her vagina. That was like putting clothes on a dog—cute but pointless. And secondly, if she were to name it, you could bet it wouldn't be a moniker that sounded like Betty White's nearly ninety vadge.

Lena continued.

"My 'sausage' of choice is Polish because Ethel likes her kielbasas big and wrapped in leather. I prefer my sex toys solar operated and the idea of a threesome with Brangelina turns me on. I hate having sex in the bathroom because it's messy and you have to do it every week, but I'd love to lick Beyoncé's ice cream cone while Jay-Z watches."

This time the spontaneous tingle in her panties caused Liv to smile. Lena's joke brought the hot thrill of her pseudo-group sex scene rushing to mind. For a hot second, Coco and Beyoncé were one. Livia felt the wet release of arousal and crossed her legs to stop the heat from spreading through her body. This was all too confusing. She was definitely a 100% penis girl but ever since today's matinee, girl-on-girl action topped the hot meter. The flush must have showed on her face because the next thing she knew, Jasi was calling her out.

"Livia, are you okay? Looks like the thought of tasting Beyoncé's ice cream has you all hot and bothered. Look at her smiling! Livi, are you turned on?"

More teasing howls. Livi buried her head in her hands. Yes, it was a joke, but talking about her sex life in public was embarrassing. Hell, the ex and she had rarely talked about it in private. That's why she'd decided not to tell Aleesa, Jasi and Lena about what had happened that afternoon. She didn't want to be teased about it or have it come up at some inappropriate time. Liv had no idea what came over her. She could only chalk it up to some kind of extreme nutritional deficiency (according to her friends, vitamins s.e.x. should definitely be a recommended daily requirement), akin to the kind that makes you do crazy things like eat dirt or dry wall.

Dearth aside, her actions today were so out of the norm that Livia knew they would never be repeated. Therefore, she wanted to keep them private, her own delicious secret that could be pulled up and savored in the privacy of her own fantasies.

"Move on," Livia insisted, blaming her pinkish tint on the champagne.

"Cuz, you are such a prude," Aleesa teased. "Don't you dare waste that fabulous new rack of yours on baking cupcakes day and night. Promise you'll take the twins out on lots of play dates."

"That's right. And you better dress them up in all this new stuff," Lena insisted. "Don't suffocate those beauties in those tired old lady brassieres and sports bras you usually throw on."

"In other words, it's time for you to really do the whole *la dolce vita* thing," Jasi chimed in. "And that includes taking your no-sex-havin' self out to the club and getting into all kinds of yummy trouble. I'll bet you've never had a one-night stand, have you?"

Livia shot Jasi her practiced, slit-eyed, you're-kidding-me-right look. Jasi already knew the answer to that question, as did nearly everyone in the room. Livia was a virgin the day she got married at age twenty; spent twenty-five years with a husband who'd exhausted his bag of sexual tricks about three years into the union; had been divorced four and fighting breast cancer nearly two. When the hell was there time (or the desire or courage) to have a freakin' one-night stand? Even if she wanted to, which she didn't. Good sex was hard enough to come by with a mate, let alone a perfect stranger.

"Come on, Jasi; Livia doesn't even own a vibrator. Do you think she's going to have sex with a man she just met?" Aleesa asked.

"When and where does she meet any men? She's always up to her armpits in flour. We have to start her off slow," Lena added.

"I tried to hook her up with an eHarmony membership, but

between the mad texters, white thrill seekers, and young boy toys, she couldn't hang," Aleesa recapped.

"She gave up too easily," Jasi chimed in.

So much for not hanging your private sex life out on the line flapping in the wind for everyone to witness. Was it any wonder that Livia refused to let these blabber mouths in on her secret?

"You need a fuck-it list," Jasi announced.

"A what?" Livia asked for all of them.

"A fuck-it list—like a bucket list—but instead of being about skydiving or climbing Mt. Everest before you die, it's a list of all the sex stuff you'd like to try before your pussy dries up," Jasi explained.

The squeal of approval nearly shattered the chandelier.

"She's got a point," Aleesa said. "This should be easy for you. You're always making those damn lists."

"Girl, let those new fabulous hooters be the start of a hot, new, sexy you," Jasi continued. "Promise that before your next birthday, you'll put on one of those pretty new bras and let some sexy, handsome stranger peel it off of you while the night is still young and the bubbly still cold."

"That's right. Preach, Jasi," Lena said as she stuck out her left hand and crooked her little finger. The channel-set blue diamond band that the four of them bought after Liv's diagnosis and wore as a sign of their lifelong friendship sparkled in the light. "Pinky-swear right now in front of all the women here, who you love and who love you back, that before your fiftieth birthday rolls around, you will have compiled your fuck-it list with at least ten entries of those deep, dark, sexual fantasies you keep safely locked up in your imagination."

"And make them come true!" Lena added.

"Ten?" Livia asked in open-mouthed disbelief.

"Let's get real," Aleesa interrupted. "Make a list of ten and fulfill at least one."

"Three," Jasi countered.

"Two," Lena compromised.

Livia hesitated. They were all pretty serious about the pinky swear. Once given, there was no taking it back. Her birthday was in less than six months and she didn't want to promise her girlfriends, or herself for that matter, something that she couldn't live up to. Liv took in a deep breath and let out a noisy exhale before extending her hand. Nervous excitement bubbled up from her toes and through her body, causing a wide, though shaky, smile to break out across her face.

What the hell! Cancer makes you bold, right? Plus, in reality she'd already fulfilled half the promise. None of these women could argue that getting off in the hallway of a stranger's house, while watching a sexy thigh in a yellow leather chair masturbate to the sight of an interracial couple of lesbians, did not qualify as a genuine act of sexual outrageousness. She could come up with one more simple act of lust and be done with it. Knowing she had them beat, Livia laughed aloud, reached out and hooked her diamond encircled little finger into Lena's.

"I swear, within the next six months, that I will make my fuck-it list and find two situations of, as Jasi says, yummy trouble to get into."

"And tell the rest of us about it," Jasi added.

Livia shot her the look again.

"Well, then what's the point? I mean, how we will know if you don't give us a full report," she said, her eyes including the rest of the group.

"She's right," Aleesa and Lena concurred.

"Okay, okay, okay. And I promise to give my report to Jasi, Aleesa and Lena, which I am sure they will promptly share with you," Livi added, turning to include the rest of the guests. She'd purposely left out the word, "full." After all, it was her list to share or not.

"To Livia," Jasi exclaimed as everyone picked up their champagne flutes, "as she works to find her inner freak. Own it. Work it. Use it to grab all the happiness you can and above all, take no prisoners and make no excuses."

Livia raised her glass with the others, a tad annoyed that she now had to do something to fulfill her promise when she already knew that her inner freak did indeed exist. Two questions remained, however. One, could she coax her out to play again or had she packed up her marbles and gone home for good? And two, did she even want to play with her again?

The Fuck-It List

Aleesa, Jasi and Lena had done such a great job of cleaning up after the party that there was nothing left for Livi to do but pour herself another glass of champagne, gather up her lacy loot and go upstairs to unwind.

She walked into her room, kicked off her shoes and plopped down on the queen-size bed. Livia loved her bedroom. After the divorce, she'd totally redecorated, turning it into a private sanctuary. It was her sensual oasis, full of soothing earth tones, glowing scented candles, touchable textures and pleasurable sounds—a great space specifically designed for one to relax and reflect.

And tonight she was in a reflective mood. This had been a crazy ass day and she needed some quiet time to wrap her mind around everything that had taken place, particularly that morning. Livia wanted to review (and revel) in her behavior at her client's home but the echo of female voices filled her head with an incessant barrage of unsolicited commentary.

You're such a prude…your no-sex-havin' self…yummy trouble…one-night stand…doesn't even own a vibrator…start her slow…you're such a prude…prude…prude.

Her best friends' statements repeated themselves over and over like a bad hotdog. Liv couldn't disagree with them; technically, they spoke the truth. And their comments, insensitive as they might have sounded, were wrapped and delivered in true love. But still, was tonight really the time and/or place for their onslaught?

Tonight was supposed to be about celebrating her life and good health, not highlighting her sad, hide-and-go-seek sex life.

Livia glanced over at the pile of lingerie, her eyes settling on Lena's Queen Kong brassiere. It looked strangely out of place among the colorful purveyors of seductive suggestion. Each, with their CFM qualities, belonged on the chest of a sexual predator, not a divorced cake baker whose taste in over the shoulder, boulder holders ran toward the boring and sensible.

Jasi, not just certifiably insane but extremely organized as well, had placed adhesive dots with the giver's name on each item so Livi could write thank you notes. She inspected them, one by one, realizing that each represented the giver's taste much more than her own, but through each, a snapshot of who she was, or more accurately who she wasn't, began to develop.

She slipped out of her rhinestone-encrusted halter dress and into Jenny's gift of a velvet balcony bra. And in yet another untypical move, padded over to the mirror for a head-to-toe inspection. For Livia, the mirror was merely a feng shui decorating move. She never looked at herself in a full-length mirror with more than a passing glance while fully dressed, so standing there semi-nude was a rare happening, and completely in the buff a non-event.

Even knocking on the door of her fifth decade, the demi-gods in charge of youthful aging had been kind. Liv's perpetually tan complexion was relatively unlined and despite a few little age spots around the eyes and a couple of pores on her nose that you could plant tulips in, it kept secret her true age. Every feature of her heart-shaped face—pouty mouth, narrow nose and almond-shaped brown eyes—still hung together in a pleasing, deserves-a-second look mosaic, and now their collective beauty was highlighted by the wise glow that comes with life experience. Her golden brown halo of hair, highlighted blonde to hide the gray, was full of healthy, spiral curls that framed her face like honeycombed fingers.

Livia did a slow pirouette in the mirror to inspect her five-foot, ten-inch frame. Dressed in a hot bra and her usual Fruit of the Loom granny panties, the visual before her was definitely a tale of two biddies. Hot chick versus old babe. A classic yay-and-nay scenario. The yay was her bust, which, showcased in this up-and-at-em, fuchsia-colored bra, was freakin' spectacular. The new girls were perky and upright, and because she'd had the best plastic surgeon on earth, looked totally natural and not like someone had super glued half a cantaloupe on each side of her chest.

The nay was also her bust. This hot set of knockers looked noticeably out of place on the rest of Liv's nearly half a century old body. Her new boobs were now part of a premenopausal size eight torso that on any given day fluctuated to a size ten just because it felt like it. They looked down on her pudge of a tummy, which on a daily basis, mocked her inability to have children by keeping her looking "slightly" preggers.

Livia dropped her drawers to the floor, turned to inspect the rear view, and cringed. From the front, she was a hottie; from back, a nottie. Her breasts no longer drooped but her cellulite-kissed butt sure did. Definitely too much time spent taste-testing cake batter and not enough doing squats.

Note to self: Add a gym membership to your "fifty and fabulous" birthday list.

She was definitely soft. A comfortable, rumpled bed at the end of a hard day kind of soft, but soft nonetheless. But you know what? Her friends didn't lie. She was still kind of sexy. That self-realization made Livia smile. She blew herself a coy and campy kiss, which made her laugh. And then for some unexplainable reason, she started imitating the looks of erotic bliss she'd seen this morning on the wall of Naomi Maddox's den. Livia slowly licked her top lip like she'd seen Coco do and released a seductive "ooh." She closed her eyes and with open, welcoming lips, let her head fall back with an aroused moan, just like Nilla had done while Coco had sucked her nipples. Before she knew it, Livia was in the throes of a hot and heavy *When Harry Met Sally* meets *Debbie Does Dallas* display of faux orgasmic delight. Feeling silly and spent, she climbed back in bed, confused by her feelings.

The orgasm may have been fake, but the desire it stirred up definitely was not. She was horny. Again. Still. And not run-of-the-mill horny, but Maxwell, *Til the Police Come Knocking* horny. Prince, *Do Me Baby* horny. Livia was craving sex tonight more strongly than she'd ever craved it before in all of her sexual life. And it wasn't just the fact that she hadn't had sex in over four years. This was different. More raw. More urgent. Less quick fix, and more long-term satisfaction kind of desire.

You had sex for years but never with any real passion.

Whoa. Where did that bolt of enlightenment come from?

Sex had not been a problem in her long marriage, but it had never been a particular highlight either. Even up to the end, Dale and she still had relations at least once a week, but always at his prodding. Truth be told, she'd been a sex-by-request wife. Rarely initiating but hardly ever turning down any advances either. Still, with all that marital action, Livia had always thought of herself as a perfectly adequate lover. Having no other experience to compare it to, she'd even go so far as to say a good lover (Dale never complained), but certainly not an adventurous one.

For twenty-five years, she had lots of sex. Sex on request. Sex by appointment. Sex by the numbers way inside the box. But never crazy, passionate, paint outside the lines, drive me crazy sex. She liked sex and would even venture to say she enjoyed it, but she never actually craved it. For her, sex was a lot like potato chips. She rarely bought them, but if offered, she'd help herself and engage in some mindless snacking. It occurred to her that she'd been a trained performer who followed a sexual script that had been written throughout the years by the tastes and habits of a man whom she'd finally come to realize wasn't too sexually interesting either.

Jasi and the girls were right about me, Livia thought. *I am a no sex havin' so and so whose vagina should be named Ethel for all the action I've gotten.*

But Livia didn't want to be an Ethel anymore. She wanted to feel hot and sexy now and always, like she had all day today since fingering herself to orgasm within earshot of a strange man in a yellow chair. She wanted a bold, confident, bad girl vagina. A vagina named Suzy, Lola or Sadie—a vagina that was powerful and sexual, one that knew what she wanted and took it. Lola wasn't afraid of sexual energy. She fed on lust like a vampire feeds on blood. Desire was the magic elixir that made Sadie feel alive.

After twenty-five years of monogamous monotony, and before her Suzy shut down and turned into a senior citizen, Livia wanted to be a sexually confident, bad girl who had a full and sassy sex life. Yeah, that's exactly what she wanted. The only issue was how did she turn a lifetime of paralyzing, judgmental morality into delicious, albeit respectful decadence? How did she go from being straight-laced, sexually conservative Livia, to a grown and sexy woman who embraced her libido and lived an amorous life on her own terms? Who was that woman and where was she hiding? Livia knew she was somewhere deep inside because she'd emerged this afternoon to introduce herself, only to disappear again. But she was still there. Livi could feel her.

Start with the fuck-it list, she decided. Make a list of all the sexual fantasies that had been previously shot down and/or ignored for being outlandish, sluttish or scandalous by Grandma Ethel. A list that fulfilled her promise to her girlfriends and, at the same time, set her inner slut free.

Purposefully, Livia sashayed down the hall to her office and sat Ethel down. From the drawer, she pulled out the pink-and-black flocked journal Caroline had given her for Christmas. It seemed an appropriate journal for this particular inventory. Livi thought for a moment and quickly realized that first things being first, she needed to make two lists—both personal, but one more defining than the other. She pondered for a bit and then, under the heading of *Sexy Sidekick*, added names that in one word, exuded sensuality and sexiness.

Sexy Sidekick
1. Lola
2. Tina
3. Suzy
4. Quincy
5. Trixie
6. Sophia

Lola, she liked a lot. She thought of the song, *Whatever Lola Wants*, and liked the thought, but it sounded way too cliché so Livia eliminated her. Tina, her inspiration being the incredibly sexy and timeless Ms. Turner, didn't quite do it either. She didn't have that raw, smoky sensuality and no matter how hard she tried, never would. Suzy sounded way too sexy girl next door. Trixie was too *The Honeymooners*, and Sophia, while the surname conjured up the hot, *molto* sexy Italian legend, it sounded too sophisticated for her vadge. Livia needed a handle that when spoken, felt like her, but a different part of herself. The sexy, adventurous part.

She kept coming back to Quincy, which sounded like a modern, fun, adventurous and mischievous lover.

It took Livia twenty minutes, but after careful consideration, her vagina had a first name and a whole new attitude. Goodbye, Ethel. Hello, Quincy.

She decided to move her second list-making task to the bathtub. Liv drew a warm bath, adding vanilla-scented bath salts to the water. It was the baker in her. The hot water mixed with the salts, releasing a calming, satisfying scent into the air. With candles ablaze, Michael Buble singing in the background, and a fresh wine spritzer sitting on the edge, Liv slowly submerged her body into the tub. She sat back and relaxed into the water, releasing her stress and unleashing her imagination for the task ahead. She titled this one the *Fuck-It List.* But once that was done, she had no idea where to start. Livi quickly drained the spritzer and let the buzz go to her head and pry loose whatever sexual fantasies were there hiding behind a lifetime of appropriate and ladylike behavior.

"What would Quincy do?" she wondered aloud, delegating the task to her newly appointed sexier side.

Toys, Quincy answered, remembering Aleesa's comment.

Her cousin was right; Livia didn't have any playthings, never did. Her ex had never been big on sex toys. He didn't like the idea of bringing anything into their bed that could in any way be construed as competition. He'd told Livia that if she had a need for pleasure toys, then she must feel that he wasn't man enough. Even after their divorce, largely because of her health issues, sex had been so far behind the back burner that the idea of buying a vibrator had never been considered.

"But Quincy was about to change all that," Livia informed the butterflies flitting around the tile.

Fuck-It List
1. Buy and play with toys
2. Vacation on a nude beach and go skinny dipping
This is all you've got, bold Quincy interrupted to chide. *You only pinky swore to actually do two. Go for it!*

That dare wrapped in a reminder released an imagination that Liv never realized she possessed. The cocktail was fueling her imagination and releasing pent up frustrations. She thought about conversations Jasi, Lena, Aleesa and she'd had about sex; about movie scenes she'd enjoyed; sex scenes she'd read in books that had turned her on. Livi remembered how much she'd enjoyed the HBO documentary, *Real Sex*, and took inspiration from that. Before she knew it, Quincy had quite a fuck-it list awaiting her.

There were nine "action items" on the list and one to go, but the now tepid bathwater was killing her wine buzz and slowing the creative flow. Livia put the journal down and turned on the hot water, making a sensual game out of directing the warm water over her shoulders and bosom. The strong cravings she'd felt earlier, strengthened by her concentration on erotic ideas, were back with a vengeance. Quincy needed relief. And with no man in sight, that left the job up to her.

With Michael Buble's sexy Rat Pack voice begging Livia to tell him, *Quando, Quando, Quando,* (when, when, when) in the background, she reached for the bottle of body oil. She tipped it slightly over her body, letting the warm oil drizzle down the full and fleshy mounds of her chest. For the first time since the surgery, Livia manually inspected her breasts, experiencing their nubile firmness with proud excitement. Did her first set ever feel this firm or look this sexy? No longer incubators of disease, they'd become brand new and more lethal than ever weapons of mass seduction. As the delicious vanilla scent seduced her nasal passages,

Livi cupped her breasts with both hands, gently pushing them together and watching as one thick fragrant drop traveled down her left breast and hung clinging to its tip. She captured the drop on her fingertip and slowly massaged it into the nipple, feeling the slightest bit of sensation as they began to well under the slippery smoothness of her oiled fingers. They were definitely not as sensitive as they'd been before surgery, but there was now more sensation than there'd been weeks ago. In Livia's book, any sensation at all was a good thing.

Her nipples between her fingers and her head full of her fuck-it list and all the erotic possibilities awaiting her, caused a rush of heat that had nothing to do with sitting in a bathtub full of warm water. Livia closed her eyes, and slipped effortlessly into fantasy. She was back at Naomi Maddox's house, but this time inside the room and sitting in the tall, yellow leather chair. He sat across from her on the foot stool. The man her mind created was fine, friendly and vaguely familiar. Terrence Howard's eyes, Denzel's smile, The Rock's chiseled body. A DNA bonanza of Hollywood star features. All imagined. All good. And for all intents and purposes, all hers.

"You want to touch them, don't you," she teased, looking him straight in his hazel eyes.

"Yes, they're beautiful. May I? Please," he begged.

"No. Not yet. I want you to watch me. Would you like that, baby? Would you like to see me fuck myself?" She emphasized her query by parting her lips and placing her finger in her mouth. Her digit became his penis and she erotically treated it as such. Her tongue wrapped the tip in circles of bliss before her lips clamped down and, with a seductive rhythm of varied speed and pressure, sucked. She could feel the erotic pull both in her fingers and clit and she could tell that the visual, in combination with her increasingly obvious arousal, was getting to him.

"Yes." His voice was but a deep whisper as he fought to maintain his

cool. But the sight of her naked breasts, released from their satin confinement and showcased by a half-unbuttoned blouse was rendering his efforts ineffective.

"Okay. I promise to let you watch me but only if you abide by my rule— no touching yourself or me until I give you permission. Agreed?"

"Yes."

"Good boy," she said before treating him to the sight of her lifting a breast to meet her bended head and taking her nipple into her own mouth. She circled her areola before lapping her nipple with a wide, firm tongue. "You like that, huh? Me too," she told him, seduced by her own bawdy behavior.

He said nothing, just sat licking his lips and trying to keep his hand away from his rising dick.

Her vagina was wet and juicy and crying out for attention. Slowly, she did a full body stretch, shifting her weight to her feet and arching her torso away from the cool, smooth leather, and raised her skirt until it was high in her lap. Then, in a classic Sharon Stone, Basic Instinct *move, she slowly separated her legs, revealing her hidden treasures, which were conveniently unfettered by fabric.*

"Come closer," she commanded and watched as he obediently leaned his face into her hot crotch. She gently spread the lips of her pussy, revealing Quincy's lovely pink underside and stiffening clitoris. "Blow on it."

A steady stream of warm breath hit her wet nib, tantalizing her with a fire and ice sensation and taking her desire up a notch. "Hmmm," she moaned. "Isn't she pretty? Wouldn't you like to give Quincy a kiss?"

He did, and moved to respond, but she wasn't quite ready yet.

"No, keep blowing," she called out.

Back in position, he continued to blow while moving his hands, which had been clutching the sides of the ottoman, to stroke his engorged member.

"Ah-ah-ah. No touching," she decreed, painfully enforcing her own rule. Every nerve ending in her body wanted, needed, demanded that he touch her, but delayed gratification was still proving to be a powerful aphrodisiac.

"That feels nice, baby. Now taste it," she commanded, gently opening the folds of her vagina wider.

He dropped to his knees, and with his face directly in her pleasure zone, lapped up her creamy middle with his tongue. Wanting to make the best of this opportunity, he began to tickle her clit, first at the tip and then with the broad whole of his tongue. She felt weak with want and grabbed his head, pushing him deeper between her legs. Without instruction (ya gotta love a man who thinks quickly on his knees), he began to suck her clitoris like a pacifier, pulling the blood from the rest of her limbs and causing it to pool at the very tip of her sexual universe.

Her hands, answering the call from a jealous chest hungry for more attention, kneaded her breasts before concentrating his attention on rolling her nipples until they were as stiff and engorged as her clit.

"Stop, stop," she demanded, pushing him away before he could make her come. *Despite the throbbing, telltale signs of an approaching orgasm, she wasn't ready to come.* "Stand up."

He complied, rising to his full six feet four inches, which placed his dick squarely in her face. She ran her fingertip against the tender underside of his head, causing his rock-hard shaft to bounce in her hand.

"What do you want me to do?" *she asked.*

"Suck it," *he managed to squeak out.*

"You'd like that, wouldn't you? You want me to take that pretty, hard dick in my mouth and suck it until you come?" *Her voice cracked. It was getting harder and harder to remain composed.*

"Yes, baby. I would. Please. Suck it. Kiss it. Touch or let me touch it. Do anything. I can't stand it anymore!"

"Or do you want to fuck me? Would you rather I suck you off or fuck *you off?" She was getting bolder and nastier as the arousal escalated.*

"Either. Both."

"Kiss me first," she demanded, giving him permission to touch her.

Happily he lowered his face down to hers and filled her mouth with a hungry tongue. There was no façade of romance or love. This was a kiss fueled by pure lust. Primal desire. She loved it and it released all sense of control. She grabbed his dick and pulled it toward her. Fucking in that chair was an absolute impossibility and she damn near threw the two of them to the floor in an attempt to get him inside of her as fast as humanly possible.

"Fuck me!" she demanded.

She spread her legs in welcome and he grabbed his dick with one hand and pushed it inside her. Her body and mind gave a collective sigh as he glided in and out, hitting every nerve ending he could find on both the up and down stroke. After several moments of glorious poking, he placed his hands on the floor on either side of her head in order to lift his body and adjust the angle. Once again, he began to thrust and grind with mounting intensity, this time with his dick hitting her ready-to-burst bud.

Livia couldn't hold her pleasure at bay any longer. Her body tensed and she heard herself scream as wave after wave of orgasmic pleasure washed over her. The release was strong and powerful and seemed to last blissfully forever. She lay back, spent and happy, feeling lost and languid in her own watery afterglow. A few more minutes of lollygagging and Livia took a deep breath and lifted herself out of the bathtub. She quickly dried off, grabbed her journal and climbed into the bed and under the sheets.

Pen in hand, Livia opened her journal to finish the list, inspired by her rub-a-dub-dub-in-the-tub activity.

Fuck-It List

1. Buy and play with toys.

2. Vacation at a nude beach and go skinny-dipping.

3. Get a sexy tattoo

4. ~~Sex with Kiss a woman~~

4. TBD act of outrageous sexual behavior

5. Have a one night stand with a stranger

6. Have sex in a public place

7. Have *9½ Weeks* sexy food play

8. Find and fuck Bobby Jeffries

9. Make love on a boat

10. Buy a yellow chair.

There it was, the fuck-it list. Giving herself a break, Livia checked off number six. It might have been sex with herself, but it was no doubt in a public place. Well, public enough, as she wasn't at home, and there was a crowd involved, though technically they were in another room.

You're cheating.

"Shut up, Ethel," Livia demanded, as she erased the check, and her old, conservative alter ego from her mind. Okay, so technically the crowd was in another room. Shushing Ethel, she moved on to finding and fucking her first love, Bobbie Jeffries. This would definitely be a challenge, but she was intrigued by the idea of sexually experiencing the man who, then a hot and horny teenager, she'd stupidly kept her legs crossed for because they weren't married. Number ten was going to be the hardest to pull off, but the scene at Naomi's place had burned itself into her memory and that man had captured her imagination. But finding a suitable chair was now a mission.

Looking it over again, she also questioned sex with a woman, crossed it off and wrote *kiss* before striking that off the list too. Like the chair, Livia figured adding it had everything to do with that afternoon, but while it might be the fuel of many fantasies to come, she doubted she'd ever have the courage to actually be with a woman. Sure, Lena had only good things to say about her experience, well, that is until it momentarily blew up her world, but Livia wasn't trying to become heiress apparent to her father's broadcasting empire.

She downgraded that fantasy to a "to be determined" expression of outrageous sex and immediately checked it off. "There, Ethel, you satisfied?" she asked, happy that she could now legitimately check off that afternoon's escapade. "One down and nine to go." But Livia's moment of satisfaction was short-lived as she looked over her list one more time.

"Who are you kidding, Livia Charles? You are no more going to fuck someone in a public place or have a one-night stand than Jennifer Aniston is going to get Brad back."

Making the list had been fun, but in actuality, the only thing Livia knew for sure was going to get accomplished was number one. She was going to go online, buy a few toys, spend a weekend exploring herself with a vibrator, water down her version of what had happened at the Maddox house, report back to the crew and be done with it. And while she was definitely going to do what she needed to do to rev up her sex life, Livia sincerely doubted that the fuck-it list would be any more than an inventory of exciting fantasies for her naughty alter ego to explore within the safety of her head.

And that's what Livia would do. All talk no action. With a defeated sigh, Liv reached over and turned out the light.

"Goodbye, Quincy. Welcome back, Ethel," she said, before punching up her pillow and flopping over onto her back. As her head hit the pillow, Livia felt a tempting twitch between her legs—a silent but powerful tingle that spoke loud and very clear.

"I don't think so, bitch."

Double AA Lovin'

"You were with him last night, weren't you?" Chris accused Jasi once the throbbing in her pussy began to subside.

"You are a real BK," Jasi announced, reaching down to the floor to pick up her panties. *Damn, how did she find out?*

"BK? Is that some new hip lingo you picked up from your boyfriend? What the hell does that even mean?"

"Buzz kill. As in, instead of being able to bask in the fucking afterglow of the amazing licking you just gave me, I have to hear this shit. And for the last time, it's not what you think."

"So he's just another beard to make your mother happy?"

"Not exactly," Jasi said, giving Chrissie her 'don't go there' look, as she zipped her jeans. She had no intention of discussing either Todd or her mother.

"So you are fucking him."

"And what if I am? We're not exclusive, remember? I made that perfectly clear when we first hooked up." Jasi felt her tone turn cold, which she hated because Chrissie was sizzling hot and really knew her way around a pussy, but Jasi was definitely not in the mood to get into this territorial bullshit today.

"I *know* we're not *exclusive*," Chrissie shot back, spitting out the word like the nail in her heart that it was. "But you should at least decide which team you're going to play on. Either you're a lesbian or you're not."

"Are you really going there again?" Jasi got up to retrieve her

T-shirt and pulled it over her naked chest. The sexy mood between them had evaporated and the only thing she wanted to do was get the hell out of Dodge. "You've known I was bi from the very beginning."

"I'm just saying, Jas, it's not fair."

"Chrissie, how in the world does my liking both dick and pussy make this an unfair proposition for you or anyone else?"

Chrissie stood and tugged at Jasi's turquoise nugget belt buckle, pulling her lover close enough for her to see the tears pooling in her brown eyes. "Because if you don't have a preference, then nobody has a chance with you. There's no way to compete."

Jasi unleashed her "you're precious" smile and fought to resist the temptation to say something sweet and comforting. She also resisted the urge to reach down and suckle those delicious, coco brown, 34D's staring up at her. She didn't want to give Chrissie false hope by either flattering or fucking her. Besides, Jasi was scheduled to meet Livia downtown at three, and according to her watch, even if she left now, she was going to be late.

"You're sweet," Jasi said, touching Chrissie's forehead with her lips. It was the kiss of death because while she had no issue doing boys or girls, Jasi did not do cling-ons, and this sad sister was beginning to reek of Velcro. "But I have to go. I'll call you."

Chrissie fell back on the couch and watched her lover pull on her boots and head for the door. Jas could tell by the look on her face that Chrissie clearly understood what had been left unsaid—she was never going to dial her number again.

Livia stood in front of Tickle Me Pink uncomfortably shifting her weight from foot to foot, too chicken to go inside by herself, and getting progressively more embarrassed while waiting for her chronically late friend to arrive. Livia's intent had been to fulfill her pinky promise by partaking in a little online shopping spree. Her mistake had been calling and asking Jasi to recommend a good website. So instead of remaining an anonymous cyber freak, here she was in public. When it came to Jasi, good intentions, like Livia's diet plans, often got shoved to the wayside.

To tell the truth, Livia would rather be taking this excursion with Aleesa or Lena, who both were much more sexually free than she, but who would handle her with kid gloves through this. No such luck with Jasi. She was always so full steam ahead about everything, especially when it came to anything sexual. Livia had never met another woman who defined herself through the pleasure principle as much as Jasi did. She viewed sex through a man's mindset—there was no such thing as too much or too often. Depending on what eye you looked out of, Jasi could be viewed as an insatiable freak and borderline slut, or simply a sexually evolved woman who saw the pursuit of her own pleasure as an inalienable right.

Livia was a wee bit cross-eyed when it came to how she felt about her friend. She was indeed awed by Jasi's self-confident sense of sexual entitlement while, at the same time, a bit taken aback by her lack of moral certitude. Jasi's moral compass seemed to always point in the direction of N—for nasty.

Still, in the end, it was probably a good thing that it was Jasi on the task. Livia was certain she'd push her beyond Ethel's old lady tendencies, or at least try. Livia wasn't quite sure how far down Jasi's road to sexual freedom she was ready to travel at this point.

Livi tried to settle her nerves and bubble up some bravado by channeling Quincy.

So what would Quincy do? For Quincy, this would be no big deal. Just like going to the drugstore to pick up tampons. No, condoms, she corrected herself. Quincy would walk into this place, proud to let the clerks know that she was about to get seriously busy. Yeah, that's what Quincy would do.

Livia felt her body pull itself up to its full stature and turned to see Jasi speed walking up the street.

"Hey, doll!" Jasi's voice called out. "Sorry I'm late! Let's go buy you a dildo!"

The guy walking past broke out into laughter and Livia felt Quincy disappear, crushed by the weight of the ginormous cringe that had enveloped her body. Before Livia could die of embarrassment right there on the sidewalk, Jasi grabbed her elbow and whisked her inside.

Tickle Me Pink was nothing like she'd imagined. She'd pictured in her head a seedy, dusty porn shop atmosphere, full of cheap sex novelties like blow-up sheep and sex dolls. But Livi was pleasantly surprised. This store was open and airy, and set up more like a high end jewelry store. The décor was definitely boudoir chic, carried out by black, flocked wallpaper and flourishes of hot pink. Two crystal chandeliers shed soft light on the elegantly showcased merchandise. Lining the walls were black bookcases stocked with various products grouped together by purpose.

Okay. It was obvious she had misjudged the entire adult toy industry on the basis of days gone by when sex shops were sleazy stores peddling to pervs and predators. The whole ambiance of Tickle Me Pink bubbled with feminine pleasure.

"So, where do you want to start?" Jasi inquired with an amused bend to her lips.

Livia shrugged her shoulders while taking a quick check of the inventory. Vibrators and dildos in one corner. Handcuffs, crops, feather dusters and other bondage and fetish toys in another. Anal play, water play items in one section. Candles, oils, body paints and lubricants to get you in the mood, were shelved in another. There was something on these shelves for every appetite.

"What's a Clone-a-Willie?" Livia asked.

"It's a kit for you to make the perfect copy of your man's penis," the store clerk, who'd suddenly appeared at her side, informed them. "It comes in white and brown. Would you like to see how it works?"

"No thanks," Livia replied, not wanting to reveal that she didn't have a dick at home to clone and even if she did, she'd yet to find a willie pretty enough to duplicate forever. "I'll just look around for a bit."

From the corner of her eye, Liv saw Jasi mouth the words, 'first time' to the clerk as she walked by. Apparently, Livia decided, embarrassing her in front of every stranger they encountered was Jasi's mission for the day.

"It's been a month since your party. I gotta give it to you. I didn't think you'd actually go through with making that list," Jasi said.

"Oh, I made the list that very same night," Livia admitted. "It's just taken me this long to act on it. But I promised, so here I am."

Livia walked over to one of the two, tall, glass display cases. It was well-lit to showcase a bevy of glass dildos and other high-end sex toys inside. A sparkle caught her eye. Were those jewels? People actually blinged out their vibrator?

"Are those real diamonds?"

"Yep. Twenty-eight round cut VS1 diamonds. Well over half a carat. It's available in both pure platinum or 24K gold," the sales-girl said, unlocking the case and putting it in Livi's hands.

It had a nice heft to it and Livia couldn't help sliding her hand up and down its smooth shaft before handing over to Jasi.

"It's called the JimmyJane Eternity."

Jasi laughed.

"What?" Livia asked, amused by her amusement.

"The name—Jimmy, Jane. It's like they wanted to make sure they'd covered both bases."

"It's completely waterproof and the motor is replaceable, thus the name eternity. It's the ultimate hybrid of luxury and decadence."

"And how much does this ultimate hybrid cost?" Jasi asked the question Livia had been thinking.

"The gold is two thousand seven hundred and fifty and the platinum is three thousand two hundred and fifty."

"Dollars? For a vibrator?" The shock in Livia's voice matched the look of disbelief on her face. Wow! The adult toy industry was a lot more lucrative than she'd imagined.

"It will last you forever, plus it's pretty enough to display if you wanted to. Kate Moss and Mary-Louise Parker each have one."

"Well, it sounds like a real star fucker, but this is her first toy; let's make sure she likes it before we bring out the big guns," Jasi declared, handing the JimmyJane back. "Let's say we start her off in the rabbit hutch."

Livia followed the two of them over to the shelves designated to the rabbit vibrators. Even though she didn't own one, she'd heard about the Rabbit and knew it was popular, information gleaned both from conversations with her friends and also seeing it on reruns of *Sex and the City*. How sad is it when you're still getting your sex education from a television show at nearly fifty?

"I got this," Jasi said, dismissing the sales girl as she pulled a purple dick off the shelf and handed it to her friend. The slightly curved shaft, with its helmet looking head, resembled a penis and was textured and grooved, but that's where the lookalike qualities ended. Below the head, the shaft was filled with pearls, and jutting out below the beads was this odd-looking, double-tipped probe (thus the rabbit). It looked more like the clone of some alien's willie, and unlike the simple dick-and-balls dildos on the next shelf. With the attached control box sporting multiple sets of buttons and flashing indicators, this was a pretty complicated piece of apparatus. And heavy, too. With this thing, Liv could definitely multitask—work on her biceps as well as her orgasms.

"Lots going on here," was all Livia managed to say.

"You've got in your hand the best-selling and most popular vibrator sold. It twists and turns, and these little vibrating ears, whoo, girl, will become your clit's BFF! Trust me, there's a reason bunnies are always screwing!"

"What's up with the beads?"

"They spin to stimulate the vaginal walls," Jasi said, pushing a few buttons and setting the thing off in a noisy frenzy of shakes, shimmies and swirls.

"What else do they have?" Livi asked, not sure if even Quincy was ready for such an assault.

They spent the next twenty minutes checking out the Tinkle Me Pink inventory. Jasi showed Livia everything from vibrating ben wa balls to strap-ons to G-spot stimulators. Liv was feeling confused and rapidly getting bored with the whole sex toy escapade. Jasi's tastes were too out there for a beginner like herself. The term 'simple pleasure' seemed an apt description for her needs. By the time they ventured into a small side room full of lingerie and other small novelty toys, Livia knew what she didn't want, but was no closer to knowing what she did. She might have been less adventurous and reluctant to explore her sexual side than her friends, but Livi did know a thing or two about her body. If it came down to clit stimulation or penile penetration, the clit won every time. In fact, she'd never even experienced a vaginal orgasm, so Jasi's suggestions didn't appeal to her.

Jasi's phone rang, and based on the tone of her "hello" and her quiet departure from the room, this was a private conversation. As soon as she left, Livia beckoned over the sales girl, all the while hoping that Jasi would be on the phone long enough for her to make some kind of promise-keeping purchase and beat a hasty retreat.

"I'm really looking for something kind of simple and discreet. All of this is new territory. I need to start slowly."

"Absolutely," she said, moving toward a nearby shelf and pulling from it several items that looked nothing like the weird sea creature-shaped vibrators and huge pearl-stuffed dicks Jasi had been throwing Livi's way. The clerk put on the glass counter in front of her a silver tube of lipstick, an egg, a fig leaf and a pair of lace panties. "Most newbies start with vibrators."

"These are vibrators?"

"Yep." She removed the top from the lipstick, twisted the bottom and placed the top of the red "lipstick" into Liv's palm. She could feel the vibrations in her hand and through her arm.

"It's pretty strong," Livia commented.

"Yep, feels great when properly applied," she quipped. "Very discreet and folks would never suspect."

"I like that." Suddenly a rush of naughty ran through her. This was a dirty little secret she could handle. "This one is definitely going home."

"You might also like this as well," the clerk said, putting the fuchsia fig leaf in her hand. "It's extremely discreet, and you can use it with the bullet inside or not. She lightly caressed the back of Livia's hand with the velvety textured leaf. "You can also put it in your panties or stimulate your nipples. It's great with a partner for an erotic massage, and you can use it with any kind of oils. Very versatile."

As the clerk rubbed this nontraditional toy up Livia's arm, she could feel the vibrations throughout the entire leaf and imagined what it would feel like in her underpants. The idea alone got her feeling all tingly down there.

"Okay. I'll take that as well," Livia announced, suddenly on a spree and getting excited over her new toys. "And what's this?"

"These are remote control panties. Really lovely, black lace bikini, with a little gusset in the crotch that holds a bullet vibrator."

"And the remote?"

"Well, you can use it to activate it yourself or give it to your lover to get your attention with a little illicit buzz."

"Oh, sounds fun but, uh…I don't have a lover—"

"At the moment," Jasi returned to finish her sentence. "These sound fun. You should get a pair."

"They're expensive, ninety bucks to be exact. They'll just sit in my drawer. It's a waste of money."

"Consider them my gift to you. We'll take them," she told the clerk. "And some batteries, please."

"And use them with whom?"

"Well, later, when you start going down your list, these might come in handy," Jasi said. Livia could see the light of another crazy idea shining through her eyes.

"Right now, we might as well give you a kick start on whittling down that list. Is there a place she can put them on?" Jasi asked the sales girl.

"Jasi, what the hell?"

"Oh come on, let's go hit a bar and have some fun before we go."

"Jessebelle's is right on the corner," the sales girl offered before going to ring up their purchase.

"Perfect. We'll go there and have a drink. I'll buzz you a few times, get you good and horny and you can go home and play with your new toys. Come on; it will be fun."

"You are damn crazy, girl. Your twists are apparently way too tight." Livia looked at Jasi in total disbelief. To be one of the tiniest of women she knew, barely five feet and one hundred pounds, Jasi Westfield had the audacity and boldness of a gladiator three times her size.

"What's the big deal? You said that number one on your fuck-it list was to buy and play with toys. Well, we've done the buying; now let's get on with the playing. Jeezus, Liv. You're not getting naked. Not screwing anyone. You're not doing anything but revving up your coochie and having a little fun. Lighten up. New lease on life, remember?"

Livia took a deep breath and didn't even bother to ask the question. She knew what Quincy would do, so she grabbed the panties and headed to the dressing room. Ready or not, Quincy was about to make her debut.

Girl Interrupted

Livia and Jas departed Tickle Me Pink and walked up half a block toward the bar. Snug in its cotton pocket, Livia could feel the hard, cylindrical pocket vibrator pressing up against her lower lips. She tried to keep her stride looking as normal as possible, but Liv felt like she was walking with a tube of lipstick jammed down her underpants.

"I've really been meaning to go see that play," Jasi commented, as they waited for the light to change and a yellow cab advertising *Sister Act* zipped past them. "Lena and Aleesa want to see it, too. We should go for your birthday."

"Sounds like a plaaaan…" Livia replied, her voice rising in pitch, as what could only be compared to an electrical jolt buzzed her pussy lips. The shock and awe of it all caused Livi's body to stiffen and jump slightly while she tried to don an extremely unconvincing poker face.

Jasi attempted to swallow her laughter as she pushed the remote again. This time, Livia sucked in her breath, trying to internalize the pleasurable vibrations with no external indication. She took a quick peek around her, convinced that, despite the city noises going on all around them, everyone could hear the buzzing sound coming from under her skirt. She cut her eyes in Jasi's direction, only to be met by the teasing laughter of her mischievous friend.

The light changed and the humming stopped, so Livia stepped off the curb and followed the crowd of tourists and New Yorkers into the street. She'd taken only a few steps when her knees slightly buckled, weakened by the delicious, nonstop assault to her vagina. Livia heard Jasi giggle behind her as she kept her finger steady on the trigger.

"Keep it movin', lady," the guy behind her grumbled, after nearly colliding with Livia.

"Omigod," Livia offered her breathless apology with a slight chuckle. "I'm so…so sorry."

Jasi momentarily let up from the remote, allowing Livia to take another couple of steps before blissfully battering her crotch again. She continued chuckling as Livi tried to navigate the crosswalk without stopping or bumping into anyone again. Walking had slightly shifted the bullet and each stride shook her rapidly swelling clit and sent a pleasurable vibration across her pelvis and lower extremities.

Once Livia stepped up on the opposite curve, Jasi stopped the torment and witnessed her release a tense exhale. Jas stepped beside her friend and smiled as Livia punched her playfully in the arm.

"I can't believe you did that!"

"Who are you trying to kid? You loved it. I thought you were going to get off right there in the middle of the street."

Livia's response came in the form of an exaggerated eye roll followed by a toothy grin. She hadn't told Jasi about her alter ego, and she would never admit it out loud, but just like she had following Naomi's cake delivery, Livi was feeling rather bold and scandalous. And much to her surprise, she, aka Quincy, liked it. "You're crazy," was all she offered.

"Yeah, well you know what Jimi Hendrix said: 'Craziness is like heaven.'"

It was a minute or two past four-thirty when they walked through the doors of Jessebelle's. It was small, but its high, vaulted ceiling made it feel open and airy. Booths built for four lined either side of the horseshoe-shaped bar. Everything, from the walls to the barstools, was covered in burgundy leather, lending a dark, decadent sex appeal to the place. Seating options were plentiful, as the after work crowd had yet to descend, so Livia headed over to a prime booth, one where they could witness the comings and goings around them.

Jasi knew all about Jessebelle's, but didn't want to freak Livia out. She'd figure it out for herself soon enough—or not. Either way, Jasi figured it might be amusing to watch her friend squirm, both from the jolts to her pussy, and the one to her head once she realized that despite Jessebelle's coed appearance, it was a bar that quietly catered to the undercover, girl-on-girl crowd.

"What can I get you ladies?" the waitress sauntered over to inquire.

"I don't know what to order. There's so much here," Livia said, checking out the drink menu.

What would Quincy drink? she wondered to herself. No way would hot and spontaneous Quincy be drinking a fuddy-duddy wine spritzer. "I'm kind of in the mood for something new."

"One very dirty martini, and my friend here will have a green teani," Jasi told the waitress, with a flirty smile.

"Really? A green tea martini?"

"Yes, doll. You really need to get out more. There is a whole world out here that you have yet to discover."

"I know. I know."

"So how's your list shaping up?" Jasi inquired, giving her friend a shot in the clit for emphasis as the waitress arrived with their drinks.

"Ummmm. Thanks." Gratitude, rolled up in a quiet moan, slipped between Liv's lips. She reached for the glass and downed half the drink, a useless attempt to put out the fire in her panties, and quiet the noises in her throat.

"Okay, now slow down so you can taste the damn thing," Jasi suggested.

"Sorry, you and that damn remote have got me all discombobulated," Livia said before sipping the martini and letting its taste settle onto her tongue. "Ooh, this is strong, but really good!"

"I figured you'd like it. Since green tea is your favorite hot drink so it stands to reason you'd like the cocktail version."

"You're a good date," Liv complimented her.

"I know this," Jasi responded, punctuating each word with a buzz to Livia's clit.

Nicely liquored up, Jasi relaxed and let Quincy enjoy the ride. She let her body relax into the cushy leather upholstery. She pressed her pelvis into the seat looking for relief from the delightful agitation. Quincy responded by exploding into a thousand micro orgasms, prompting Livia to cross her legs, squeeze her inner muscles, and hide her moans in a cough.

Jasi could tell by Livi's flushed face that their friendly sex play was getting to her. Jasi also recognized that it was firing up her own girl dick as well. How could she not get turned on? She was clit-buzzing a beautiful woman and watching her squirm with pleasure. Damn that Chrissie for getting all personal and possessive before she'd been adequately satisfied! Now the raggedy remnants of Jasi's unquenched lust were intruding on what should be a fun-filled, platonic outing with one of her best, and most unavailable, friends.

"This is so wicked."

"Wicked is good, especially for a girl scout like yourself."

Livia sipped on her drink, responding in her head. *Humph! Livia might be, but Quincy's no girl scout. Quincy gets herself off watching other people get off. Quincy has orgasms while another girl masturbates herself from afar. Quincy would totally consider fucking that hot ass bartender behind the bar simply because she thinks he's cute. Quincy's a quietly wicked little slut!*

"Damn, a Benjamin for your thoughts," Jasi said, watching the lustful expressions traipse across her friend's face. She gave Livi five seconds of nib stimulation, taking pleasure in the fact that she was keeping Livia dancing on the razor edge of a truly powerful, and extremely public orgasm.

"Stop. Seriously. I'm about to come again right here."

"Again? Go for it, you little freak!" Jasi said, buzzing her again.

"Stop!"

"Okay, I'll stop if you tell me what you were thinking about."

"I was admiring the guy behind the bar. He's definitely a cutie."

Jasi turned to check out the honey who'd caught Livia's attention. She managed a good investigative look before locking eyes with the extremely hot Latina sister sitting at the bar. "I thought you didn't like the youngins."

"Not ordinarily, but doesn't he look just like—"

"Rick Fox."

"Exactly! Well, maybe his son or little brother."

"So are you telling me you'd like to hit that?" Jasi asked, simultaneously teasing Liv's crotch with an electronic tickle.

"Maaybe," Liv replied in singsong while going with the flow. The alcohol was definitely mellowing her mood.

"Interesting. These magic panties must really be getting to you. So, what else is on your fuck-it list?"

Livia took a swig of her cocktail, buying time while she decided how much to reveal to Jasi about her list. She wanted to keep things close to the vest, mainly to avoid ridicule and a barrage of specific questions about how things were proceeding. Quincy, however, was insistent on full disclosure. Livi decided to meet her spunky vajayjay somewhere in the middle.

"Well, besides buying toys and playing with them, which we've already done here today, I want to go to a nude sunbathing beach and get a sexy tattoo. Oh, and don't ask me why, but I'm obsessed with finding a yellow leather chair to make love in."

"Okay. I don't even want to know what that's about," Jasi said, and much to Livia's relief, dismissed the leather chair revelation. "I mean, those sound nice, but this is supposed to be your damn f-u-c-k list—as in sex, intercourse, layin' pipe. I'm hearing about vacations and furniture shopping, but there's nothing on that list that has anything to do with fucking."

"Remember, I only have to do two."

"Fine, and today you've crossed off one, but the other one has to at least involve another person."

"I don't believe that was ever specified as part of the pinky swear."

"Well, I'm amending the rules," Jasi informed her.

"I do have other stuff on the list," Livia replied, deciding not to argue the fairness of this deal.

"Like? Come on, give me just one good one."

"Like getting caught up in the moment and doing it with a stranger."

"Okay, now we're talking."

"And I always wanted to go back and do it with my high school boyfriend," Livia continued.

"That sounds like it has promise. Why him?"

"Because I regret that we never made love, even though I was crazy about him."

"And why didn't you?" Jasi asked, discreetly looking over to the bar and sharing a flirtatious look with the object of her desire.

"Because I was young and convinced by all the powers that be that sex was a no-no if we weren't married."

"Damn, I was wondering how you managed to stay a virgin until you got married."

"Bobby Jeffries. God, he was so hot! A basketball player," Livia said, closing her eyes and smiling at the memory. "I wonder if he still is."

"Still is what?"

"Hot."

"Only one way to find out, doll."

"I have no idea how to find him," Livia admitted.

"Google. Facebook. You have heard of a little thing called the Internet, haven't you?

"Don't be stupid. Of course I have, but it doesn't feel right stalking somebody in cyberspace. It's like an invasion of privacy."

"So you never looked up any of the guys you dated from eHarmony?"

"Nope, I don't even go online that much. My assistant does all the research for the bakery."

"Wow. You and my mom," Jasi joked. "I'm going to get another drink. Want a refill?"

"No thanks. I still have some sketching to do when I get home. Got a couple of big events coming up—both referrals by Naomi Maddox. In this messed up economy, all I can say is thank God for her and her Glitterati friends."

"So that will be another green teani?" Jasi insisted, ignoring Livia's refusal. "Naomi Maddox and her friends can wait. The only work you have to do tonight is playing with yourself and the rest of the toys in that bag."

"You know what, you're right," Livi said, giving voice to Quincy's demands. "I've earned some down time. Let's run a tab. I'm buying!"

Jasi laughed as she took Liv's credit card. She was legitimately happy to see Livia feeling so light and free. Apparently, this freaky little adventure was agreeing with her. She'd never witnessed her friend feeling so loose and willing to shrug off work in the name of having some sexually mischievous fun.

"Be right back," Jasi said, pressing the remote to add some physical to her emotional pleasure.

"Give me that thing!" Livia demanded, holding her hand out.

"Not a chance. The night's still young." Jasi laughed, giving her one last clit-buzz before heading over to the bar.

Jasi, casual but determined, headed straight to the side of the woman with whom she'd been eye-fucking. "Can I get another dirty martini, a green teani, and another for my friend here?" she asked Livia's sexy bartender, gesturing to the bronze-skinned lovely next to her.

"Thank you.

"You're welcome…"

"Belinda."

"Jasi. You know, Belinda, I've been sitting over there trying to help my friend, who's going through a tough time in her love life, but my mind and eyes keep wandering," Jasi said, making clear two things. One, she and Livia were not a couple; and two, she found Belinda very attractive.

"And exactly where were they wandering off to?" Belinda asked suggestively, licking the salt rimming her Margarita glass.

"Ahh, that information is private. Definitely not for public revelation," Jasi said, getting her flirt on.

Belinda laughed. "Well, maybe we should hook up sometime and you can whisper it in my ear."

Jasi's face broke out into a wide smile. It was definitely good news that this beautiful honey was as smokin' as she looked. "Definitely, sooner than later, I hope," Jasi responded, shifting her eyes toward the bathroom as an invitation.

Belinda RSVP'd with a sexy, lip-biting smile.

"Be right with you." Jasi's left eye winked while her mouth addressed the bartender. "Thank you," she said as the bartender slid the drinks in front of her. "I see it's still pretty dead in here. I was wondering if you might have the time to do me a favor," Jasi asked, slipping the fox a fifty-dollar bill and the remote control to Livia's panties. "See my friend over there? Could you keep her occupied for a while?"

Jasi leaned in to explain the remote and share with him some need to know information so he'd know exactly what needed to be done for Livia while she took care of more pressing, and personal, business.

"I think that's entirely possible," he said, giving her a conspiratorial smile.

"Treat her nice," Jasi insisted as the bartender smiled and nodded.

Jasi picked up their drinks and headed back over to join Livi at the booth. From the corner of her eye, she watched as Belinda finished her drink, slipped gracefully off her barstool, and headed toward the unisex bathroom.

"A toast," Jasi said, raising her glass. "To the fuck-it list. May all your fantasies come true!"

They tapped glasses and as Livia raised the cocktail to her lips, her clit began to tingle. This time, the pace was different, more syncopated and rhythmic. It was delightfully confusing her vagina with a delicious buildup of vibrations, followed by seconds of stillness before revving up again. The tempo was maddening and Livia crossed her legs again, trying to stunt the pleasure before she exploded right there in the booth.

"Stop it!" she demanded, before gulping down half of the smooth-tasting martini. "Oooh. Se..seriously, give me that th..thing!" Livia demanded, holding her hand out. "I caaa…n't take it much longer, and I refuse…mmmm… to embarrass myself."

"Can't, and wouldn't even if I could." Jasi laughed. "I'll be right back," she said, and headed off to the bathroom to get some quick nib teasing of her own.

The zinging stopped and camouflaging her peek at the bartender behind a sweeping view of the bar, Livia looked around the small establishment. Still awaiting the after work crowd, Jessebelle's remained nearly empty. Her eyes came back to the bar, catching Mr. Fox's eye. They exchanged brief smiles before Liv looked away, and Quincy started singing again.

"Omigod!" she blurted out as her body nearly jumped in her seat. Out of the corner of her eye, she saw the Fox chuckle. *Damn it, Jasi!* She wished Jas would stop, because her vadge could not take much more of this blissful torture. Livi quickly downed the rest of her cocktail, trying to cool the heat creeping between her legs and up her neck.

"Another drink, miss?" the waitress strolled over to the booth to ask.

"Yes, please," she said, her eyes following the server back to the bar so she could steal another look at the Fox. She was both relieved and disappointed to see that his shift must have ended; a new bartender was now mixing her drink.

Livia sighed and closed her eyes, resorting to her imagination to bring back the hottie drink slinger. In the bedroom in her mind, he was sucking her nipples and running his hands between her legs. Quincy clutched hard at the thought before shedding tears of desire. Her new panties were beginning to feel soaked and it took everything Livia had not to slip her hands between her legs and give herself a quick rub.

Just as the Fox's imaginary tongue was leaving her belly button and traveling down toward her hungry clit, Livi felt a tap on her shoulder. Her embarrassed eyes flew open as she wondered what expressions had been traipsing across her face.

"Excuse me, miss," the waitress interrupted, "but there is a problem with your credit card and the manager needs to see you in the office."

"Uh, thanks," Livia replied, her head turning in the direction of the server's pointed hand.

Concern pushed her sexual urges to the side. Just like her bakery, Livia's credit was pristine. It had to be for Havin' Your Cake stay in business. There must be some error. As she jumped to her feet ready to find out, her boozy head forced her to sit again. Liv reached for her glass of water, hoping a quick dilution would help sober her up a bit and allow her to talk business. She finished her water, pulled herself together, picked up her purse, and walked along the bar to the manager's office.

Livi knocked, and instead of hearing a welcoming voice, she felt three, quick and tingling shots to her bud. The surprise assault caused her to steady herself against the wall as more tiny orgasms exploded like fireworks in her pants. She looked around for Jasi, who had yet to emerge from the ladies' room. What the hell? That remote had more range than she imagined.

Feeling the dampness between her legs, Livia exhaled, and knocked again. This time she heard a deep sounding, "Come in," and pushed the door open, only to find herself in the Fox's hole.

"Hi. There's a problem with my card?" she asked, gently squeezing her legs together in an effort to shut Quincy the hell up.

"Actually, your card is fine, Livia. But apparently you need some help with a certain…list," he said, holding up the remote and pushing the button.

"How did you get that?" Livia said as it dawned on her what Jasi had done. "Omigod, it's been you?"

"Your friend asked me to take over for a while. And I've enjoyed watching you squirm, so to speak," he told her, coming close enough for her to smell cloves on his breath. "So I was wondering if you'd care to cross off another item on that list tonight. You know the one about getting lost in the moment with a perfect stranger." Fox put his fingers in her hair and pulled one of the blonde, springy curls across her cheek, tickling her lips.

Damn! Jasi and her big mouth! What else had she told him?

"May I?" he asked, bringing her thoughts back into the moment.

For one split second, Livia's usual conservative self tried to protest, but she was quickly shut down by Quincy, who was now taking full control of the situation. Livia's alter ego was horny, ready and willing for some hot sex. And truth be told, so was Liv. She was so tired of trying to curb her desire with self-pleasuring that Jasi's intercourse rider to her pinky swear was looking like a very doable mandate.

Making a mental note to address Jasi later, Liv pushed her friend out of her mind, and lifted her lips to his. She proceeded to first lick, and then suck his lower lip before accepting his tongue in her mouth. It was a smooch hot enough to suspend time and melt opposition. Livia felt herself getting lost in a pool of familiar but nearly forgotten sensations, when Fox engaged the vibrator again.

"No more," she pleaded, tired of the metal stimulation and craving manly flesh. She made her point clear by pulling away long enough to step out of her panties and let them drop to the floor. Fox smiled, and reached around to the zipper on her skirt, separating the teeth and sending it flitting to the ground to join her drawers. Feeling inebriated and emboldened, Livia reached for his hand and placed it between her long and shapely legs. It was a move that effectively aroused both of them to an impassioned pitch.

Fox's fingers dipped into Quincy's gushy well and swirled her pussy pudding around her fully engorged clit. He massaged her nib with his index finger while taking two others and finger fucking her with a promising rhythm. Livia allowed her pelvis to buck against his hand, as desire overwhelmingly conquered any sense of decorum. Her desperate kiss became a torch, igniting their physical need to go further, faster.

Again, Fox pulled away, this time to unbutton her blouse and reveal her perfect breasts. His action caused Livia's breath to catch in her throat, but she had no time to worry if he thought her boobs were real or faux, as his actions revealed it really didn't matter. He peeled the lacy fabric away and directed his hot mouth to her protruding nipples. He nibbled them with expert technique until Livia heard a lazy moan escape her lips. They still worked! Her nipples were back to being scrumptiously sensitive and responsive to the tongue. Hearing her excitement, Fox lingered there, rolling her erect nibs gently between his teeth. Livi continued to moan, arching her back and pressing herself against him, letting him know she was oh so willing for more.

They stumbled across the floor, in an awkward dance that added an additional layer of wanton lust to their encounter. Fox pushed her back against the door, providing the support needed to withstand this delicious ravishing.

Livia closed her eyes and took a deep, satisfying breath. It felt so damn good to have a man's hands and mouth on her body again. For the first time in such a very long time, she felt alive and sexy and vibrant. She'd gone so long without sex that she'd begun to wonder if she even liked it any more. Today, she had her answer. HELL FUCKING YES!

She could hear the bar filling up outside, but instead of being put off, she was turned on. At that moment, Livi didn't care about the strangers beyond the office door, her friends, her moral convictions or anything other than having passionate, spontaneous sex with this sumptuous black brother.

Livia's pelvis pushed forward toward his. She felt his thick erection jump through his jeans as his lips returned to her face. Their kiss became more urgent as Fox's lips devoured hers and his tongue tickled the inside of her mouth. His hand continued to massage her pussy, dipping, sliding, poking and teasing it into madness.

"Yeah, bitch, I'm gonna fuck you good," Fox said under his breath, but loud enough to catch Livia's ears.

Bitch? Did he just call me bitch?

Livia raised her hands to his chest and pushed him away. Calling her out of her name was a definite turn off. For some women it may be a new school term of endearment, but Liv was not one of them. She felt offended and used. She may have not had intercourse in over four years, but did she really want to get reacquainted with dick in some bullshit office with some disrespectful bullshit artist.

"Why? What?" he asked hoarsely. He held his now hard as a rod dick in his hand, clearly confused by what had just happened.

"I'm not a bitch," Livia told him as she sidled across the floor to retrieve her skirt and panties. Suddenly feeling humiliated, she tried to ignore the Fox in the room as she dressed quickly, removing the vibrator from its pocket and holding it in her palm as she fluffed out her blonde halo of curls.

"Baby, I didn't mean anything by that. For real."

"I'm not your baby either."

Livia scooted past Fox, avoiding his eyes and opening the door.

Suddenly, she heard a buzz and felt the vibrations from the bullet climb up her arm.

"Don't forget this," he said, holding up the remote.

"Keep it," she said, dropping the bullet on the floor and walking out.

The internal chatter of disgust provided the soundtrack to her departure as Livia made a beeline to the bathroom to clean up, gather her thoughts, and find her sneaky friend. She was a mix of divergent emotions. Livi wanted to curse Jasi for setting her up like that, and herself for allowing some strange man to ravish and then insult her all in the name of some stupid covenant between friends. Quincy, on the other hand, was still revved up and now pissed at Liv for refusing to end her miserable sexual drought.

Livia got to the unisex bathroom and once again, behind door number two in this joint, she was met with a shock. The sounds of sex in the making greeted her before her eyes fell on the couple in mid-lick. There stood an attractive brunette, back to the wall, skirt pulled up around her waist, with Jasi's head bobbing up and down between her legs. Livia's gasp broke the ladies' concentration. Six eyeballs ricocheted around the space as the three traded confused and embarrassed looks. Jasi and Livia locked eyes, engaged in a split-second conversation heavy with confusion, betrayal and embarrassment, before Livia turned on her heels and walked through the bar and out of the front door.

Girls Just Wanna Have Fun

Livia sat at the table, anxiously awaiting Lena's and Aleesa's arrival. She'd arranged this emergency lunch meeting so they could discuss everything. Well, almost everything that had happened at Jessebelle's. A week later later, she was still shocked and confused by both her and her friend's behavior, and had yet to answer any of Jasi's multiple calls or texts. And now she was back in the city, in need of help sorting out her feelings, and knowing that the always forthcoming, IMDO (in my damn opinion) team would do just that.

It had been Livia's intention to open up with the Jasi scandal, but she was now having second thoughts. She'd learned about Jasi's alternative lifestyle by accident, not admission, so did she really have the right to out her friend? One's sexuality was a big deal. If Jas had wanted the three of them to know about her sexual preferences, she would have told them.

Instead of lying to us all, and pretending to be someone she isn't, Liv thought, but didn't share. It suddenly occurred to her that at the center of her confusion was pure anger at Jasi for not trusting them enough to love her, whatever her desires.

And could you? Would you still love her knowing that she lived a lifestyle that you'd been taught all your life was wrong and perverted? Livia queried herself. She honestly wasn't sure. She wasn't homophobic in that evangelical, conservative, Southern kind of way. Liv didn't think that gays would be damned in hell, and she truly believed that they should be treated like everyone else when it came to their civil liberties. But still, it didn't seem *normal*.

Livia's thoughts continued to baffle and anger her. Before she caught her with that woman in the restroom, Jasi was one of her dearest, and definitely go-to friends. But this new knowledge put an entirely different, and rather ominous, slant on Jasi's entire life. It was no secret that they all lovingly referred to Jasi as a slut with a heart of gold, but was she gay as well?

Gay or not, she was still a liar, and fraud. There she was, making all of her bullshit demands for me to work it, and own it, and make no excuses, when she couldn't even do those things herself.

And what kind of friend sets another friend up like that? That bartender could have been a crazy rapist or something. But Jasi, with her cavalier, fuck and be fucked attitude about sex, had sent her in that office like a lamb to the slaughter. As the old adage went, with friends like that, who needed damn enemies?

Livia's thoughts switched over from her confusion over Jasi to her own bawdy behavior. She hadn't exactly walked out once she'd understood what was going on. In fairness, she couldn't hold Jasi completely responsible. She'd been willing to play the game until the rules changed.

Liv checked her watch. The girls were running late, which was unusual for her always punctual crew. To pass the time, she pulled out her list for review. Aleesa had already informed her that she expected a full report on her progress thus far. Happily, she could report that she'd fulfilled her end of the promise and be done with this. It was clear from her experience at Jessebelle's, she had neither the guts nor the disposition to be even a part-time ho.

Fuck It List

1. ~~Buy and play with toys.~~

2. Vacation at a nude beach and go skinny-dipping.

3. Make love on a boat

4. Get a sexy tattoo

5. ~~Sex with Kiss a woman~~

5. ~~TBD act of outrageous sex~~

6. Have a one night stand with a stranger

7. Have sex in a public place

8. Have a 9 1/2 Weeks Sexy Food Play

9. Find and fuck Bobby Jeffries

10. Buy a yellow chair.

Going over the fuck-it list, Livia was satisfied that the items she had managed to accomplish could definitely be listed under the spontaneous, adventurous, and bold columns.

Not bad for a good little Catholic girl like yourself.

Livia took her finger and symbolically drew an invisible line across the rest of the sexual scenarios on the list. She was hoping to feel the same sense of accomplishment she'd experienced with every other list she'd ever made and completed. Livi had literally stumbled into realizing two of her fantasies, thus fulfilling her promise and, in her mind, rendering the list defunct. But even though she'd held up her end of the pinky swear, the sensual side of her, Quincy to be exact, wanted to complete the journey. Somewhere between the fingering herself in the shadow of the man in the yellow chair and getting fingered by Mr. Fox at the bar, Livia's sleeping libido had been awakened. Quincy wanted to complete her mission and strut into fifty feeling like she and sex were satisfied peers.

However, being called a bitch by a man she didn't know, but was ready to fuck, and seeing Jasi going down on that girl in a public bathroom had squashed the appeal of sexual vagabonding for Livia's more sensible side. Forget Jasi's deep, dark secret that Livia's barging in had unintentionally revealed, witnessing her friend doing publically, what should done in private, had convinced Livia she had neither the appetite nor the disposition for the potential humiliation that could accompany living and loving scandalously. Fifty or not, she cared about what her friends and family thought about her. What if Jasi had walked in on her? Or one of her clients? She would have been mortified. Some things were not meant to be shared, even among friends.

"Hey, girl," Lena's voice interrupted.

Livia quickly folded the list and tucked it in her palm while she stood to welcome her girlfriend and cousin with a kiss.

"Sorry we're late. You know it wasn't me," Aleesa said, scooting into the booth across from her. "Miss Large and in Charge here got held up in a meeting."

"And I'm sorry. Contract negotiations. I have to get back," she informed them. "I only have an hour."

"No worries," Lees commented as they both picked up menus.

Livia checked out her girls while they perused the lunch selection. The three of them were quite the exercise in compare and cotrast. Aleesa Davis, with her dark hair and chocolate skin, had an effervescent energy that was approachable and friendly, and served her well as a television marketing executive. Lena Macy, on the other hand, from her hazel eyes and long, fine hair, bore all the telltale signs of a biracial family tree. And Lena carried herself like the wealthy, powerful CEO that she was. She might appear aloof and intimidating to strangers, but to those who knew and loved her, Lena was a warm, crack up of a loyal friend who was as generous as they come.

Where the other two were height-challenged, Livia, with her perpetually tan complexion and honey-colored bushel of hair, stood a regal and commanding, five feet ten inches. She was the shyest and most conservative of the three in both look and action, but as her past health issues had proven, she was a fierce fighter and survivor. Together, they were a cache of midlife magnificence and each still had what it took to cause men to want to stop, drop and take a lustful roll.

"So what was so important? Is this about the list? It hasn't even been six weeks. Don't tell me you're ready to make your report?" Lena asked once lunch had been ordered.

"Shouldn't we wait for Jasi?" Aleesa asked.

"Uh, she's not coming." Livia took a quick sip of her lemon water to avoid having to elaborate on why Jas had not been invited.

"Okay, so what's up?" Lena asked, pushing the meeting along.

Livia unfolded her list and handed it over to Aleesa, who shared it with Lena. "And as you can see I've already made good on my promise to do two."

"Details," Aleesa insisted.

"Lees is right. We need the down and dirty. How do we know you didn't simply cross this stuff off to shut us up?"

"Yeah, like this 'to be determined act of outrageous sex.' What the hell is that all about?" Aleesa probed.

"I got busy with myself in the hallway of one of my client's homes while this guy was in the other room watching porn and jerking off. There, outrageous enough for you?" Livia asked, smiling broadly at the memory.

"Ah, hell's bells! Livia's a freak and she likes it!" Lena chuckled. "Did he see you?"

"Hell no! I would have died."

"When?" her cousin asked.

"The day of my party."

"No wonder you were willing to pinky swear so readily," Aleesa said. "You gave in way too easily. I should have known you had something up your sleeve."

"So what about the other stuff? How'd that happen?"

"Well, that was all Jasi's doing. We started at Tickle Me Pink. Hey, did you know there is a diamond encrusted vibrator that costs over three thousand dollars?"

"I have one," Lena revealed while the other two looked at her in disbelief. "What? It was a gift."

Livia went on to tell them all of the events in which Jasi had conspired against her. From the toy store, to walking the streets of New York with a vibrator down her pants to her sexy high jinx in Jessebelle's, she gave them all of the sorted details, watering them down to quiet the embarrassment that was tiptoeing through her.

"Oh you've been a busy little slut," Lena teased. "Toys and strange boys! Go on, girl. I'm proud of you, though you still haven't actually done the nasty."

"Yeah, well, Jasi already tried to amend the pinky swear to include intercourse, but it's too late."

"Well, now that you've tiptoed outside the box a little, how do you feel about yourself?" Aleesa queried.

"For the most part, good," Livia admitted. "It was kinda hot and sexy being spontaneous like that, even if I didn't do the deed. Him calling me a bitch when we were about to do it turned me off. He didn't even know me. Why would he call me something like that?"

"Sounds like it was heat of the moment lust talking. Kids these days use the term *bitch* like we use *baby*," Aleesa schooled her.

"Well, he tried that too and I found both offensive. I'm too old school for all of this, but I am glad that I have the memories to take into the next decade."

"Omigod, have you already gone back to being the boring old cake lady?" Lena accused.

"I did what I promised to do."

"And admitted feeling good doing it. So why not go through with the whole thing? Most of these things don't involve sex anyway," Aleesa pointed out.

"That's what Jasi said. So, really, what's the point?" Livia argued. "As you've all noticed, half of my fuck-it list doesn't even involve fucking! I'm obviously not very adventurous."

"Don't look at it that way. Look at them as places to start," Lena offered. "Who knows where they'll lead you."

"Now on *my* list, I'd definitely have to include a threesome with two guys. I love the idea of it being all about *me*. Double the pleasure, double *my* fun," Aleesa revealed. "Walt can watch if he wants, but that's all."

"Oh, so now you're ready to take Walter up on his offer?" Livia remarked, referring to Aleesa's husband's misguided anniversary gift of no-questions-asked sex with a stranger.

"My man watching someone else get me off does add a lot of heat to the situation," Lena agreed, remembering her time with Jason in the Champagne Room. "The idea of a stranger watching me have sex is pretty hot, too."

"Okay, top three fantasies?" Aleesa dared Lena, not even bothering to look at Livia.

"Fantasy or for an actual fuck-it list?" Lena asked for clarification.

"Either. Both."

"That's tough. My go-to are, number three, an orgy. Do you ever think about what that would be like? All those sweaty bodies rolling around fucking their brains out?" Lena asked. "Hot, but would it actually go on my fuck-it list or remain a fantasy? Don't know. Number two, a little exhibitionism. I read about this erotic art show where guests get to finger paint naked models before getting their brushes dipped, if you know what I mean. Sometimes if I need a little push over the edge, I think about that. But my number one fantasy—don't laugh—is getting spanked by my old English Lit professor. I discovered that my good girl likes to be punished for being bad. Now, that's one fantasy I've incorporated into my actual love life—without the costume. The whole plaid skirt and knee-highs look is too over the top for me."

Livia sat listening, feeling both intimidated and embarrassed by her weak ass fuck-it list. A sexy tattoo? Buying toys and playing with them? Compared to these two, most of her fantasies could be part of a Disney double feature.

"Your top three?" Lena asked Aleesa.

"Well, my number one is definitely the threesome. But that's only for the head, because Walter would never agree to that."

"Unless it was two women and you!" Lena laughed.

"True that! Number two is me dominating him and using a strap-on. Again, head games only. And number one, without a doubt, is being with another woman."

The visual of Jasi licking that girl's pussy popped up in Livia's head. And just like it had when she'd watched Nilla and Coco go at it, her vajayjay clutched. What was going on with her? Why all of this fascination with girl-on-girl action?

"So you fantasize about…you know…doing it with a woman?" Livia queried.

"All the time," Aleesa admitted. "When I was writing the freak book for Walt, I had so many fantasies about me with women. I discovered that I definitely have a bi-curious mind, but a strictly dickly pussy."

"I won't lie, that stripper was sexy as hell. When she was sitting on my lap and grinding on me, I was so turned on I kissed her! I'm getting hot right now just thinking about it! But ultimately, all I wanted was to get to Jason. That said, it's still a go to vision when I'm alone and trying to get off."

"So fantasizing about it doesn't mean you might…you know… be…" Livia attempted to ask.

"Gay? Girl, you have got to get your head out those Betty Crocker books and into some other seriously hot reference materials," Aleesa replied.

"Having sex with another woman is like one of the top four fantasies for straight women. It doesn't make you gay or mean you want to do it for real," Lena added.

"Then why do we get turned on seeing two women together?"

"Because from advertisements in the magazines to those *Girls Gone Wild* videos, the sexy images of two women together now seems like forbidden but natural fruit," Aleesa explained.

"What do you think Jasi would say about it?" Livia asked, fishing to see if they had any idea about their friend.

"It probably turns her on, too, and that girl is all about the penis," Aleesa replied. "I think that's why she's never been married. Too many dicks, too little time."

"What about Todd?"

"An open, commuter relationship? He's perfect for her," Lena chimed in. "You know Jasi. Variety is definitely the spiciest part of life."

Livia took a bite of her salad and pondered this dilemma as she chewed. It was crystal clear that the two of them had no idea about the double life Jasi was leading. Livia had to wonder if Aleesa and Lena would be as angry as she was by Jasi's deception. They were a pretty liberal, you-do-you, group of friends, and unlike herself, Liv was pretty certain that they could not care less whether Jasi was bisexual or a lesbian. And truly, aside from her own confusion about the morality of alternative lifestyles, it wasn't the idea of Jas possibly being gay that upset her most. It was that she didn't respect their friendship or trust them enough to be honest. It seemed a sad commentary on their relationship that Jasi felt the need to deceive her friends. She'd been fronting all these years, and now Livia had no idea who Jasi Westfield really was.

"So, Livia, back to you and your list. Did we give you any ideas?" her cousin queried.

"I don't know. While I was doing the stuff it did feel kind of fun and liberating, but once I got home and really thought about it, it's just not me. I bake cakes and have sex in committed relationships with men who call me beautiful, not bitch. I'm almost fifty. I can't get rid of the church girl just like that," Livia said, snapping her fingers for emphasis. "And…I'd be mortified if anyone found out what I did. I was embarrassed telling you two."

"Then keep it to yourself, but don't stop growing and discovering yourself," Aleesa said, sounding more like a life coach than a cousin.

"Lena, look what happened to you. You ended up on the Internet, well sort of. Even though that video of the girl in the strip club wasn't you, people thought it was, and you were humiliated. Look how long it took you to set things straight with your family and the public."

"That was probably the most humiliating thing that ever happened to me. I felt like I'd totally disgraced myself and my family. I thought the scandal was going to kill my father. But that crazy relationship with Jason was the best thing that ever happened to me. Can I tell you, making all those bets and paying them off with amazing sex has not only made me a better lover and woman, but a better business woman. Seriously. Those months of having sex on my own terms were so damn liberating. It gave me confidence to face anything and anyone, and be a fine ass sexy woman doing it."

"Long live Pocahontas!" Aleesa cheered.

"Exactly. That's what you should do, Livia. When I was Pocahontas and Jason was Mr. Big Johnson, it was like hiding in plain sight. I felt like somebody else was doing all of those sexual things that I wanted to do, but couldn't bring myself to actually do."

"Well, I already have Quincy."

"Girl, you are way freakier than you admit." Aleesa laughed.

"Who is Quincy?"

Livia lifted both hands and pointed down to her crotch, sending the other two women into a hysterical laughing fit. As Lena and Aleesa exchanged a fist bump, Livia went on to tell them how their teasing at the party had caused her to rename her vagina, losing Grandma Ethel and replacing her with hot and spontaneous Quincy.

"Great! Now make her real," Lena told her. "Give Quincy a personality and life and put her in charge of getting your fuck-it list done. Every time a chance to cross off an item on your list comes up, let Quincy take the lead. That's what I did. How else do you think I'd ever wind up in a titty bar with a stripper on my lap?"

"I did that when I was out with Jasi. I kinda let Quincy take over."

"See, and look what happened! You nearly banged the hottie behind the bar."

"Yeah, but if one of my clients had seen me? Or Adin and Ashri?" Livia asked, speaking of Aleesa's boys and her godsons. "My reputation and business would be ruined."

"Then what you need to do is take your fuck-it list on the road where you don't know anybody and nobody knows you," Lena advised. "There is no way your uptight behind is going to do anything at home."

"There's an idea. We can make that the theme of this year's trip," Aleesa suggested, referring to their annual girlfriend getaway.

"No. Unh, uh. She needs to do this on her own," Lena argued.

"You're right." Aleesa retracted her initial opinion to concur. "She doesn't need any voices, other than Quincy's, whispering in her ear and confusing her.

"You're awfully quiet. What do you think about a little pleasure trip?"

Livia was surprised not only to find herself warming up to Lena's suggestion, but feeling grateful to her for providing her this solution. The idea of being away from the known so she could anonymously delve into the unknown intrigued her. And while she wasn't sure how much she'd actually accomplish, she wanted to try. Thanks to a perfect storm of age, desire, and a dare, what had started as a joke was turning into a quest.

"I'll think about it," was all she would commit to.

"And don't go asking Jasi," Lena told her. "You know that little ho will have her condoms packed and be on the first thing smokin'."

"You got that right. And then after she climbs off the dick between her legs, she'll catch the next plane to meet you!" Aleesa said, making all three of them laugh.

Don't be so sure it's a dick, Livia wanted to tell them.

"I know exactly where you should go," Lena announced with all the excitement of an Idris Elba sighting. "If you want to go skinny dipping and incorporate any other upgrades on this sheet, go to Saline Beach in St. Bart's. Best nudie cutie beaches in the Caribbean. Stay at the Christopher Hotel. Great rooms, great service, great time!"

"Nudie cutie? Really?" Livia asked, rolling her eyes.

"Honestly, though, do you think she can handle being by herself? You know, alone in active pursuit mode? We are talking about

Livia Charles," Aleesa asked, ignoring Livia and speaking to Lena as if her cousin wasn't sitting at the table.

"True. It is a bit like sending the Little Red Hen into Colonel Sanders' kitchen. There's a good chance she's gonna get devoured."

"Hello. I am sitting right here," Livia protested. "What are you two so worried about? It's not like I'm fresh out of high school and headed abroad on my own."

"Yeah, well, here's the thing, Livi, Aleesa's got a point. If you play in the big girl leagues, you've to be ready to handle the attention that comes with putting yourself out there like that," Lena explained.

"What she's trying to say, Cuz, is that you're beautiful and the more you bloom, the more men are going to want to sniff your bud. Especially down there in the islands where the universal rule of 'what happens on vacation, stays on vacation' applies."

Livia could feel a mix of confusion and concern color her face. Her desire was definitely piqued, but maybe this whole going away alone to get her groove on wasn't such a good idea after all.

"So are you now saying that you don't think it's a good idea for me to go?" Liv asked, her head shifting from side to side so she could gauge both their reactions.

"No, not at all. What we're saying is that you need to be prepared for the attention," Aleesa replied. "And have a few guidelines to follow."

"Like what?"

"Like always listen to your gut. Don't go with anyone or do anything that doesn't feel one hundred percent right," Lena said.

"And always let someone know when and where you are."

"Take your own supply of condoms. No cover. No lover," Lena told her. "And have an exit line," she added.

"An exit line? Okay, now what's that?" Livia asked as her head ping-ponged back and forth between the two.

"You know, a line to let someone down easy, so they walk away feeling good and not pissed at you."

"We're scaring her to death," Aleesa remarked. "Look at her face. She's not going to go alone."

"No, you haven't," Livia said, surprising them both. "True, I might be a little nervous, but I really want to try this. Besides, you're forgetting one important detail. Quincy's got this. I'm merely going along for the ride."

Mama Don't Preach

Jasi kissed Belinda on her forehead before pulling back the covers and putting her feet on the floor. She turned to gaze down at her still sleeping lover. The beauty in her bed made her smile, both with happiness and disbelief. Jasi couldn't remember the last time she'd spent two, let alone seven nights in a row with one lover—man or woman. But ever since their tryst at the bar, keeping Belinda Rodriquez off her mind, and out of her arms, had been a mission impossible. If Jasi didn't know better, she'd swear she was falling in love.

There was nothing more she'd rather do than stay in bed all day and find out, but it was Sunday and that meant getting her ass up and dressed so she could get over to Staten Island before eleven. Belinda stirred and turned over, exposing her beautiful naked ass. Jasi felt her pussy start to cream again and it took everything she had not to jump back in the sack and gently fuck her awake, but being late for Sunday brunch at her parents' was not an option. Not even if it meant walking away from the juiciest apple ass this side of the Hudson.

Her mind was a muddle of thoughts as she undressed and stepped into the shower. The fact had not escaped her that finding this new love had cost her an old one. True, they were not equal in nature—one was gift wrapped in romance, sex and intimacy, while the other was cloaked pleasingly in friendship. Different yes, but both involved a dedicated, heartfelt love. She and Livia had not spoken since that fateful incident at Jessebelle's, but it certainly was not for her lack of trying. Jas had called, emailed, texted and even ambushed her at the bakery so they could talk this out. Other than the three or four sentences she'd managed to blurt out, Livi had refused to talk to her, but the disapproval on her face had said it all. Confusion and silence had solidified into anger and taken the fate of their friendship hostage. Jasi had no idea what to think. And until the two of them could sit down and talk, she would remain clueless.

Jasi sudsed up her new pixie cut and tried to wash thoughts of Belinda and Livia out of her head so she could concentrate on the task before her. The curtain was about to go up on her role as a committed lover to her "significant other" of 13 months, sports photographer, Todd Derrick. One-part boyfriend, three-parts beard, Todd was an interesting man—intelligent, cultured and delightfully clueless. They'd met at a Knicks game, and attracted to his Johnny Depp-like good looks and artistic mind, Jasi had gone home with him. With the help of some serious fantasizing, along with his talented tongue and half a bottle of tequila, he'd proven himself to be a sweet and adequate lover. She'd taken him to Sunday brunch with her the next morning, where he turned out to be the perfect foil, and the answer to her mother's prayers— a potential son-in-law and father to her unborn grandbabies.

Todd and the Westfields fell in love with one another, and thanks to his crazy travel schedule, he became Jasi's ideal boyfriend, around just enough to keep her sleight-of-hand show running, but too wrapped up in his career to realize or even care that his committed relationship with Jasi was little more than a sham. Best of friends for sure, with Todd she had the best of both worlds, the look and feel of a dutiful daughter, and the freedom to live her undercover life. For this reason alone, she had to love him.

Jasi rinsed and turned off the water with a sigh. The bottom line was that she was tired of pretending to be in love with Todd so she could continue to perpetuate the lie for her parents that she was a happily heterosexual woman. Falling for Belinda had certainly complicated things big time, but it was the fall out with Livia that worried her the most. The fact that her relationship with a dear friend was teetering on the edge of collapse was bad enough, but now someone knew her secret and, intended or not, had the power to destroy the delicate balance of her life with one whisper.

While Jasi pulled on one of her "only on Sunday" dresses, it saddened her to think that not one person whom she professed to love—not her parents, her boyfriend, lovers, or friends really knew Jasi Westfield. Hell, she was no longer sure she did. Her parents, now in their late seventies and ready to be grandparents, thought she was straight and would be announcing her engagement any day now; her lesbian lovers thought her to be a bisexual vagabond, while her career-driven boyfriend, Todd, loved her "freedom rules" attitude, and was perfectly happy with their no-strings attached relationship. Meanwhile, her platonic girlfriends knew her to be a crazy, bold, man-eating, insatiable but loveable ho whose personal mission was to stay single and fuck her way through life.

Funny thing was, Jasi was none of these things, and yet if asked, she wouldn't know exactly how to describe herself. All she could say with total honesty was that the sad phrases practiced "liar," "lost soul," and "emotionally exhausted" certainly applied in some form or fashion. But now, with the potential of having her secret life exposed, "deathly afraid" was applicable as well. Jas was utterly terrified of losing everything. Good, Southern Baptists, an alternate lifestyle would not be understood, let alone accepted, and it would absolutely destroy her conservative, God-fearing mother and father. Livia's reaction to shut down and shut her out, was as disappointing as it was hurtful, and made it clear that even the best of friends could put ideology over alliance. And what about her students and their parents? What would be their reactions to their daughters spending time in the classroom with a lesbian? For some idiotic reason, teachers were expected to live the pristine lifestyles of monks and nuns to prove themselves worthy of passing on their knowledge to the children of strangers whose family lives were usually much more dysfunctional and outrageous than any teacher she knew.

Jasi reentered the bedroom and stopped to take a long look at her lover. Opening her eyes to the new day, Belinda looked sexy as fuck with her just woke up bed hair and lazy smile. Jasi leaned over to give her a loving kiss. "Good morning," she said after their last smooch.

"Morning, *Mamí*. Where are you off to so early?"

Jasi smiled. She could listen to Belinda talk forever. She loved her sexy Puerto Rican accent. Fuck, she loved everything about this damn girl!

"Staten Island to see the folks. Standing Sunday date."

"Want me to come with you?"

"Not this week, doll, but soon, okay?" Jasi promised, knowing full well it would be months and months before she'd ever introduce her to her Jasper and Harolyn Westfield. Maybe after her infatuation died down. When they couldn't read the love and lust her eyes held each time they fell on Belinda. And after she'd found the guts to tell Belinda the truth—that she lived her life deep in the closet with the rest of the pathetic skeletons.

"Okay. I'm going back to sleep. I'm so tired. You wore me out, *Mamí*."

"Stay as long as you want," Jasi said, and leaned over again and gave her lover a long, passionate, reassuring kiss.

Belinda snuck her hand between Jasi's legs, searching for the magic button that turned her on, and after some tender loving care, always turned her out. Belinda's fingers slyly maneuvered around the edges of Jasi's panties and wiggled inside her warm, moist pussy. Jas pressed her crotch against Belinda's open palm, looking for pressure. Belinda lubed up and fingered her lover's pearl with one hand while the other pulled Jasi's braless tit from her bodice and latched on, bathing her already hard nipple with morning saliva.

Jasi's moans mingled with the sunshine streaming in through the window. Sound and light danced around their heads. It took everything Jasi had to force herself to disengage from this hot and horny miracle in her life. "I thought I wore you out."

"Second wind," Belinda said, giving Jas a wink and a smile. "By the way, you should wear dresses more often. Easy access goes both ways, *Chica.*"

"Where's that handsome fella of yours?" was the first question to leave Jasper Westfield's mouth once Jasi crossed the threshold and he gathered her into a big, papa bear hug.

"I told you he was in South Africa covering the World Cup," Jasi said, not mentioning what a happy coincidence his leaving town for weeks and she meeting Belinda had been.

"That young man of yours is always on the road. Well, come on in and sit. You know your mother has everything ready to go," her father said, taking her hand and ushering her into the dining room. Just like it was every week, the table was set with the good china, crystal, and silverware. It was the traditional setting for Sunday brunch for the Westfields and their very untraditional, only child.

"Jasilyn Westfield, what have you done with your hair?" asked Harolyn, coming over to give her daughter a warm hug.

"Cut it. I was tired of the twists."

"Well, me too, but at least you had some length. This looks like a boy's haircut."

"Leave her alone, Harolyn. As long as Todd likes it, that's all that counts."

"Where is Todd?"

"South Africa. He says hello," Jasi replied, watching Harolyn's smile dim. Even though her parents were thrilled to see her, it was clear that they, particularly her mother, was disappointed the Todd hadn't accompanied her. Apparently, there'd be no engagement announcement today.

The three sat down to their weekly dinner, this week roast beef, garlic mashed potatoes and string beans, followed up by her favorite dessert, German chocolate cake. Between courses, parents and child caught up on their individual comings and goings of the past week. Jasi invited them to her school's upcoming art show, proudly describing the work of her star students and how incredible it made her feel to see their talents progress. Harolyn filled her in on their trip to Jasper's upcoming college reunion at Prairie View A & M, and her decision to begin a Zumba class at the local senior center. By dessert, it was clear that, for at least another week, all was well in the Westfields' world.

Her crazy, deceitful personal life aside, Jasi felt lucky to have landed in the very loving arms of Jasper and Harolyn. Unable to conceive for years, Harolyn became pregnant well into her late-thirties, and years after she'd given up on having a family. Forever grateful, they dedicated their lives to serving the God who had blessed them with a miracle. Labeled with the crazy blend of their names, Jasilyn Haro Westfield had been treated like the wonder child her parents believed her to be. They'd doted on Jasi her entire life, educating her at the finest private schools, encouraging her budding interest in art through classes, study abroad programs and tuition to the prestigious Rhode Island School of Design. When Jasi burst her mother's dream of having a daughter who was also a world-famous artist, Harolyn had managed to rally her emotions and support Jasi's decision to teach art to middle school students at the esteemed Flint Place Girl's Academy. With every life plan Jasi came up with (and discarded), they'd found a way to encourage and cheer her on, making it clear that the only thing they expected in return was for her to stay close to them and God, and eventually have a family of her own for them to love and nurture until their deaths did they part. Jasi felt like a failure on every count that mattered.

"So, Jasilyn, when exactly will Todd be returning from his trip?" her mother asked over coffee.

Jasi cringed at the mention of his name because it meant only one thing, the personal inquisition was about to begin.

"Not for another week or two," she said, feeling the jump in her gut. Once Todd returned the juggling of him and Belinda would begin.

"Will he be around for your birthday?" Harolyn asked. "It is the big four O."

"I don't know, Mom. That's like another eight months from now."

"I realize, but this is a big year for you, both of you. It's getting time to make some serious decisions. You understand how hard it was for me; you need to get started sooner rather than later."

"Mom, not the 'when are you getting married and giving me some grandbabies' conversation again," Jasi whined.

"Your mother is merely trying to make the point that women can't wait as long as men can when it comes to having families. Todd can't keep dragging his feet about this. You don't want to wake up and discover it's too late, baby girl. Your mother and I were truly blessed that it happened to us," her father said, offering his soft but precise summation.

"I understand and we have been talking about it," Jasi lied. "But honestly, I'm not sure that a marriage is in our future," she said, planting the demon seed without looking her mother in the eye.

Harolyn gasped for air like she'd been sucker-punched.

It killed Jasi that she was unable to live up to her parents' expectations in this one, totally reasonable area. Every Sunday without an announcement was another hairline fracture in her mother's heart. Her parents were correct, time was running out. And the telling tick of her biological clock was being drowned out by the very loud, psychological sobs of Harolyn's profound disappointment.

"I'm beginning to believe that Todd isn't really interested in settling down," she explained, quickly spinning the facts into a sorted fabrication of the truth. "His work is so important to him and he's always traveling. I'm only saying that it might be time to face the fact that Todd might not be the one for me."

"It's been a year. You're only now discovering this?" The words "at this late date," though unspoken, came through loud and clear in her mother's question.

Jasi chose to reply with a simple shrug of her shoulders.

"What about a family?"

"I don't know right now. I still have some time, and if it comes down to it, maybe I'll have one on my own," Jasi said, testing another pool of tepid water.

The shock on her parents' faces immediately let her know that

Plan B was a bust right from the start. "By yourself? Without a husband?" her father said, looking for clarification.

Jasi nodded, unable to verbalize the word that would only make the cracks deeper.

"But having a child out of wedlock is a sin, Jasilyn. I won't let you bring a bastard child into this world," Harolyn informed her. "It's not fair and it's not right. I don't want to hear another thing about this. You and Todd will find a way to work this out," she said, falling back on her faith in all things righteous, whether they were realistic or not.

Jasi didn't know what made her want to cry more, the fact that giving her parents the one thing they wanted most was looking further and further beyond her reach, or the fact that if they couldn't or wouldn't even consider the idea of her having a baby on her own, what would they think if they learned that instead of a husband she was coveting a wife?

A Real Pick Me Up

Livia stepped onto the beach, wearing a sarong over her new bikini, and immediately felt grossly overdressed. Saline Beach was liberally dotted with the tanned hides of the island's naked sun worshipers. It was interesting to note that the gorgeous, bronzed bodies she'd been expecting to see were few and far between. Liv let out a big sigh of relief. The good news was if she was going to get naked, she didn't need to be worried about being the only tonally challenged body swimming in a sea of perfect physiques. This was going to be more like Arielle bobbing around in an ocean of inner tubes. There were more forty ounces than six packs, more saggy tits than grand tetons, and more doughy buns than those of steel walking around not giving a damn about their form or being fit.

If they don't care, neither do I, Livia decided.

Ultimately, it really didn't matter because she was taking this whole journey one step at a time. Right now, all she was concerned about was finding some isolated spot to disrobe, catch some rays, cross another item off her list, and head back to fully clothed civilization. Livi was there to see, not be seen. But now, based on the jiggles, wiggles, sags and bags kicking up the clean, white sand, she wasn't even going to be doing much sightseeing either.

Feeling a bit braver about the whole nudie cutie (to coin Lena's term) thing, Livia headed over to the beach hut to rent a lounger, and then led the handsome islander carrying her rentals over to a quiet patch of sand, not far from the water (in case she wanted to make a mad dash to take a cooling dip), but away from any fellow beach dwellers. Despite her vow to get butt naked in public, this was a personal exercise in private scandal. Livia wasn't ready to be any kind of exhibitionist.

She spread her towel on the chaise, sat down and began removing the necessary beach essentials from her bag. She pushed sunglasses into her curls and began to apply oil on all of her exposed skin, while mentally preparing herself for the unveiling. Liv was still debating between the slow ease versus quick rip technique. Not wanting to look like what she was feeling—a total punk—she decided to go for it. Thirty seconds later, Livia Charles was nude and lying on her stomach with her ass in the air.

She closed her eyes and released a relaxing breath as the slight ocean breeze whispered sweet nothings across her backside. Livia smiled into her towel and congratulated herself for having the guts to go through with this. She'd always shied away from anything new or remotely scandalous. Little about her or her life reeked of true adventure or spontaneity. Thinking about it, Livia realized that only thrice had she voluntarily taken major, life-altering chances—marrying, and then filing for divorce, and starting Havin' Your Cake. She was surprised how liberating this relatively minor show of boldness made her feel. The girls had been right; taking a few daring risks here and there did make Livia feel more vibrant and alive. She had to wonder, if four minutes of public nudity could make her feel this way, what was the rest of the week going to bring?

Lena's suggestion to come to St. Bart's had been spot on. It was everything she'd described and more. At that moment, Livia wished Aleesa and Lena were there with her. It would have been nice if they'd made a girl's trip out of this, adding more shared memories to their sisterfriend journey together. But she understood their point. Some things one really needed to do on one's own, and if Lena and Aleesa had accompanied her, even this simple trip to the beach would have taken on an entirely different vibe. With familiar eyes watching and assuming, Livia didn't know how free she'd feel about doing just about anything—from wearing her new wardrobe to satisfying the deep-rooted wanderlust that seemed to be bubbling to the surface. They were right to realize that she needed some alone time to reflect and reinvent herself for this next chapter of her life.

Livia would be fifty in less than four months and as Jasi so succinctly paraphrased, "if not now, then fucking when?" Yes, Quincy and the fuck-it list might have brought her to this place, but her newly unearthed desire to find herself was keeping her here.

The sun was bearing down on her behind, but Livia wasn't quite comfortable with the idea of being sunny side up. Lying out on her back would leave her feeling open and vulnerable, two things, truth be told, she'd spent most of her days consciously avoiding. Liv had to giggle. Here she was hiding her perfect new bosom while exposing her raggedy old behind. She sighed—a typical move in Livi World.

Feeling ever so emboldened, Livia decided to flip over and change vistas. Immediately she received a valuable lesson about missing things in life by operating out of fear. Yes, she was sitting totally exposed, but the beauty of what lay ahead of her was absolutely breathtaking. Before her was a huge and spectacular cove, unmarred by hotels and villas. The beach was sandwiched between green bluffs that sloped gracefully into the calm, pool-blue waters. Out in the distance, she could see dots of white as sailboats made their way across the horizon. The sky, with its various shades of blue, tinged with white clouds, mimicked the beauty of the sea and the wavelets below. The instruction was not lost on Livia. Paradise was stretched out before her, and had she not been bold enough to open up and expose herself (pardon the pun), she'd have spent the day staring at sand.

Livi sighed into the sea air as she thought about her relationship with courageousness. While she could pat herself on the back for having the guts to battle cancer into remission, when it came to the little things, like being brave enough to face her emotional and sexual boogeyman so she could move on to a full and emotionally expressed life, she choked. Everyone else around her seemed to be capable of finding their truth and living it. Why was it so difficult for her?

"Well, not everyone," she addressed the gulls walking the sands.

Livia's mind went back to her "conversation" with Jasi before leaving for St. Bart's. In actuality, it was an ambush, with Jasi showing up at the bakery and trying to force a discussion—one she wasn't ready to have—about what had happened. But Jasi, being Jasi, couldn't, or wouldn't, accept her decision not to talk and had continued blurting out her mind's thoughts, even after Livia had slammed her office door in her face.

In hindsight, Livia felt badly about treating her friend with such angry disregard. It wasn't that Livia thought their relationship to be over, or that she didn't want to speak to Jasi ever again, just not until she'd sorted out her own anger and feelings about the subject. But Jasi's bullheaded insistence only made things worse. Now there were even more lies to overcome, in addition to Livia's irritation over Jasi putting her in stranger danger by arranging that sordid hook up with the bartender.

She couldn't believe that Jasi had pulled the same, "it's not what it looks like" move that most men try to put over on their suspicious women. Livia might be a bit naïve and inexperienced when it came to carnal adventures, but she wasn't stupid. If this had been, as Jas declared, a one-time attempt to satisfy a curiosity, wouldn't the other girl, the expert, be going down on her, the novice, and not the other way around?

All of Jasi's blustering about taking control of Livia's own desires was a bunch of bull. She had lied, both directly, and by omission, to all of them. For all of Jasi's "I do it my way" convictions, she was as scared and insecure as the rest of them, but at least Lena, Alyssa and Livia put their fears on the table. Jasi hid hers away behind a veneer of over-the-top bravado.

"Let it go; let it go," Livia commanded herself, willing away her friendship troubles. She expelled a deep breath and closed her eyes, settling into the lounger. She was here to revel in her rebirth, not worry about Jasi's problems.

The soft roar of the waves hitting the shore was so relaxing it was easy to clear her brain. Lulled into a state of total relaxation, Livia closed her eyes, ready for a yummy nap, as the soft caress of the ocean breeze blew over her. She sat still, smelling the salty sea air while allowing herself to feel the sexy mix of heat and cool caressing her naked skin. Suddenly, every nerve in her body was on high alert, turning her relaxed state into one of delicious agitation. She recognized the feeling. It was the same sensation she'd had sitting in the hallway of Naomi Maddox's home, and stepping into the manager's office at Jessebelle's. A montage of bodies, lips and tongues from her day at Jessebelle's flew into her head and settled on the serious almost sexing that had gone on between her and the Fox. That quick taste of male "hands on" attention had stirred up her appetite and been a source of craving ever since.

Livia felt the need to move, do something to break the surge of sexual energy that was suddenly overtaking her body and making her feel both uncomfortable and insatiable. Trying to snap the tension, she bent her knees to her chest, which only made matters worse. Like a lover's tongue, the gentle wind snuck between the slight space between her legs and lightly licked her newly trimmed cooch. Immediately, Livi tried to shut down the pleasurable sensation by straightening her legs.

DON'T! Quincy screamed.

Livia took a quick look around. She was still alone on her tiny stretch of sand. Why the hell not, she decided. She was here to stretch her wings and step outside of her sexual self. Might as well start right here and right now with a little natural masturbation.

Gingerly, she drew her knees back toward her chest and cracked her legs. Once again, Livia felt the air creep between her lower lips as her eyes surveyed the scene. Relieved to see that she was still all alone, she spread them wider, welcoming the wind's kiss. For a woman who didn't like to feel exposed, Livia felt deliciously vulnerable, splayed wide open, as elements seduced her tender, naked skin. She could feel her pussy tingle and her clit jump as her nipples hardened in response.

Livi's brain released a moan, but her mouth refused to give it voice. She gently lifted her butt off the chair and squeezed, pushing more blood into her clit. Both it and her breasts were screaming for attention. With her bottom lip tucked between her teeth, Livia covertly gave each of her nipples a quick tweak, causing her jealous pussy to rise higher in protest. Her actions felt sexy and slutty and fabulous as hell! Livi was definitely aroused, and had to force her hands to stay still and away from a begging Quincy.

She closed her eyes and let her mind drift off into fantasy land. It took her back to Jessebelle's and replaced Mother Nature's kiss with Mr. Fox's. She could feel his hot mouth on hers while his hands worked her clit, rubbing and teasing it into stiffness. Her imagination took their dalliance to the next level, causing her hips to once again push away from the lounger, shoving her pelvis into his, and forcing his imagined cock deeper into her snatch.

Livia's defiant hands refused to remain still. She reached into the middle of her sexual grotto and dipped into the pleasure puddle that had formed. She smeared her clit and discretely began to rub, feeling it grow tall and stiff. Both her left eye and tiny dick began to twitch with the anticipation of approaching orgasm. The pleasure was so intense that Liv bit down on her bottom lip to silence the groans, as she rubbed and tickled her nib to the point of no return.

Her massive orgasm felt like a swarm of fireflies flitting across Livia's nether regions. It was the biggest one yet, and was powerfully sweet, though ultimately unsatisfying. Between the cake delivery incident, toy shopping, Mr. Fox, and planning for this sexcation, fucking was constantly on Liv's mind. And it was true what they said, the more you think about sex, the more you want it. Orgasm or not, she was still feeling hot and horny and totally unsatisfied. Livi wanted more relief than she could get from playing with toys or a quickie hand job. Livia was tired of fantasizing and masturbating. Quincy needed some serious, prolonged penetration, and for once, Livia was in total agreement.

"Damn, I really want to get laid," Livia revealed to the birds, as she clenched her ass. Her scandalous behavior out here on the beach, coupled with the knowledge that her willingness and apparent ability to climax using her mind and wind as stimulants, was a huge turn on.

Livia closed her eyes, took a deep breath, and counted to ten before exhaling. It was a sad attempt to calm the demands of Quincy's dissatisfaction. She'd been on St. Bart's for three days, with nothing to show for it but a few tan lines and some pricey souvenirs she'd picked up while sightseeing in Gustavia, the island's capital city. She only had four more days on the island, and today

was the first day she'd accomplished anything on her list. Nothing
and no one thus far had piqued her interest enough to allow her
to make any progress. Livia plucked the crinkled list from her bag,
happy to be able to at least cross today's adventure—though yet
another that had nothing to do with intercourse—from her list.

Fuck It List

1. Buy and play with toys.

2. Vacation at a nude beach and go skinny-dipping.

3. Make love on a boat

4. Get a sexy tattoo

5. Sex with Kiss a woman

5. TBD act of outrageous sex

Masturbate in ear shot of a perfect stranger getting off

6. Have a one night stand with a stranger

7. Have sex in a public place

8. Have *9½ Weeks* sexy food play

9. Find and fuck Bobby Jeffries

10. Buy a yellow chair.

With mixed satisfaction, Livia drew a line through number two
on the list. She'd only half-fulfilled the requirements, but with the
sun bearing down on her, she planned to take her skinny dip in a
few. As for the rest of the list, she couldn't go home without making
a concerted effort to achieve at least one sexual escapade. She was
here in beautiful St. Bart's, an island full of sun, surf and sailboats.
It only made sense to concentrate her effort on number six, making
love to someone by the sea. Livia lifted her eyes from the paper and
looked out into the ocean. She immediately focused on the white
sails of a boat bobbing on the Caribbean Sea. She smiled at the
thought of being out there, naked and spread eagle on deck, while
the tantalizing Old Spice man seduced the fragrance from between
her thighs as they rocked the boat doing the nasty on the high seas.

The combination of solar and sexual heat hit Livi with a hot flash of epic proportions. She dropped her list into her beach bag and quickly head down the beach. The sounds of approaching voices sent her legs into a trot into the cool blue water. Livia couldn't believe how wonderful the warm water felt on her naked skin. The combination of sea and sun was invigorating. She felt freer than she had in years and suddenly Livia found herself laughing and frolicking in the ocean like a three-year-old.

Livi dove into the water and emerged belly up, floating on her back. Enjoying the seductive feel of oil, water and wind on her naked skin, she closed her eyes and allowed the sun to kiss her face.

This must be what heaven feels like. At this moment, whether her list got completed or not, Livia was so very happy she'd listened to her friends and taken this trip. After so many hardworking years of building her business, and then cancer, this down time was a welcome, and much needed respite. Right then and there, Livia decided to start a new list: Things I Need to Do on a More Regular Basis. 1) take more vacations…

And have more sex, her vagina threw in.

And maybe fall in love again, countered Livia's heart.

Feeling cool and surprisingly collected, Liv was ready to move back on shore and let the ever present breeze blow her dry. She started forward, but nearby voices, a mix of masculine chuckles and feminine giggles, kept her shoulder deep in the surf. Livi took a quick spin around to see that her formerly uninhabited stretch of beach was undergoing a population boom. The rental guy was busy setting out chaises and picking up stray garbage as a group of Lookie Lou's, four bathing suit-clad black men and two blonde women, settled into their chairs. The practical Livia wanted to bolt to her own lounge and protect her orphaned valuables, but modesty kept her grounded. The always playful Quincy, however, saw a parade in her immediate future.

Livia knew exactly what Quincy would do, and unless she was going to hide in the water all day, she had no choice but to indulge her willful vagina. Besides, she was here for a purpose and it was time to get to work.

Funny how the ones with the good bodies are the most afraid to go nude, Livia thought. Feeling surprisingly confident, and slightly smug, Livia imagined herself to be a gorgeous mermaid, and emerged from the sea, stretched to her full five feet, ten inches. She began her leisurely stroll toward the beach when she caught movement from the corner of her eye and turned to see that she had definitely been noticed.

"Omigod, I think I've just been ogled," Liv informed the airborne gulls from the corner of her mouth. On the surface, Livia felt calm satisfaction spread through her. The same delight in being decadent she'd felt at Jessebelle's had resurfaced. Livia realized that she actually liked the idea of men thinking of her as hot and sexual. Good thing too, because that's exactly how she felt.

Her left foot was about to leave the water and touch dry sand when Livia released a blood-curdling scream. An intense stinging in her ankle caused her to drop to the sand, writhing in pain. Immediately, two of the men left their chaises and came rushing over.

"Are you okay? What happened?" the shorter, rounder gentleman inquired.

Livi was unable to answer, as a mix of tears and intensifying hurt rendered her mute. The fact that she was butt-naked didn't help matters either.

"It looks like she got stung or something," the taller, better-looking man calmly suggested. "Probably a jellyfish."

Both he and Livia managed to ignore her nakedness as he scooped her up in his arms and carried her over to her lounger. He laid her down and gallantly pulled her sarong out of her bag.

His action caused much of the contents to spill out, but Liv was too grateful for his thoughtfulness to care. While he quickly caught up with the windswept papers from her bag, she put all her attention on wrapping the tropical print around her naked body, happily stunting one source of her agonizing pain.

"It doesn't look too bad," he said, after retrieving and replacing the things in her purse. He took a moment to inspect the raised red welts forming on the side of the sting, which made her ankle look like it had been hit with a whip. He began picking away the gossamer strings wrapped around her leg. "Are you okay? No shortness of breath? Your throat isn't tightening up, is it?" he asked, checking to make sure she wasn't in danger of having an anaphylactic reaction.

"No, it just hurts."

"Okay; that's a good sign. No severe allergy. So, I don't suppose you happen to have any vinegar in your beach bag?" he asked, causing a slight smile to appear on both their faces. Livia silently shook her head, gritting her teeth, trying to keep both her embarrassment and agony in check.

"Kenny, fill something up with salt water, and ask one of the others to go get the rental guy. See if he has any after-sting ointment up there."

"Ahh," Livia cried out, her face and body wincing in pain.

"Not that I'm trying to see what you're carrying around in your handbag, but if you have any Tylenol or Motrin, you might want to pop a couple to manage the stinging. Even though this is a pretty small one, these bites can be pretty nasty."

"They're in my cosmetic pouch," Livia informed him with implied permission to retrieve them for her. He was already unzipping the little black bag when Livia remembered the condoms and lipstick vibrator she'd stashed inside.

Great! He meets me on a nude beach and now this. He must think he's hit the whores-a-plenty jackpot!

As he pushed aside the Trojans to get to the Tylenol, her vacationer slash paramedic tried to hide an amused smirk behind a concerned smile, while Livia buried her humiliation under a real cry of pain.

"Here you go," he said, handing her four pills and her bottle of water.

"Are you a doctor?" Livia asked after swallowing the pills. Embarrassed or not, she was impressed by his knowledge and cool under pressure demeanor.

"No, actually I'm a slave to Wall Street. Mitchell. Nice to meet you."

"You too." Livia paused, trying to decide whether to tell him her real name or go with her diva alter ego. "I'm Quincy," her vajayjay blurted out, deciding for her.

"Here you go," Mitchell's friend, Ken, said, returning with a small beverage cooler full of sea water.

"You'll want to soak your ankle in the sea water for about half an hour," Mitchell informed her. "That will keep the venom from releasing."

"Thank you," Livia said, speaking to both of the men.

"Well, dog, it looks like you've got this," Ken said, sharing a smirk and an ocular fist bump with his boy. "Quincy, nice meeting you. Hope you feel better soon."

"Thanks again," Livia told him before turning her attention back to Mitchell. "So, how do you know so much about caring for jellyfish stings?"

"Experience. They're a recreational hazard. I'm the anecdote to the myth that black people don't swim. I love the sea and all seaworthy activities—fishing, snorkeling, jet skiing."

The happy bells went off in Livi's head. His list of playtime preferences definitely piqued her interest. While he shoved the things back into her beach bag, Livia shamelessly scoped him out, noticing that this attractive, good Samaritan was in great shape. His walnut brown face was an alluring blend of worldly experience and boyish charm. His arms and legs were long and toned. His swimming trunk-clad ass, tight. From her current angle, she couldn't see his package but could only assume that it was proportionate to his height (tall) and weight (good).

Not a day over thirty-five, Livi decided as she watched him glance down at his hands and then around, catching Livia's surprised gaze. He smiled broadly and gave her a curious, knowing nod.

"So, is there someone here on the island I should call to come get you?" Mitchell asked, fishing for information.

"Ah…no."

"So, Quincy, you're down here by yourself for a little R & R?"

And S & M and T & A, her smart-aleck hot box chimed in.

"Uh…yes, until Sunday. And yourself?"

"I came down for my boy's pre-wedding festivities."

"What? A week long, out of sight, out of mind, bachelor's party?" Livia joked.

"Something like that," Mitchell admitted with a cute, "ya got me" smile. "I'm leaving next Monday. So, I was thinking that we give you a couple of days to recuperate and then maybe do a little sightseeing together."

The fortuitous arrival of the beach attendant and his first aid kit allowed Livia to delay her response. It appeared that in the quirkiest way possible, the universe had teed up this handsome stranger as a possible vacation playmate. He was good-looking, obviously kind and had a sexy swagger that was hard to ignore. All in all, he looked like the perfect candidate to help Livi further her very personal mission.

"I cleaned it up as best I could, though your friend here did all the right things," the beach attendant told her as he finished treating her sting. "I'd check in with the hotel doctor when you get back."

"Thank you so much," Livia said, grateful that the pills had kicked in, taking the edge off the pain. "Would you please call me a cab?"

"So what do you say, sightseeing on Friday?" Mitchell asked, reissuing his social request with a hard-to-ignore smile.

"What about your friends?"

"They'll understand."

"How about we have dinner together on Friday and see how it goes?" Livia said, buying both her injury and her indecision a little more time.

"I'll call you then. Where are you staying?"

"I'm at the…" Livia stopped in mid-sentence when she realized that Mitchell would not find Quincy registered at the Christopher. "Why don't I call you?" she suggested.

"Not a problem," he replied, misinterpreting her secretiveness for security, and in fact, deciding to follow her lead. The woman was gorgeous and based on the contents of her purse, seemed quite interesting, but there were plenty of beautiful crazies in the world.

"I'll tell you what, there is a small hotel in Pointe Milou called the Christopher," Mitchell said. "It's about fifteen minutes from here. Why don't we arrange right now to meet on Friday at five-thirty."

"For dinner? Isn't that a bit early?"

"Not if you want to see the sunset, which I promise you, you do."

Livia tried to keep a straight face as her brain raced. She didn't want to tell him that she'd spent the past few evenings watching the sun go down in the very spot he was speaking of. More important than that were her questions. Did he know she was staying there or was this another coincidence, a sign from the universe that she and Mitchell were in the right place at the right time for a racy reason? "Okay, I'll find it," she told him.

"And I'll find you."

"You're very sure of yourself, Mitchell," Livia said, giving him a small grin of her own.

"Only when I see something I want. It's a nasty habit I picked up from childhood."

Livia smiled, happy to have someone flirting with her after so long. "My cab's here," she said, acknowledging the gesturing attendant. "Thanks again, Mitchell."

Livia picked up all of her belongings and stood up to head for the taxi. Putting weight on her ankle sent a searing pain shooting up her leg and radiating through her body. Without a word, Mitchell gathered Livi up again into his arms, and carried her across the sand. Not quite sure what to do with her arms, Livia wrapped them loosely around his neck, lightly resting them on his sturdy, muscular shoulders. This time, Livi was uncomfortably aware that the only thing between her naked, and his half-naked body was a thin cotton sarong. It confused her that before he'd shown up, she was feeling risqué and ready to find a stranger and fuck him. But now, face-to-face with a real possibility, her shy old ways were reemerging.

Dagnabit! Livia thought as Mitchell helped her into the cab, *Love may be complicated, but damn if lust isn't just as confusing.*

Guess Who's Coming at Dinner?

Friday, promptly at 5:15, Livia left her suite and headed down to the lobby of the Christopher Hotel. Nestled into Pointe Milou, on the quiet northeast side of St. Bart's, it was an intimate and sensual hideaway, a perfect spot for whatever this vacation brought. Surrounded by both luxurious, fragrant gardens and the romantic lull of the nearby surf, it was hard not to be seduced into wanting to experience pleasure in this paradise.

Did Mitchell know this, too? Is that why he'd picked this as their rendezvous spot?

She wandered into the gift store, which provided a perfect view of the lobby comings and goings. She was to meet Mitchell at five-thirty, but didn't want to risk getting caught coming down from her room. Besides, this spot gave her the perfect opportunity to catch a first glance and, if necessary, adjust her assessment of the man, who on the Saline Beach had become her hero. But between the sun, stinging pain, and embarrassing nudity, Livia didn't quite trust her judgment. What if he was nothing like she remembered?

Livia passed a tanned gentleman of European decent, who stopped in his tracks to shower her with an appreciative smile.

"De toute beauté."

Livia wasn't quite sure, but it sounded like he'd called her beautiful in French. His compliment made her decision to wear the slinky orange sundress that highlighted her strengths and camouflaged her weaknesses, the right choice. She was especially happy she'd put on the stiletto sandals Aleesa had forced her to buy and bring. Always tall, Livi never understood the need for wearing heels. At this moment, she totally recognized their appeal. The sex was in the heel.

"Go Livi; go Livi," she sang under her breath, enjoying the fact that another man in the shop was checking her out as she inspected the swimsuits near the front window. She had to admit that she was really enjoying this mini whirl of attention.

Ten minutes later, Livia's initial assessment was solidified and bolstered when a cool breeze came through the lobby doors in the person of Mitchell the Marvelous. He was dressed in well-fitting tan slacks and a collarless, white linen shirt. His gorgeous eyes were hidden by the golden lenses of aviator sunglasses, but his smile, framed by succulent lips bearing just the slightest sheen of ChapStick, was on public display.

Livi watched with admiring eyes as he strode further into the lobby looking for her. A metallic flash of gold glinted from his wrist as he lifted his arm to remove his sunglasses. Mitchell was the epitome of superman, supermodel, masculine chic.

Her vagina tweeted in agreement.

"Game on, Quincy. Game on," Livia murmured to herself as she stepped out of the gift shop and into the lobby so he could see her. In the wash of the lobby's white décor, her pumpkin-colored halter sundress was an immediate beacon.

Livia watched with silent thrill as Mitchell stopped a couch length away, and let his eyes take her in. He'd obviously left his emotion filter with his boys, as his expressions translated every positive thought racing through his head. Mitchell started at the top of her sexy mass of unruly golden curls, loving the way they blended so well with her honey-tanned face. She saw his eyes pause at the round tops of her spectacular breasts while his lips puckered slightly, allowing a nearly undetectable exhale of excited breath.

Moments later, they were on the move again, taking in the nip of her waist, the flair of her hips and the length and curves of her toned and tanned legs. Approval was etched all over his face.

In Mitchell's mind, he'd hit the cougar jackpot! Guessing her to be about six to eight years older than him, Quincy, on the surface, looked like a beautiful, classy woman. While her appearance definitely did not read conservative, neither did it reek of wild woman. But it was obvious that there was a rip tide bubbling under her cool and sophisticated exterior. Any woman who would vacation and visit a nude beach alone, sporting a purse full of condoms, no less, was looking for the kind of action he was ready and able to provide. Not to mention that crazy-ass sexual wish list of hers that had fallen out of her bag. He hadn't intended to invade her privacy, but when a document entitled, Fuck-It List, belonging to a fine and naked sister, falls open, any red-blooded man with a working dick is going to check it out. He'd only gotten a quick glance, but it was enough to confirm that Quincy was obviously a freak on the make. You had to love that in a woman.

"Quincy, you look beautiful."

"Thank you. You look great yourself."

"How's your ankle?" Mitchell asked, taking the opportunity to look down and admire her legs once again. The vision of those long legs and stiletto-clad feet wrapped around his waist caused him to shift his weight.

"It's okay. The Tylenol is managing the pain and the hotel doctor gave me something for the itching, so it's all good."

"Glad to hear that. I hope you don't mind eating here at the hotel. They do have a great restaurant, but I also figured after traveling here, you might want to stay put."

"That was very thoughtful of you," Livia said, smiling. It was clear to her that he didn't know she was a guest.

Mitchell took her arm and led her outside to the Mango Bar. They were greeted by the hostess, who took them to a small table for two on the far tip of the bar area. It was the perfect spot for a couple of lovers, or a couple contemplating becoming lovers, to watch the sun go down on their inhibitions and welcome the moon's silver lust.

"This is really quite incredible," Livia said, looking out on the sea as Mitchell helped her into her chair. "How did you find this place?"

"We thought about staying here, but decided to rent a villa instead," he confessed.

"Probably for the best. You know, boys will be boys and all," Livi teased.

"Okay, you can lose the visions of *The Hangover*," Mitchell replied, referencing the now classic bachelor party movie. "Nobody's trying to trash hotel suites or kidnap a tiger."

"Ah, I see, you and your friends are a party of gentlemen."

"Your usual, Ms. Charles?" the waiter interrupted their conversation to ask.

BUSTED! Livia thought, grateful that the server didn't know her first name.

"Yes, please," she said, avoiding Mitchell's eye as the waiter wrote down her green teani and Mitchell's rum on the rocks order.

"Your usual?" he said, both confused and amused.

"I have to confess. I'm a guest here," Livia said. "I mean, we were strangers…and I wasn't sure it was a good idea you knowing where I was staying." Livia felt a self-conscious blush heat her face and accompany her laugh. "You know, you are the first man who's literally picked me up on the beach."

"Sounds like the *naked* truth," Mitchell said with a flirtatious lift to his lips. "But this revelation begs the question: what other secrets are you keeping from me?"

"Well, I'm probably older than you think," Livia revealed, wanting to address that whale in the fish tank. It was such an obvious fact, but one she felt needed tackling before the night moved forward. "And if you don't mind me asking, just how old are you?"

"I don't really care how old you are. I'm hoping you feel the same way, but to answer your question, I am thirty-three."

Sixteen years! Livia's shocked mind did the math. It wasn't that she was really surprised; she'd guessed as much, but still hearing it confirmed—sixteen years! What was it about her and younger men? She'd taken herself out of the disastrous online dating pool for the very reason that the only men who contacted her were either grandpa or grandson, and she had little in common with either. What was she doing wrong that she could not for the life of her attract age appropriate men?

Well, we're not trying to date this honey. We're trying to fuck him! Quincy reminded her.

"What?" Mitchell asked, confused by the look on her face.

"Let's just say, I was throwing my sweet sixteen party the year you were born."

"So 1979 was a very good year for many reasons," Mitchell said, not buying into her passive aggressive argument about their age difference. "I meant it when I said you are beautiful. Trust me, your face, that body, you put the young girls to shame, Ms. Charles, is it?"

Trust me. His words hit her ears at the same time her own left her lips. "Yes, but just then you sounded like you were talking to your biology teacher. Quincy is fine," Livia said, feeling more and more at home with her alter ego.

"Quincy Charles. It fits you," Mitchell said, letting his fingers tiptoe closer to a spring of curls near her chin. "Very hot and happening."

"Thank you." Livia had to smile, not only because even though

Quincy was no more real than the bling in her ear, she was enjoying sporting Q's attitude.

The arrival of their cocktails, accompanied by the dip of light in the sky, made for a natural pause in the conversation. Within a few awesome minutes, the blue sky over St. Bart's turned fire red with streaks of pink and a burst of orange dropping below the horizon.

"A toast," Mitchell offered, raising his glass. "To jellyfish."

"Jellyfish? Really?"

"Absolutely. First of all, that jellyfish obviously knew fine and delicious when he saw it, and if not for him finding that sexy ankle of yours irresistible, I would not be sitting here right now enjoying the sunset and trying my damndest not to get caught up in the romance of it all, and lean over and kiss you."

Livia was both taken aback and intrigued by Mitchell's very direct flirting style. It teetered on the line between polite and presumptuous. It made her feel desired and delightfully off balance.

"So, what idiot let you come here to this gorgeous paradise alone?" Mitchell asked, careful not to reveal what he'd already seen on the beach.

"I wanted to regroup. Sometimes when you travel with someone else it becomes a trip, instead of a vacation, if you know what I mean."

"For sure, trying to synchronize schedules and interests and incomes, it can get to be a bit much."

"Exactly, so I decided to treat myself to a real vacation. No worries, no one else's timeline but my own."

"What do you do back in the States?" he asked, curious but really more interested in establishing a comfortable vibe between them.

"I'm um…I'm a chef."

"Oh, a foodie. You apparently don't eat much of what you cook," he said, with an admiring glance. "Do you work in a restaurant?"

"No. I'm more on the catering side." Livia really didn't want to be any more specific about her personal information or the miracle of fashionable camouflage. "What's your favorite dessert?" she asked, turning the questions back on him.

"Peaches and cream," he answered, looking her straight in the eyes before taking a swig of his rum and Coke.

Livia lowered her eyes to avoid broadcasting her emotions. Okay, perhaps she should be insulted by his bold, and some might think, nasty insinuation, but she wasn't. This sexy stranger was getting to her, but she wasn't quite sure if she was ready for him to know how much.

Flirt back, Quincy demanded. *DO NOT pussy out on me this time.* Clearly, her vagina wasn't about to stand for Livia letting this yummy dick get away.

"Peaches and cream—a simple but tasty treat," Livia replied, with a Quincy wink in her voice.

"Yes, and it's amazing how every recipe is different."

"That's because every chef has her own secret ingredient," Livia said, giving him a sideways glance.

Mitchell's response was a deep exhale and seat adjustment. Clearly, she had upped the ante and Livia could tell that he was enjoying every moment. She bit her lower lip as she contemplated her own feelings. Maybe this wasn't what she was used to, but wasn't that why she was here? Not to be courted or charmed, at least not this time. Liv was here to be open and sexually spontaneous, and Mr. Opportunity was staring her in the face, and knocking at her coochie's door.

"Don't do that," Mitchell said, his request wrapped in an enticing whine.

"Do what?" Livia asked, confused but curious.

"Bite your lip like that. I find it sexy and damn near irresistible. You have beautiful lips. Very kissable lips."

Livia smiled into her glass while looking at him over the rim. "Thank you," she said, after taking a nerve-quenching sip from her drink. *And so, hot damn, do you!*

The two sat in companionable silence, enjoying their cocktails and the twinkling night sky as they each deliberated their next move. Mitchell was reluctant to push much harder, afraid of going too far and putting a damper on Livia's smoldering interest. He'd made his desires known. It was time to sit back and let her make the next move.

"Mitchell, did I thank you for rescuing me on the beach?" Livia asked, making a decision and putting the rest of the evening in motion.

"Yes, between the oohs and ouches, I believe you did."

"But you deserve more," Livi said, before leaning in and surprising him with a quick touch of her lips. "Remind me to properly thank you when I get back from the ladies' room."

An intrigued Mitchell stood and pulled out Livia's chair. As she turned to exit, her body brushed up against his. "I can't wait that long."

Livia felt her entire body tingle as he moved in and kissed her. The moment their lips met, Livia's ego kicked into overdrive. She may have had only one lover in her life, but she was a gold medal kisser. She immediately took control, determined to lead with her strengths and give Marvelous Mitchell a taste of her own brand of sweetness.

Head-to-head, with only a breath separating them, Livia slipped her hand between their faces and lightly explored the soft cushiness of his lips, first the top and then the bottom, with her fingertip. This simple action briefly prolonged the inevitable, allowing him to experience the delicious, split-second thrill of anticipation. In one smooth motion, she lifted her other arm and placed it behind his neck, applying gentle pressure as she tilted his lips to hers. Livia momentarily touched her mouth to his before allowing the tip of her tongue to penetrate and circle the edges of his lips. Mitchell released a throaty moan as Livi retracted her tongue and gave his lips a warm, sensuous stroke.

Slowly, she began to disengage but was stopped by the force of Mitchell's full-on kiss. His body pressed against hers as he slid his tongue between her lips and lingered as if asking for permission. Receiving no resistance, he searched her mouth until their tongues collided and began a frenetic dance.

The sound of a disapproving throat being cleared broke the spell and separated the couple. Livia giggled, a nervous response to both her usual embarrassment and uncommon audacity.

"That was quite a check you just wrote," Mitchell said with a new huskiness to his voice.

"When I get back, I'll let you know if you can deposit it," she replied, proud of her flirty, return quip.

Livia smiled broadly as she walked away. She could feel Mitchell's eyes on her moving tail as she floated toward the bathroom. Omigod! He was such a turn-on in every way frickin' way possible. As he'd shown on the beach, Mitchell could be a chivalrous white knight, ready and able to come to the rescue of any damsel in distress. And as he was steadily proving tonight, he was also a thoroughly desirable boy toy. Age be damned, Mitchell was turning out to be the perfect combination for a no-strings, vacation lover.

In the bathroom, Livia readjusted her curls as she gazed at

herself in the mirror. She bit her lip and smiled, trying to determine what about that move seemed to thrill Mitchell so. And then she saw. It was a tempting mix of innocence and allure. The perfect "good girl gone naughty" smirk. Liv stayed a few more minutes and practiced her new signature grin, building muscle memory in her mouth for future reference.

One more coat of lip gloss and Livia was ready to go see what the evening, and Mitchell, would bring. She headed toward the door, turned the handle, only to find him waiting on the other side.

"Mind if I join you?" he asked, with an "I dare you to say no" fire in his eyes.

Livi gave him one of her practiced smiles in response, while mentally checking numbers five (one night stand with a stranger) and six (sex in a public place) off her list.

"Lock the door," she said, not wanting to repeat Jasi's error in judgment.

Not another word was exchanged between them, as their mouths were too full of each other for conversation. Mitchell decided it was his turn to prove himself as the ultimate cougar master. His lips pressed against Livia's softly at first and then slipped down to pull her lower lip between his. He sucked her lip like he it was her clit before sticking his tongue in her mouth and giving her a preview of his hopes to come. His tongue jetted in, out, and all around, varying in speed and rhythm, and driving Livia into blissful madness. If he could do with his dick what he was doing with his tongue, Quincy was going to be a very happy vajayjay.

The sexy Buddha Bar lounge tunes piped into the restroom faded away as Mitchell's mouth burned into Livia. This kiss held none of the polite pretense of their earlier kiss. This kiss was fueled by an overwhelming hunger in search of satiation. He began to dine on Liv's eyes, nose, cheeks and earlobes before once again devouring her mouth.

Livia's breath became short and labored as she instinctively pressed her body against his. She could feel the hardness on Mitchell's thigh and it excited her. A whimper of desire escaped her lips, giving him cause to push forward.

Mitchell's hand gave her breasts a grab and a squeeze before reaching up and pulling the orange tie around the back of her neck, releasing the bow and causing the front of Livia's halter to fall away. She stood frozen with anxiety as he stopped what he was doing to stare at her breasts. As she'd been with the Fox, Livia felt self-conscious about her bosom, waiting for Mitchell's reaction to her spectacular silicone breasts.

"You are beautiful, every bit of you," he murmured in admiration, proving once again, that when it came down to doing the do, tits were tits, real or fake.

Mitchell lowered his head so his hands and tongue could inspect them up close and personal. He latched on, bathing her nipples in warm saliva, while simultaneously drenching her panties. He continued his erotic tongue and hand massage. Mitch nibbled and kneaded with practiced expertise until Livia announced her escalating excitement with a primitive groan. Encouraged, he lingered, pushing her breasts together and rolling both nipples gently between his teeth until Livia signaled her need to go further by arching her back and pressing her groin against him.

His hand lifted her dress far enough for his fingers to latch on to the sides of Livi's panties and release them from her hips. He used his foot to push them to the floor and kicked them away. It was Mitchell's turn to moan as his fingers reached between her legs and dipped into the well of her desire. The scent of pink boomeranged around the room, exciting them both. He used her peaches and cream to lube up her nib and massage it into near orgasm.

"I need you inside me now," Quincy spoke through Livia's mouth.

"My pleasure, baby."

Now that's what I'm talkin' about. Finally a young stud with class, she giggled to herself.

Mitchell stopped hand fucking her long enough to pull a condom from his pocket and drop his pants to the floor. Livia watched with delight as he gloved his long, caramel-colored dick in latex. Taking him into her hands, she guided Mitchell into her salivating pussy. His hands grabbed her hips and he lifted her effortlessly off the ground. Livia leaned her back against the wall as she wrapped her long legs around his waist. As his thick rod penetrated her, Quincy and Livia's breaths combined, releasing a gush of air into the room.

Together they rocked vigorously, his hands on her ass, their lips locked in a "can't help the way that I feel" kiss between strangers. Mitch's hard dick pounded the walls of her grateful pussy, awakening every sexual nerve ending in her body. After weeks of steady clit-teasing, she was primed and ready, and came almost immediately. They both could feel the powerful contractions of her pussy grab his member. Livia held the screams wanting to escape in her throat as she let herself be still and enjoy the delightful sensations running through her body.

"Yeah, baby. Let that shit go," Mitchell encouraged her.

They were interrupted by a knock on the door. Livi felt her body jump as she broke out in nervous giggles. Mitchell immediately covered her mouth with his hand, smiling back at her as he continued pumping his dick into her.

"Be…right…out," he called out.

The knowledge that only a one-inch plank of wood was keeping her from becoming a public spectacle excited her. She could feel Quincy revving up again, pushing and pulling the blood to her clit, wanting to detonate again. She ground her pelvis into his, feeling the ridges on his head rub up against all of the nooks and crannies of her pumped-up pussy.

"I'm gonna cum, too, baby. Right now. I'm gonna cum, too."

With his hand still covering her mouth, Mitchell and Livi bucked up against each other, increasing the friction between them to the point of no return. Finally, his body shuddered, and Mitchell held Livia so tightly against him she could hardly breathe. As he withdrew, she let her legs slide to the floor, her heartbeat slowly returning to normal.

"Thank you," he said, discarding the rubber full of his spunk.

"I should be thanking you," Liv said, feeling the seeds of awkwardness begin to bloom. All this politeness felt odd, while at the same time sweet. Never once had her ex-husband expressed gratitude for experiencing an orgasm in her presence.

Knock. Knock. Knock, the rapid succession of knuckles on wood cut short their afterglow.

"Just another minute," Mitch called out while they both scurried to clean up.

Livia chuckled in response as she scooted across the floor to retrieve her panties. Suddenly feeling shy, she tried to ignore the Mitchell in the room as she tied her halter straps around her neck, and fluffed out her blonde halo of curls.

"They're standing outside. They're going to know," she said, turning to face this now familiar stranger and trying not to sound panicked.

"Probably, but who gives a fuck?" he said, giving her a big, conspiratorial smile.

"You're right. Who gives a fuck?" she repeated, thinking that Jasi would be so proud of her right now.

"Ready?" he asked, his face wearing an amused grin as he reached for the knob.

Livia nodded and took a nervous inhale. Mitch opened the door and without making any eye contact, she walked past the same woman who had caught them kissing.

"Get a room," the woman hissed as they walked by.

"And what fun would that be?" was Mitchell's cheeky response.

Livia remained silent as she continued walking. She was such a jumble of divergent emotions. Exhilaration and confusion rushed through her head at once. Within the secret confines of the bathroom, the thrill of doing the forbidden had left her feeling sexy and liberated. But now, steps away from the restroom door, Liv felt the heat of embarrassment and second guessing burning away her excitement.

What exactly was the proper etiquette when it came to boinking a stranger in a public bathroom? What did Mitchell think of her now? And should she even care? Now that they'd done the deed, and both had gotten from the other what they wanted, what would they talk about? Just like at Jessebelle's, once the moment ended, Livia was back to feeling uncertain and embarrassed about who she was and what she'd done.

Mitchell and Livia sat back at the table and both downed their drinks—much needed refreshment after such an energetic workout. Mitchell took her hand and interlaced his fingers with hers. Livia allowed herself to become reacquainted with the feel of holding hands with a man. It felt so good it scared her, causing her to slowly pull her hand away. It felt right but for all the wrong reasons.

The silence between them while easy, was also nerve-wracking.

Conversation was called for, but honestly, the less she knew about him and vice versa, the better. It was what it was—an intimate meeting between strangers, and that was all it was supposed to be.

"Mitchell, I think I'm going to take a rain check on dinner," Livia said, still feeling awkward about her wanton ways, and thrown by the post-coital handholding. Mitchell had fulfilled his mission as her give into the moment, one-night stand. It was time to say goodbye. "My ankle is kind of bothering me."

"Really?" he said, his disappointment broadcasting through his eyes. After such an exhilarating appetizer, Mitchell was ready for a full-course meal. "But I haven't even tasted your peaches and cream, and you haven't had the full-on experience of my pudding pop," he joked with a nearly straight face.

The absurdity of his description caused a cascade of nerve-melting laughter from Livia. "No grown, self-respecting man should ever utter the words, *pudding pop*, when referring to himself," she said between chuckles.

"You're right, and I usually wouldn't, but I'm just so upset. True, I don't know you well, but I would have never figured you for the screw 'em-and-run type, Ms. Quincy Charles. I'm hurt and feel terribly used," Mitchell told her, feigning anguish and dismay.

Livi smiled. His theatrics were amusing and effective. She could feel her resolve begin to wane. "I'm sorry. I certainly didn't mean to make you feel used."

"Well, you can make it up to me, by answering no to the following three questions."

"I can't wait to hear these," she said between giggles.

"Number one: do you have plans for tomorrow night?"

"Uh…no."

"Excellent. Number two: do you get seasick?"

"No," Livia replied, her interest piqued.

"Number three: You won't turn me down when I ask you to come with me to *The Contessa's* party tomorrow night, will you?"

"The Contessa?"

"It's a yacht."

"Just the two of us?"

"No. It's actually a big party sponsored by a well-known local, who also happens to be a friend of a friend. He's invited all of us onboard to party with his party."

"So this is one of the bachelor party events?"

"Yes."

"I know what kind of shenanigans go on during a bachelor party," she said with a crooked smile. "So, wouldn't having a date be like bringing sand to the beach?"

"Maybe I want to bring you as my personal shenanigan. Please don't say no, Quincy," he begged, his words and eyes coming together in a perfect storm of flirtation.

"I've never been anyone's personal shenanigan," Livia replied, letting Mitchell know by her tone that the position appealed to her. The man. The boat. The list. How could she not say yes?

Mitchell smiled broadly as he brought her hand to his lips and kissed it. "I'll pick you up at nine-thirty. Wear white."

"Okay, good night," she said, once again reclaiming her hand before the butterflies in her stomach caused her to change her mind.

"You're sure you don't want me to come up and tuck you in?" Mitchell asked.

"I'm sure. Besides, it's only eight-thirty. I'm not quite ready for bed."

"Hey, the floor, the balcony, the shower wherever you want me to *tuck you* is fine with me," he said, once again twirling her curls.

"Go join your boys."

"You're a mean lady, Ms. Charles," Mitchell teased as they both stood and walked arm-in-arm through the lobby and to the front door. Just as it had when he'd held her hand, the subtle intimacy between them, while it didn't feel forced, did strike her as odd. She and Mitchell, basic strangers, had just had sex in a public bathroom, and now they were strolling to the door like longtime lovers. Was this how Jasi and Lena and the rest acted after a "hit it and quit it" experience?

"Thank you again," Mitchell told Livia, pulling her close.

Their lips met in a "to be continued" kiss before Mitchell climbed in a cab and closed the door. He watched Livia turn and walk back into the hotel, admiring her regal bearing.

As the cab pulled away, Mitchell threw his head back with a laugh. Quincy had said yes, like he knew she would. There was definitely a very mutual and very physical attraction between them, and he was going to take full advantage. She wanted to make love on a boat and he was going to make that, and any number of other feel good things on that list, available for her. Quincy Charles had stumbled into his life, wanting to fly her freak flag. He was the man to make her dreams come true. If nothing else, Mitchell Maddox was always ready and able to serve.

Mitchell looked out the window, happily blessing his good luck, and wondering who he thought he was kidding. The truth was that they'd both stumbled into each other's lives. Quincy may be trying to find her inner freak, but Mitchell was in desperate need of restoring his swagger. Divorced less than six months, his cheating backstabber of a wife, Toris, had not only stripped him of most of his wealth, but nearly all of his damn ego. She'd left him gun-shy and homeless and wary of relationships in general. Here he was, a grown ass man, back at home with his damn parents. Celibate and jacking off to beat the band, simply because Toris had gotten into his head and convinced him that the only reason she'd strayed with their mutual friend was because he wasn't satisfying her in the sack. So, whether she realized it or not, Quincy was the perfect anecdote for his sagging ego. A beautiful, older woman, grateful for the attention, and ready to play with no eyes on the future. They had two days to use and amuse each other to the best of their abilities, before going home and getting on with the rest of their lives.

All Talk and A Little Lipstick Action

The sound of her room phone ringing broke through Livia's quiet snores, waking her. Opening her eyes forced Liv to leave the arms of her hunky dream lover and focus on the glowing green numbers on the clock next to her bedside. Three-seventeen a.m. Who in the world would be calling her at this time of the morning?

She reached out, her sleepy hand fumbling around in the dark until it located the phone. The receiver dragged clumsily across the nightstand and pillow until it reached Livia's one visible ear.

"Hello?" she managed to squeak out past the cobwebs in her throat.

"I can't get you off my mind."

At the recognition of Mitchell's deep and smoky voice, a chill ran down Livia's spine.

OMIGOD! Is this a booty call, she wondered, suddenly fully upright.

"How did you get this number?"

"I called the hotel operator and asked for Ms. Charles. They put me right through."

Close one! Quincy lives another day.

"I can't sleep because every time I close my eyes, I see us in the bathroom and I get hard. You know, women like you turn me on."

"Women like what?" Livia asked, hoping to learn exactly why Mitchell was ringing her in these wee hours.

"Bold, sensual, fun-loving women."

Livia felt her sleepy lips lift in proud surprise. NEVER had she, or any man, ever used those words to describe her, especially when it came to sex. It was clear that Quincy had already made quite an impact, not only on Mitchell, but on Liv as well.

"And how do you know that about me?" she asked, intrigued that he'd read her that way.

"You vacation alone with a purse full of condoms. You go solo on a nude beach, and when so moved, give into your desire with amazing gusto. I'd say your actions speak louder than any conversation, wouldn't you?"

"Uh, yes, I guess they do," Livia said, yawning to hide the embarrassment coloring the edges of her voice.

"Quincy, please don't be embarrassed. Not around me. There's no need. Like I said, you turn me."

Again, Livia smiled. All he said was true, and like a potent, double espresso, his acknowledgment instantly melted her anxiety and put her libido on alert.

"Thank you. And I certainly could say the same about you. Bold. Sexy. Fun-loving, and a true gentleman."

"Quincy."

"Yes."

"I really want to come over and finish what we started earlier tonight. Wouldn't you like that, baby? To feel me inside of you again?"

Those last five words, spoken in Mitchell's deep, buttery pillow talk voice, were both provocative and compelling. Fox had called her baby and she'd been offended. Mitchell said it and Livia could feel the walls of her pussy begin to sweat and her clit awaken. What was it about this man that made her ever ready to drop not only her Girl Scout ways but her panties as well?

YES! YES! YES! Quincy screamed.

"It's late," were the words that jumped out of Liv's mouth instead.

This is you first official booty call and you're trying to hang up?

"I know it's late, but my tongue is craving all of the places it would like to taste on your body," Mitchell's sexy voice revealed. "I will put it anywhere you want it to go."

FLIRT WITH HIM! Quincy demanded.

"Anywhere?" Livia asked, following both Q and Mitchell's leads.

"Yes, baby, anywhere. Deep in your hot, juicy pussy or around the rim of your pretty ass. I'll give those spectacular tits of yours a tongue bath and make your nipples stand up tall and hard until you scream for me to move on."

Oh shit. This man…his voice…those words. Mitchell was a total provocateur. A boy toy assassin whose combination of playful enthusiasm and manly desires was a lethal combination. He was steadily, albeit softly, killing all of Livia's residual inhibitions.

"Would you like that?"

"Yes," she breathlessly agreed and begged at the same time.

"Well, then tell me you want me to come over."

Livia paused to check her gut. Yes, she was horny for this man and so wanted to have a real sex session. Ever since she'd concocted that list and begun this libidinous journey, every bit of sexual satisfaction she'd experienced thus far had been either solo or a hurried, sit-down or stand-up affair. What Livia longed for at this time was hours of lazy and luxurious lovemaking. But things were moving so fast. Too fast for her comfort level. Yes, she was sorely tempted, but she also felt overwhelmed. Despite Quincy's throbbing insistence that they invite Mitchell over, Livia decided otherwise. She'd wait until this evening and see what pleasures it would bring.

"You're making it hard on me, but I have to say no," she said, softening her voice to let him down easy.

"Baby, you have no idea how hard you're making me."

"Oh, I know…" she said coyly, closing her eyes and letting herself get caught up in another carnal first—phone sex. Though a novice, she decided to delve right in and play the game by instinct. "…because I can see your dick—long and thick, and the color of toasted walnuts."

"Take off your panties," Mitchell told her, taking what he could get. "Will you do that for me?"

"Yes," Livia said, her voice dropping to a whisper. She loved the way he commanded and asked at the same time. She put the phone down on the pillow and slid off her panties and matching camisole, bought just in case Livia ended up sharing her bed. Technically, this hadn't been what she'd had in mind when she pictured herself wearing them, but in a happy revelation, having them on made her feel sexy even while by her lonesome.

"Are they off?"

"Everything is," she said, bringing the phone back to her ear.

"Thank you, baby. Just thinking about you lying there naked has me so fucking hard. I want to touch and taste all of you."

"Where first?" Livia asked, closing her eyes so her imagination could chart his course.

"I'm at your ear, running my tongue around the edges of your lobe before taking it into my mouth and giving it a little suck."

Livia could swear she felt his warm breath coming through the phone and fondling her ears and neck. "Mmmm."

"I'm glad you like that because now I'm going to run my tongue down your neck and shoulders until they find those fabulous nipples of yours. Lift them up to my lips."

Mitchell's voice was seductive and hypnotic and Livia felt herself slipping into a new and delicious version of fantasy land, complete with an audio tour guide. As requested, she lifted her breasts up to his mouth, while dropping her head down, allowing her tongue to become his, and find her own nip. Liv placed the receiver on the pillow, freeing up her hands and permitting her to act out Mitchell's words.

"What are you doing?"

What would Quincy say? Livia wondered.

I'd fucking tell him.

Yes, and proudly so, Livia decided.

"Tasting my titties," she said softly, excited by her bold move.

"You are a bit of a freak, aren't you, Quincy Charles?"

"It appears so," Livia said, feeling emboldened by his words and her actions.

"I'm jealous. I want to suck and play with your tits and feel your nipples get as hard as my dick is right now. Would you like that?"

"Yes. I would. But you know what I really want?" Liv said.

"Tell me, baby. I love a woman who says what she wants. When it comes to good fucking there's no time for guessing."

"I want you to stick your tongue between my tits and get me real wet. And then I want you to slide that magnificent dick you showed me earlier tonight in the bathroom, between them and titty fuck me."

The sound of her own mouth using such words and giving out nasty commands was thrilling. While waiting for his response, Livia bit her lip the way Mitchell liked while she tweaked her nipples and imagined his tongue running up and down between her breasts.

"Gladly, baby, but first I have to loosen my pants so I can breathe."

"No, take them off, drawers too, so I can feel you rubbing up against me. I want to feel that hard dick up against me," Livia responded.

"All for you, baby. I'm straddling you now. I'm kneeling over your chest. You like my dick hanging in your face, don't you, Quincy?"

"Yes, I do," Livi said, visualizing his tight brown body over hers. She could see his waiting and willing cock while in her mind she lifted her head to take in the tip.

"Then taste it. Suck on it a little bit and make me drip some pre-cum to lube you up."

Pre-cum? What the hell was that? Livia wondered. The only stuff she remembered dripping from Dale's penis all happened post intercourse. This was definitely something she'd have to learn about later, but right now whatever it was, it sounded hellishly sexy.

"Oh, yeah, I can feel your hot mouth covering the tip and sliding down my shaft," Mitchell said, his breath getting slower and his voice huskier. Livia could hear that he was getting just as turned on as she was, and his desire was fueling her bravado.

"Oh yeah, it's drippin' now. You got my dick drippin', Quincy. You sexy freak. Mmm, girl, now I'm rubbing it between your tits and it's getting all shiny and wet."

Livia could feel the aroma of pink rising from her sheets. This play-by-play bout of aural sex with Mitchell was keeping her in the moment, and she was consciously, and blissfully aware of every reaction her body was experiencing.

"I'm squeezing my tits together around your dick," Livia told him. "I can feel every ridge of your cock as you rub against them. Can you feel it?"

"Yeah, and it feels fucking great. I'm going to fuck your tits and then give you a nice, gooey pearl necklace when I'm done," Mitchell told her.

Gooey pearl necklace? What the hell? Was she really that sexually inexperienced and naïve? She didn't dare ask. After all, Mitchell thought Quincy was a freak. Why burst his bubble now?

"On second thought, I need to fuck you first. I can't spill my cum all around your neck before feeling that hot pussy again."

Thank you for giving me a clue, Livia thought as her hands traveled south to check out the condition of her feminine floodplain.

"Good, because my pussy is so wet right now."

"I know. I can smell that delicious peaches and cream of yours. I want to taste it. I want to lick your twat until you explode in my mouth."

"Then eat me," Livia said, boldly uttering words she'd never said before.

"How, baby? Tell me how to eat that delicious pussy of yours."

"Lick my clit. Soft and slow first, and then faster. And then suck on it so it gets long and hard in your mouth, like your dick gets in mine," she muttered as her hands got busy between her legs. A noise from the next room interrupted her groove and forced Livia's eyes open. She gazed around, seeing nothing, until her eyes settled on her pocketbook sitting on the desk.

Lipstick was exactly what she needed! She slipped out of bed, grabbed her purse and quickly returned to bed, pulling from her bag the cosmetic pouch that held the silver tube she was looking for. Seconds later, she was back on the phone, allowing Mitchell to wrap his horny words around her.

"…pussy tastes so…mmm…good. It's creaming up and ready for my dick. Can I put it in? Please, baby, let me put it….uh… don't you want this hard black rod inside you?"

"Yes, I want your dick inside me, but first rub the tip on my clit," she requested, acting out her words by pressing the faux lipstick to her nib. She could hear the low buzz of the vibrator as it forced her body to go limp in order to fully enjoy the vibrations zipping through her pelvis. In her mind, it was Mitchell's cock tenderizing her clitoris. "Mmmm...oh...mmm," she moaned as the toy worked its magic.

Livi squeezed her ass cheeks together tensing her lower body, in an attempt to squeeze the orgasm that was bubbling beneath to the surface. "Stick it in and fuck me hard," she gasped into the receiver.

"I got you. Oh, shit, your pussy is dripping, but my dick can feel every groove and bump as I'm rubbing up against you. When I saw you on that beach naked, my cock almost exploded. And then last night, shit your pussy is so good. In that bathroom, fucking you, I was in heaven. I want more. I have to have more. Give it to me, Quincy. Give it to me."

Livia could hear Mitchell masturbating through the phone. His soft grunts were pushing Liv closer to her own orgasm. She pressed the lipstick closer to intensify the vibrations.

"Uh shit...uh shit...uh shit....oh yeah...oh yeah!" he screamed in her ear as he reached his climax. Livi could hear him breathing hard as his body recovered from the wake of his climax. She squeezed her ass tighter and her legs went stiff as she followed his orgasm with her own. Livia announced her pleasure break with a series of sweet "oohs" and one long, exhale as her pussy throbbed with the most intense contractions she'd ever experienced.

What the hell took me so long to discover toys. She giggled to herself, as she luxuriated in the afterglow.

"Thank you, baby," Mitchell whispered in her ear.

Livia couldn't help thinking that for a total stranger, Mitchell was such a charming, albeit confusing, lover. He barked out sexual orders, while confirming them with polite questions. His language was bawdy and bold, but at the same time, comforting and considerate. Liv had to admit that he made crazy, in the moment sex with a stranger not only exciting but endearing. It was like Mitchell had been custom ordered especially for her and her now very active, fuck-it list.

"Pleasure was mine. You really are the perfect boy toy."

"Thank you, and may I say, you really know how to take care of your toys."

"Mitchell?"

"Yeeessss?" he replied, adding another layer to their flirty banter.

"I've had just about enough of all this talk. Tonight you're gonna have to do this all again for real."

"Gladly. Damn, I love when that happens."

"When what happens?" Livia asked with a coy smile on her lips.

"When what I *have* to do, and what I *want* to do come together, complete with a gorgeous, fucking bow on top," Mitchell flirted through his yawn.

"Goodnight, Mitchell. Sweet dreams."

"You too. Rest up cause I'm planning to literally rock your boat tonight."

Livia giggled again as she replaced the receiver, flipped on the light, and pulled her fuck-it list from her purse. It was crinkled and worn, a look Liv loved because it meant things were getting accomplished. She picked up the pen by the phone and, for the second time today, proceeded to revise her list.

"The hell with a lame tattoo," she said, crossing it out and overwriting it with "have phone sex." Lena had been absolutely right; this list had become a mere jumping-off point for her and her wonderfully slutty little pussy.

Fuck It List

1. Buy and play with toys.

2. Vacation at a nude beach and go skinny-dipping.

3. Make love on a boat

4. Get a sexy tattoo

Have phone sex

5. ~~Sex with~~ Kiss a woman

5. ~~TBD act of outrageous sex~~

~~Masturbate in ear shot of a perfect stranger getting off~~

6. ~~Have a one night stand with a stranger~~

7. ~~Have sex in a public place~~

8. Have *9½ Weeks* sexy food play

9. Find and fuck Bobby Jeffries

10. Buy a yellow chair.

Livia sighed with accomplishment. With four months left until her fiftieth, she'd already checked off half of her list, and tomorrow making love on a boat would be a done deal too. Progress. You gotta love it!

Best Laid Plans

"And that's what happened," Jasi explained to Lena and Aleesa over cocktails at Lena's Manhattan apartment. "She freaked out because I set her up with the bartender." Jasi took a sip of her coffee and watched their faces, trying to discern if they'd been told the whole story.

"Yeah, Livia told us all about the Fox, but she never mentioned that you two weren't speaking," Aleesa said.

"I can't believe she's still so pissed about it that she's not talking to you. Give her time. You know how conservative our little cupcake girl is," Lena added.

You don't know the half of it, Jasi thought, but kept to herself. Conservative yes, but not a snitch. Jasi snuck out a sigh of relief. It was apparent that Livia had not said a word about what she'd seen to even their closest of friends. Though she'd proven herself to be a homophobic prude, at least Livia wasn't a big mouth as well.

"The thing is, I didn't set her up with a stranger. I've known the bartender for years. She was in very safe hands. Julian wouldn't do anything to harm Livia or anyone else."

"So tell her," Lena suggested.

"I can't. She won't talk to me."

"You'll work it out. I'll bet by the time her birthday rolls around you two will be BFF's again," Aleesa remarked.

"And where have you been hiding anyway?" Lena probed, changing the subject. "I haven't seen you since Liv's party. What's up with you and Todd, or have you moved on to the next Studly Do-Right who's caught your eye?"

"I've been caught up with a new…project. Todd and I are still hanging, but just barely. He's never around. He's always on the road chasing some ball, and it's taking its toll. Oh well."

"Girl, you're never going to settle down with one man," Aleesa remarked. "Though you should try it; you might discover that you like domestic bliss."

"Okay, Harolyn! You sound like my mom. It's killing her that her only child isn't married and pumping out the big family she could never have. She really thought Todd was going to finally be the one to give her some grandchildren."

"Excuse me. Has the woman ever met you?" Lena joked. "You're not the type to settle down with any one man."

"No shit," Jasi said with a smirk. Despite her grin, Lena's comment caused a shimmy in Jasi's stomach. Lena had no idea how accurate her comment was, but for the wrong reasons. It had been clear for years now that Jas could never settle down with any man, but the thought of becoming a one-woman, woman, was starting to have great appeal.

"Do you even want kids? I never heard you talk about them," Aleesa probed.

"Maybe. I don't know…with the right partner."

"And what would he look like?" Lena quipped.

Belinda Rodriquez! The hottest, sexiest, most incredible woman and piece of ass I've ever experienced in my life! Jasi wanted to scream out to her friends. Just like any person, man or woman, who was falling in love, she wanted to shout it from the mountaintop and share with the world her sense of newfound joy. But she couldn't. Or wouldn't because she was in love with a woman and despite the fact that they were all living in the twenty-first century, there were plenty of people in her life who had yet to cross over into modern day thinking. If Livia so vehemently disapproved, there was a chance that these two might feel the same way. And honestly, Jasi was afraid that the more people who knew, the greater the risk that her parents and employer would find out.

"God only knows," Jasi said, "but we need to get on with this. I've got another meeting at seven." As much as she loved her friends, it was Saturday, and she had an extremely hot chick waiting for her at home.

"You're still okay with going in on her gift, even though you two are *momentarily* on the outs," Aleesa asked, stressing the temporary. Lees was sure the two would eventually talk and patch things up between them. They were too good of friends not to.

"Yeah, I'm down."

"So any suggestions?" Lena asked, filling both of their glasses with more wine. "After all she's been through, it's got to be something memorable."

"I've been wracking my brain trying to come up with something unique, but I got zilch," Aleesa admitted.

"I was going to suggest we chip in on a trip, but now that seems very 'been there done that,'" Jasi told them.

"Yeah, well hopefully, she's in St. Bart's doing the wild thing and checking off that list of hers."

"Come on, Lena, do you really think she's getting much accomplished?" Jasi asked. "I mean, she may want to, but based on what I've seen, it ain't gonna happen."

"OMIGOD! Of course! The fuck-it list! Let's give her something off the list," Aleesa said, her excitement causing her to jump up. "Let's get her the yellow chair. Who the hell knows what that's about, but it's something she wants, for some kind of crazy, sexual perversion."

"Wait, you might be on to something. But forget the chair, who was that guy on her list? Bobby somebody," Lena asked.

"Oh yeah. Her high school boyfriend. She said they were in love but never had sex because they weren't married. I guess she wants to see what she missed," Jasi offered.

"OMIGOD, Bobby Jeffries!" Aleesa screamed, dancing around the table. "This is perfect. We fly him in for her birthday and Livia, if she so desires, can take it from there."

"Whoa! Hold up. I already tried providing live bait. You see how far it got me. We're not speaking," Jasi replied.

"So, we don't go quite so far," Lena said, buying into the idea

"We're merely creating the opportunity," Aleesa added. "What she does with it is her business."

"Exactly, which will help us avoid catching her ire like you did," Lena added.

"Alright, but if she pops off, you two are taking the heat on this one," Jasi said, still not convinced.

"Agreed. All right, so how do we find him?" Aleesa asked. "We know he lived in Essex County and went to Regional High School."

"Google him," Lena said, pulling out her iPad.

"LinkedIn," Jasi suggested, pulling out her Smartphone.

"Okay, you two find him, and I'll figure out what to do with him," Aleesa said.

"And find out where you can rent a DeLorean while you're at it," Lena joked.

"What the hell?" Jasi asked, trying to connect Lena's request to the task at hand.

"Oh, I get it," Aleesa laughed. "Happy birthday, cousin. We're about to take you back to the future."

"What does your gut say?" Aleesa asked, hugging the phone to her ear as she whipped the potatoes for Walt's dinner.

"To go for it," Livia informed her. "I'm probably over analyzing this. The thing is, I do feel comfortable and safe with Mitchell, but instead of feeling secure, it kind of scares me. I'm sure Natalee Holloway also felt comfortable with that crazy guy," Livia revealed as sat on the lobby sofa waiting for her date. It was bad enough she'd been caught in a lie of sorts regarding her hotel, she didn't want to risk him trying to call Quincy Charles's room again, only to learn that there was no such person registered.

"I see your point. You did say that it's a party, right?"

"Yes. He's here with friends for a week-long bachelor party."

"But your instincts say he's a good guy?"

"Yes."

"Okay, give me all of the information you have about the party. Do you know the name of the yacht?"

"*The Contessa.*"

"Okay, when you get to the marina, text me all of the particulars. Then call your room and leave a message with all of the information about where you are and who you are with. This way, if something goes down, which I'm sure it won't, you've left a bounty of clues."

"Sounds reasonable."

"Liv, you don't have to do this. We keep pushing you, but you have nothing to prove."

"I don't feel like you are pushing me. I'm actually starting to enjoy myself," she said, smiling at the memory of her and Mitchell's bathroom romp and racy phone call.

"Okay. Have fun and take your own condoms. Remember…"

"I know. No cover. No lover."

"Lena and Jasi are not going to believe this," Aleesa told her.

"Truth is, neither did I. We all kind of thought you'd get down there and chicken out."

"Well, you weren't too far off. I was very close to your prophesy coming true. I'd been down here three days and nothing happened. Then I decided to go skinny dipping and the next thing I know, some hottie is literally picking me up on the beach."

"Probably didn't hurt that you were naked." Aleesa giggled.

"No, in fact, that's the thing that got the ball rolling. Ooh…gotta go. He's here."

"Have fun!"

"Oh, I plan to. Did I mention that he's got the dick of life?"

"Twice! Okay, have fun and be safe. Don't forget to text me."

Ships A-Whore

As Quincy preceded him down the length of the dock toward the last slip, a flash of teeth broke out on Mitchell's face. With her wild, honey-colored hair and smoking body, Quincy was the picture of exotic temptation. Even wearing flat, gladiator sandals, she was looking every bit as tall, tanned and confident as the mythical girl from Ipanema. Her strapless maxi dress was both simple and simply sexy. It skimmed the dynamic curves of her lofty frame, and despite its white hue, Quincy appeared anything but virginal. Not only did the color offset her golden tan, it put on display two of her most delectable body parts—her shoulders and bust.

Mitchell could not wait to get his lips on those smashing tatas again. He was well acquainted with faux breasts. Seemed like every other woman he'd dated, including the one he'd married, had been under the plastic surgeon's knife. Like most men, he really preferred the touch and feel of real, but as fake goes, Quincy's were well-placed, naturally shaped and while firmer than real, not as hard as some he'd felt up. Her attitude about them made him curious about the reason behind the augmentation. Most chicks he knew, his ex included, couldn't wait to showcase their off-the-rack, rack. They were a badge of honor and most paraded them around with a sense of pride others reserved for their children. Quincy, on the other hand, appeared almost embarrassed by them.

She seemed surprised every time his attention, whether through a compliment or touch, turned to them.

"You look absolutely scrumptious," he said, catching up with her and wrapping his arm around Quincy's waist. This being his first experience with an older woman, Mitchell was pleasantly surprised by the admiring looks he received from both his boys and strangers. He definitely had found a vacation prize, and a big part of him wished that bitch, Toris, was here to see that just because she decided to bounce, didn't mean that he couldn't rebound—big time.

"As do you," Livia said, returning the compliment, but not really paying attention to her date. Mitchell certainly did look yummy as hell, but for the moment, her eyes were eating up the sleek vessel before her. They crossed the gangway onto the aft deck, and Livia was immediately blown away by the opulence around her. *The Contessa* was no mere boat. It was a 210-foot, seaworthy mansion. Now, this was sexy!

"Omigod," she muttered under her breath with total awe. Accepting a glass of champagne from one of the stewards assigned to greet the guests, Livia soaked in the luxurious party atmosphere. Music was blaring from the first-class sound system as waves of guests gyrated on the dance floor. Moving further onto the main deck, Liv admired the outdoor living room set up, awash in a tasteful and cool tone-on-tone, cream-colored palette. Shaded by the deck above, it was furnished with two large, eggshell sectional couches, with a large coffee table and two chocolate brown chairs adding an earthy touch.

Livia scouted the crowd. The yacht was awash in white, but for several runway-worthy women, each dressed in a different colored bikini, fishnet thigh-high stockings and heels, who were scattered throughout the crowd. Clearly, they were hired to promote something for some company, but what and for whom, Livia wasn't sure. She judged most of the party people to be a mix of twenty and thirty-somethings, with most of the women falling into the younger group and a few forty-plusers sprinkled throughout. Liv knew that she looked younger than her birth certificate would indicate, but still, she felt like a fish out of water in this sea-going group of hot, young and rich revelers.

"Whose yacht is this?" Livia asked, still ogling her surroundings.

"Some dude named Ahmed. He's the cousin of some Saudi sheik. One of my boys got the hook-up."

"This is absolutely beautiful," she replied to tell Mitchell, referring to both the crowd and the ship.

"You're beautiful," he repeated, unknowingly assuaging her insecurities.

Livia rewarded him with a toothy grin. "Thank you for bringing me."

"Had to," he flirted, smiling as he moved in close to speak in her ear so Quincy could hear above the music, and feel the beginnings of his erection. "Don't forget, you're my personal shenanigan."

"Ah yes, I seem to remember that from the invitation." She felt her stomach flutter and Quincy contract. Anticipation was truly a serious aphrodisiac.

"So right now, we party. Later, we'll take the VIP tour and finish what we started on the phone last night."

Livia smiled and bit her lip in expectation. Whether he'd intended to or not, Mitchell had managed to whet her appetite and set her imagination on fire. She had every intention of enjoying herself with this sexy man, and refused to feel guilty when the deed was done. Not this time. Since her party, with her list in hand, she'd found herself immersed in such a Jekyll and Hyde existence. It seemed that while she was in the throes of sexual abandon—whether in the Maddox hallway in Montclair, in a bar in New York City, or the hotel bathroom in St. Bart's—Livi was capable of staying in the moment and experiencing the delight of sex for sex sake. But once her lust had been tucked back into its steamy box, she was left feeling more shameful than satiated. But not tonight. Tonight, shame and guilt were not an option, because even though they were strangers whose relationship would be over when the sun came up, Mitchell didn't feel like someone Livia had recently met.

Yes, it was true that they knew very little about each other. Hell, he didn't even know her real name. But that didn't seem to matter. Right from the very beginning, there'd been an instant familiarity between them. Livia wouldn't exactly call it true intimacy, but "intimate acquaintance" certainly fit. And more than anything this evening, she felt like being up close and very personal with this hot and handsome partner in salacious crime.

"Let's dance," she suggested, grabbing Mitchell's hand and leading him happily out into the crowd. She didn't recognize the music, but she certainly loved the groove. Its rhythm was infectious and insistent on making her body move. Too fast for a slow grind, and too slow for a fast boogie, Livia let the music seep into her pores and infuse her body with seductive energy. Her hips began to sway along with her arms, sending a message to her partner that she felt alive and excited by the carnal possibilities that lay ahead.

Mitchell read her body language and responded by bringing his torso in close, placing his hand on her hip and drawing Quincy to him. In unison, they performed a sensuous lovers' dance, oblivious to the throng of partiers engulfing them. Livia enjoyed the way their bodies seem to instinctively fall into sync with one another, making her curious about whether the harmony would be the same when they were dancing horizontally.

"Glad to see you're feeling better." Mitchell's friend from the beach guided his partner over to tell her.

Mitchell grabbed Livia's hand and twirled her away, slyly putting her on display for his boy.

"Thank you," Liv replied, smiling at Ken as her eyes quickly shot between the two men. She quickly attempted to decipher their ocular conversation. Best she could translate, Ken was signaling his admiration and approval, answered by Mitchell's expression of manly pride.

Who's the man? You the man! Livia joked in her head, happy with the attention derived from their boys will be boys moment. *Who's the woman, damn it?* Quincy butted in to continue the conversation. *You've snagged yourself a fine young thing. Give credit where credit is due!*

Rihanna's groove "S & M" broke through the chatter and commanded the couple back to the dance floor. Mitchell and Livia danced with their feet planted on the floor and let their bodies do the smack talking. Livia turned her back to him, an invitation for Mitchell to press his crotch against her as she pushed and gyrated her butt against his dick. Liv relished her role as cock tease, and responding to Mitchell's hands on her hips, pushed further into his groin. His eyes stayed glued to Livi's tempting ass as he recalled each glorious stroke he'd taken in the bathroom the night before.

Rihanna's song ended, but the two remained on the floor, shaking and shimmying through several popular tunes, while enjoying the view of each other's bodies in motion, and the imaginative sex play it conjured up. Mitchell felt like his balls were about to explode and decided it was time to cool things down for a while until the real party got started.

"More champagne?"

"That sounds good," Livia told him. She was thirsty, but more so, she was ready to quench her usual inhibitions and get her sexy on. They walked over to the bar and Livi looked out onto the water while Mitchell got their cocktails.

"Toast?" he asked, handing her a glass full of bubbly.

"To personal shenanigans," Livia said, raising her champagne in the air. They touched glasses and downed their drinks, laughing at the synchronicity of their actions. Mitchell abruptly stopped laughing and pulled her in close, devouring her mouth with his. He could taste the sparkling wine on her tongue, which only made him want to taste the effervesce between her lower lips all the more.

Livia's torso melted into his. Mitchell's kiss was truly indicative of the man he was revealing himself to be. It was the sweet satisfying smooch of a horny gentleman—a promising and delightful combination in Livi's eyes.

"What was that?" she asked, as the shock of three horn blasts caused her to jump back.

"Sounds like the VIP cruise is about to get started."

"What time is it?"

"Quarter to midnight. We sail in fifteen minutes."

"Sail? We're leaving St. Bart's?"

Though her voice remained steady and calm, the seductive glaze in Livia's eyes had been replaced with bright concern.

"Yep, but we're not going far. Just out into international waters," Mitchell informed her. "But if you'd rather leave now, we certainly can. I don't want you to feel uncomfortable."

Don't forget to text me. The thought of raising anchor, and leaving the country she was visiting, jiggered Livia's memory, and brought her cousin's appeal to mind.

Livia and Mitchell stepped aside as the first wave of early revelers disembarked. Livi wasn't sure she wanted to know why they needed to head out into international waters, but frankly, it didn't really matter. What she did know is that she was horny as hell, felt totally safe with Mitchell and was looking forward spending the rest of the evening in his arms.

"So what does our VIP status get us?" she asked, snuggling up against him. "A stateroom, hopefully."

"That and so much more," Mitchell replied with a wink. "We're in the Sophia Loren. It's on the lower deck, portside."

"In that case, what are we waiting for?"

"There's a brief sail away and then we're on our own," Mitchell informed her.

"Well, I'd like to freshen up before we sail."

"Okay. Follow me." Mitchell took her hand and led Livia inside and down the narrow hall toward their cabin. After passing the beautiful teak doors labeled "Gina Lollobrigida" and "Isabella Rossellini," she determined that all of the cabins were named after famous Italian bombshells.

Mitchell stopped, opened the door to their cabin, and stepped aside so Livia could enter. Open-mouthed, she crossed the threshold, immediately impressed by the opulent nautical splendor before her. She stepped into what could be mistaken for the finest suite in any luxury five-star hotel. The interior design was an impeccable blend of purpose and pomp. The teakwood built-ins blended perfectly with the upholstery's color palette of beige, brown and gold, allowing plenty of room for the king-size bed in the middle of the room.

Surprising both of them, Livia turned and literally threw herself at Mitchell, causing them both to fall onto the bed. Her lips hungrily devoured his, making it clear her intention to have her appetite sated. Since they'd met, he'd been throwing delicious crumbs her way, enough to keep her hungry, but not enough to keep her satisfied. Tonight, she intended to full out gorge herself on some seriously sexy sustenance.

Just as her hands reached for his shirt buttons, they both heard the engines revving, a sure sign that they were getting ready to leave port.

"I really hate to break this up," Mitchell said in a voice laden with desire. "But everyone has to be on deck for the sail away. Party rules."

"Okay. Why don't you go back up on deck," Livia told him, eyeing the bathroom door. "I'll meet you back on the dance floor in a few minutes."

"Hurry back up. I've got a few surprises for you." Mitchell winked at her before quickly departing, eager to get back upstairs and finalize everything.

Livia crossed the roomy cabin and stepped into the full bath, amazed that even on the high seas, one did not have to give up the comfort of a hot shower or soothing whirlpool bath. She pulled out her phone and sent a quick text to Aleesa, letting her know all of the pertinent details, and then she called the hotel to leave the same message on her room phone. After completing that task, she made use of the bidet, before heading to the medicine cabinet, which was fully stocked with various personal sundries. She quickly rinsed her mouth with mouthwash, reapplied her lipstick and fluffed out her curls.

Before turning to leave, Livi took a long look at the madam in the mirror and smiled. There was a newfound radiance about her that had everything to do with finally letting go and letting loose. All of her life she'd played by the good girl rules and had ended up living 49 years without feeling fully alive. In these few short months, she'd begun to rectify that situation and had begun to acquire the inner satisfaction to match her outer glow.

Livia felt the earth shift below her as *The Contessa* slowly pulled away from the dock. She took a final look before turning and hurrying back upstairs and into Mitchell's waiting arms. She walked through the doors back on to the deck and was greeted by a pair of stewards, one bearing a tray of delectable looking, bite-sized desserts, the other, a tray of champagne flutes. Admitted chocoholic, and connoisseur of fine pastries that she was, Livia couldn't resist grabbing one of the brownie bites and immediately popping it into her mouth. She momentarily closed her eyes, enjoying the bittersweet taste of the velvety, rich cake on her tongue.

"Wait, one more." Livia smiled, happily consuming another taste before chasing them both down with a glass of the most delicious champagne she'd ever tasted. Definitely, a VIP upgrade in the bubbly. The combination of the two was the ultimate in decadence—a theme Liv had every intention of carrying into the rest of the evening.

A Bounty of Booty on the High Seas

Livi walked out on what, minutes before, had been a deck gyrating with guests passionate about partying. Now, most of the white hot revelers had departed, but for those who remained, their passions had morphed the dance floor into a seductive and openly sexual strip club. The models who, earlier in the evening, had traipsed around the yacht leaving a trail of sex appeal and desire in their wake, were now topless and putting on a display of erotic dancing, exciting the audience's collective imagination, and libido, with their "drop it like it's hot" performances.

Mitchell immediately spotted his date and made a bee-line in Livia's direction. He pulled her to him, whispering gruffly in her ear, "Quincy Charles, you have no idea what you do to me. I can't wait to finally give you a proper fuck." While his mouth stated his intentions, he pushed her hand on to his crotch, allowing his stiffening cock to translate his ability to fulfill them.

Livia seductively licked the inside of his ear in response. Her action sent chills up and down his back, causing him to push his pelvis into hers. Under the pretense of a slow dance, Mitchell and Livia stood on the dance floor grinding against each other like a high school couple copping a feel at a "blue lights in the basement" party. Liv could feel the hardness of Mitchell's dick against her thigh. Knowing what she had awaiting her made her pussy twitch in anticipation.

"How long do we have to stay on deck?" Livia inquired between nibbles of Mitchell's earlobe.

"Until you're begging for it," he informed her.

"You know, it's really not nice to be such a tease," she flirted back, giving his balls a squeeze, much to his pleasure.

Before Mitchell could come back with a playful response, they were pulled apart, this time by three blasts of the yacht's horn. The music stopped as stewards crisscrossed the deck with trays of Cristal champagne. Soon after, a swarthy man with an unfamiliar foreign accent began to speak. Ahmed, Livia presumed.

"My friends, welcome aboard the beautiful *Contessa*. I hope you are already enjoying the splendor of this special evening. We will return to port at sunrise. Until then, give into the night, indulge your appetites and savor your pleasures to their fullest.

"Cin, Cin," he toasted, raising his class.

"Cin, Cin," Livia and the rest of the guests echoed in response. "Now I know why folks love this so much," she whispered to Mitchell. "It's like drinking an orgasm from a glass."

"I like the way you think," Mitchell responded with a lust-filled wink.

"And I love the way you kiss." Livia tried to settle her aroused libido by drowning it in champagne. By the time her glass was empty, another steward appeared with a tempting variety of tasty bite-size desserts.

"Looks like red velvet," Livia speculated, reaching for a miniature cupcake. "You've got to try the brownies. They are yummy!"

"Be easy with those," he warned.

"I can't help myself. I'm a pastry chef. I have to check out the competition," she told him, feeling the champagne kicking in. "Besides, I'm sure you'll help me work off the calories later," she said, nibbling at the cupcake.

"It's not the calories I'm worried about," Mitchell informed her. "Those are space cakes. They all have either pot or hash in them. You don't want to overdo. You may not feel it now, but when they kick in, trust me, you'll be high as hell."

"Oh shit!" Livia exclaimed, her eyes going wide with concern. "I've already had two," she said while squishing the rest of the cupcake in her napkin. Livia hadn't smoked or otherwise consumed marijuana since college, and even then it was only once on a dare by her cousin. Back in the day, weed had made her feel light and sleepy. She had no idea how her body would react now, nearly thirty years later.

"Don't worry, baby. I'll take good care of you. I promise. This evening is all about fulfilling your fantasies. Whatever you want or don't want, it's all up to you. I got your back."

Livia gave Mitchell a grateful kiss on the lips. She did feel safe with him and secure in the knowledge that he would not push into any place she was not willing to go. "Let's go watch the show," she suggested.

The two walked over to the sofas surrounding the dance floor and cuddled up together. Since raising anchor, the ambiance had changed considerably. Clearly, the drugs and drinks had kicked in because this was no longer a throwdown; it had transformed into a public get-down. Getting into the spirit of the soiree, folks were busy getting their groove on with some serious foreplay. The VIP guests no doubt had a like mindset—fuck and be fucked.

A circle began to form and Mitchell and Liv got up and stepped in closer to see what was going on. Two of the model girls, who obviously had been hired to get the real party started, were on the dance floor getting seriously busy. The Asian girl was on her back, legs spread, fingering and tweaking her own tits while the brunette's head was bobbing between her legs, eating her pussy. Several men and women stood around, enjoying the view while stroking themselves. A few of the other models, all now topless but still wearing their itty-bitty, bikini bottoms, were working up the crowd with a variety of cock and pussy teasing actions.

"Does that turn you on?" Mitchell asked, happily noting his date's fascination with the couple on the floor.

Livia, still confused by her fascination with girl-on-girl sex, replied with a guilty nod.

"Which do you think is hotter?"

"The one with the tattoo."

"I like her too," he said, giving Livia a conspiratorial grin. "She reminds me of a curvier Zoe Saldana."

Mitchell leaned over and kissed Livia's shoulder, tracing the contours of her collarbone with his tongue, while his hands took delight in the roundness of her ass. His mouth found hers and they shared a hungry kiss. The debauchery around her was proving to be a total turn-on. Whatever level of arousal she'd felt earlier in the evening had now been intensified one hundred-fold. With Cristal courage, Livia began to rub his crotch, loving the sensation of his dick's rising response to her touch.

"Touch it."

Livia unzipped Mitchell's fly, giving freedom to his hard rod. Right there on the dance floor, she began to massage him, sliding her hand up and down his shaft, twisting and pulling, amazed at his ability to grow ever bigger and wider in her palm—even more amazed by her total lack of inhibition.

Dare to be wild, Quincy encouraged.

"Suck it."

Mitchell had the uncanny ability to request things of her without sounding demanding or aggressive. Livia took a quick peek around her. A real orgy had broken out. Nobody was paying attention to them; they were too consumed with their own behavior to judge hers. Livia knelt down and took Mitchell's cock into her hand, and then gently guided it into her mouth. First, she played with the juicy plum, circling his tip with her tongue, giving homage to the very sensitive groove on the underside. Mitchell's groans were evidence that her devotion was appreciated and that it was time to move on.

Livia bared her teeth and gently scraped the length of his dick as she made her way down from tip to base. Liv began to suck his dick, her head moving back and forth at his crotch as she varied the suction strength.

Her technique was apparently a winning one, as Mitchell gently held her head in his hands, setting the rhythm as the muscles in his legs and ass clenched in an effort to concentrate all the energy and tension to his groin.

Livia sucked and teased his dick with her tongue, listening to the rhythm of his grunts and groans. When she knew she had him at the point of orgasm, Liv gave him one last long lick before moving her face to his. She felt the ground below her shift causing her to rock slightly, and leaving her unsure if it was the yacht, or the brownies kicking in, causing her unsteadiness.

"Oh, baby, don't stop. You were getting to the good stuff."

"I told you it wasn't nice to tease. Now, you see how it feels."

"It feels like I want to fuck you right here." Mitchell punctuated his declaration by giving Livia's strapless dress a firm tug, causing it to drop and pool around her ankles. The second she was disrobed, Livi felt compelled to protest, but the only sounds that her mouth would release were those of desirous submission. The brownies had definitely kicked in because at that very moment, she stood there wearing nothing but a G-string, feeling high and horny, and convinced that she and this fine specimen of maleness, were the only two people in the room.

Mitchell bent down and began sucking her nips, massaging and playing with them with one hand, while his other traveled down her belly and got lost in her panties. His hand palmed her pussy and gave it a squeeze before slipping two fingers inside her hole, as his thumb started circling her clit.

Livia squeezed her snatch around his fingers, and then willed her body to relax and enjoy the party happening in her pants. She stood there, feeling like she was weightlessly hanging in space, bucking up against his hand and feeling Quincy getting hotter and wetter and more demanding of the insertion of Mitchell's rock-hard cock. One last flick of his thumb set her clit off in a pleasant micro-orgasm, a tiny but potent firecracker that prepped her pussy for the serious pyrotechnics to come.

"Mmmm," she murmured, falling against him.

"Go with it, baby. I got you."

"Please take me to the cabin now," she begged, falling against him. She was feeling the full effects of the space cakes and wanted to lie down, not just because her head was feeling delightfully fuzzy. The pressing need to get fucked, and get fucked hard, had become paramount. "I can't stand this any longer. I want your dick inside me. I need it inside me. But not quick like in the bathroom. I want it all night. Will you fuck me all night, Mitchell? Please. Don't make me wait any longer."

Mitchell's cock went rock-hard at the sound of her begging. There was nothing hotter than knowing that the object of your desire wanted you just as badly. And God knows, he wanted Quincy. This high-level game of stranger se*fuck*tion they'd been playing with each other was about to come to a head. Just like Quincy, he was done with the seduction and quick fucking. Mitchell was ready and way far beyond willing to tear that ass up!

But first things first, he reminded himself.

"No, baby, you don't have to wait any longer. Let's go." He managed to breeze his tongue across her pussy as he reached down and pulled her dress back up over her breasts. Livia's knees buckled slightly as the sensation of his tongue on her twat radiated through her body.

Mitchell took her hand and led her back to their cabin. Livia stepped across the threshold and out of her dress in one smooth as marble move. She kept moving until she reached her destination, the bed. She sprawled her body across it, enjoying the feel of the cool Egyptian cotton on her back.

"Come," Livi requested, her fingers brushing the short fur of her aroused snatch. The brownies had gone straight to her clit and Quincy was dying for some very specialized attention.

Mitchell smiled with great pleasure at the delectable sight sprawled out before him. He was eager to do exactly as Quincy had requested, but he didn't move. It wouldn't be long before the pleasure would be his, but first he had something special in mind for his sexy and exciting new friend.

"Do you trust me?" he whispered from the foot of the bed.

Livia opened her eyes up to stare into the face of this handsome, familiar stranger. "Yes," she replied emphatically. And she truly did.

"Good. I want to blindfold you. Would that be okay?"

"Yes." Livia could feel the butterfly wings begin to flutter and then quickly settle down.

"Quincy, this is your night," Mitchell reminded her as he slipped a sleep mask over Livi's eyes. "Like I said, if you're not feeling something just say so. Okay?"

"Okay. I'll say…uh…jellyfish!" She giggled.

"Perfect, now lay back and do exactly what Ahmed suggested—give into the night. Give into me."

"Mmmm-hmmm," she murmured, enjoying the high. "Make me feel good, Mitchell."

"Oh, baby. That is definitely my plan."

"Good, but close the door first." She giggled.

"I will."

Livia could hear the sound of feet walking across the carpet. The spacecakes and champagne were working their magic and along with her inability to sit or stand, her inhibitions were gone as well. The only plan Livi had for the rest of the evening was to enjoy her weed-induced listlessness, and take the opportunity to break through some of the limits of her reserve.

"You look totally edible," he said before making his words come true.

Mitchell's hands spread her legs and she felt his thick, juicy tongue descend onto her waiting twat. Its broad side found her plump and awaiting clit and gave it several long licks before contracting into a stiff pussy probe and clit teaser. Livia's hips rose and pressed up against his face, making sure Mitchell could not break the delicious tension building between her legs. She was thoroughly enjoying the wet, sloshing noises emanating from below, when she felt a warm drizzle of oil on her nipples. Fingers complete with long, sharp nails gently tugged and clawed at her breasts.

In her heady high state, Livi's brain didn't immediately question how her body was being pleasured from both top and bottom. Her mind had gone back to the yellow chair in Naomi Maddox's house, but this time, she was one of the women and the man was watching her fucking and getting fucked. Feeling oh so naughty on this nautical adventure, Livia's imagination directed the soft porn movie while her body acted out the parts.

"You got some beautiful titties," a soft, feminine voice off in the distance remarked.

Livia put her fantasy on pause and peeked out from under her blindfold to see Zoe Saldana's look-alike straddled across her chest. "I'm here to give you a massage." The girl gave her a blurry smile as she reached up and began to massage Livia's shoulders before sliding her soft hands back to her breasts.

Before she could wrap her head around what was going on, the wet warmth of two mouths simultaneously licked at both her nips and her nib, silencing any protest and sending every sexy nerve ending in her body into a delicious frenzy. One set of lips sucked and tugged at her clit, making it grow longer and tighter, while another set did the same for her nipples. The sexy sensations traveled up, down and all around her body, exploding in a buildup of twat tingles that threatened to explode in a full-blown orgasm. Sensing that Livia was about to come, Mitchell backed off, allowing the intensity to ebb so the teasing could continue.

As the tension between her legs lessened, teeth bit down on her nipples, adding a flash of pain to the mix. Livia felt herself try to pull away, but the mouth latched on tighter and continued to suck, causing her pussy to laugh and clench. Liv gave into the rough pleasure, as a winning combination of soft hands and sharp nails rubbed and scratched their way down her torso.

The movie in her mind continued with scenes from the Maddox house mixing with visions of the dancers upstairs on deck getting nasty with each other, all as the mysterious man in the yellow chair watched and pleasured himself. Equally high and horny, Livi sought safe haven under the blindfold, allowing fantasy and reality to swirl together and raise the lust factor to a tumultuous level.

Gratefully, Mitchell's tongue began to pulsate against her nib, driving Livia to the brink of what was promising to be a monster orgasm.

"Oh yeah. Right there. Right there, just like that. Please don't stop," she begged.

Cushiony lips journeyed their way across Livia's shoulders and up her neck. She detected the slight scents of jasmine and clove as a long, silky lock of hair brushed across her cheeks. "You really got some sexy titties," her fantasy girl repeated. "Hot."

Mitchell's tongue hit Liv's spot, causing her to suck in her breath and tense the muscles in her ass. Just as breath filled Livia's lungs, a lipstick-wearing mouth pressed against hers, and pushed a spicy tongue between her teeth. It searched the recesses of her mouth with a soft deliciousness that was addictive. Livia found herself damn near levitating, trying to stay connected by both mouth and pussy. One last suck of her clit and bliss burst all over Mitchell's face. In mid-contraction, she felt his head lift from between her legs, replaced with a stinging slap to her crotch. Livia's body went into shock for a microsecond before her brain pleaded for more. Again, a short, stinging slap was delivered, raising the intensity of her orgasm to a seismic level.

As Livi rode the wave, the kiss continued until the delicious turbulence in her body ceased. Every nerve, bone, and organ was crying out to be fucked. Liv reached up and took off the blindfold. Two sets of eyes stared back at her, their faces smiling with satisfaction.

The naked dancer, who apparently, Livia herself had unwittingly picked out to join them, knelt on the bed and began to simultaneously rub both her hairless pussy and Mitchell's stiff Johnson. An initial wave of arousal was immediately replaced by an even stronger surge of jealousy.

"Jellyfish," she muttered.

"What?" the girl stopped to ask, looking confused.

Her absurd utterance had its desired effect. Mitchell immediately backed away while the dancer looked at her like she was outright crazy. Livia could not care less if the bitch thought she was crazy, as long as she took her hands off of her man's dick—even if he, and it, were hers for only the night.

Livia excused herself and walked into the bathroom. Within minutes, she heard the cabin door open and close, her signal to return to the bedroom and satisfy Quincy's unrelenting demand for rock hard dick.

"Are you okay?" Mitchell asked, concerned that he may have crossed the line.

"Shhh. I don't want to talk. Just fuck me."

"All good," he replied as Livia pushed her body into his and the two thumped against the desk. As Mitchell lifted her onto the desk and she wrapped her legs around him, everything about her upbringing and moral code told her what she'd just done was bad, cheap and terribly wrong, but for some reason she didn't feel that way. Instead, she felt sexy and liberated and empowered. Livia let out a huge gasp of pleasure as Mitchell's latex-sheathed cock entered her still crackling pussy.

"Oooh, baby, your pussy feels so good," Mitchell declared as he pumped her. Livia pushed up to swallow his dick in pink before giving it a happy squeeze with a well-timed Kegel.

Baby, no guilt here, not tonight, Liv thought as her face broke out into a huge smile. She was damn near fifty, and for the first time in her adult life, she genuinely felt like a grown-ass woman!

Putting Genie Back in Her Bottle

O n a beautiful fall Sunday, while the rest of the world was at church or lazing the morning away drinking coffee and reading *The New York Times*, Livia sat in her office at the bakery, busily revising and refining her plans for upcoming cake orders. Business was thriving and clients wanting custom designs consulted with Livia up to six months ahead of their event to allow for design and any revisions. While their actual cakes were baked the day before, decorative elements were often created weeks, sometimes months, ahead.

Her jaunt to the Caribbean, though well worth it, had put her behind schedule, forcing her to work the weekend in order to catch up. Livi's hand stayed on-task, tweaking designs that would eventually become frosted works of art, but between the squiggles and swirls, her mind kept racing back to St. Bart's.

She'd been home almost two weeks and not a day or night had gone by without one lusty vacation memory or another interrupting her thoughts. Livia's attention kept shifting from the monotony of now, to the monumentality of then. Blue oceans, tropical winds, and lots of amazing sex, sex, sex with a fine-ass young man!

Livia pushed aside Naomi Maddox's anniversary cake design and pulled out her crinkled and scratched-up fuck-it list. She loved the revised mess it had become. In her eyes, the circled, ad hoc additions, erasures and second-thought deletions were a testament to her growth as a bona-fide sexual woman.

Fuck It List

1. ~~Buy and play with toys.~~
2. ~~Vacation at a nude beach and go skinny-dipping.~~
3. ~~Have sex on a boat~~
4. Get a sexy tattoo

~~Have phone sex~~

5. ~~Sex with Kiss a woman~~
5. ~~TBD act of outrageous sex~~ (threesome)
5. ~~Masturbate in ear shot of a perfect stranger getting off~~
6. ~~Have a one night stand with a stranger~~
7. ~~Have sex in a public place~~
8. Have *9½ Weeks* sexy food play
9. Find and fuck Bobby Jeffries
10. Buy a yellow chair.

Livia went down the list and briefly relived each of her sexual accomplishments, remembering where she was and with whom at the time. She had to giggle. Initially, the plan had been to follow through on her promise by taking care of two and moving on. She'd approached each one reluctantly, willing to partake in the bare-bone basics in order to mark them off the list. But five months later, there were only three unfulfilled fantasies left on the page. Livia was amazed by just how many of her sexy desires she'd already managed to satisfy, and how confident and open she'd become in the process.

Yes, her time in the islands had been productive to say the least. After the nude sunbathing, skinny dipping, and jellyfish affair, things had moved along quite swimmingly. The first night with Mitchell had turned into a sexual trifecta, allowing Livia to cross out having a one-night stand with a stranger, sex in a public place, plus add the bonus phone sex activity to the mix. Night two together had been a windfall of sorts, allowing her to satisfy her fantasy of making love on a boat, and garnering her, the "imagined but never thought it would happen" kiss from a woman, and the equally delightful and disturbing, threesome. Now, in addition to flying her freak flag, Livia's wonderfully bawdy activities with Mitchell had earned her the right to wave the "mission accomplished" banner as well.

Hot and sexy Mitchell. Both sets of Livia's lips twitched at his memory. Mitchell had gently led her to the limits of her passion and then gratefully showed her how to stretch them. He'd made so many of her listed fantasies come true, and in the process, created others that had sprung the hot and horny genie from her bottle. But now she was home and alone, and was left asking the questions: what next, and with whom?

Livia put down her list, opened the top drawer and pulled out Mitchell's number. She raised the St. Bart's postcard to eye level and for the hundredth time, examined his scrawled handwriting across the top, *Mitchell 917-785-5255*.

Her mind took her back to the moment they'd said their good-byes. He'd seen her back to the hotel from the yacht. Her hand in his, Mitchell had charmed her into letting him stay for what was left of the night. Worn-out from their evening, they'd immediately fallen asleep, fully clothed, and woken up to the bright light of the Caribbean sun, cuddling and spooning like an old married couple. Livia had once again been perplexed by their odd familiarity be-cause as he'd done every time they'd hooked up together, Mitchell had managed to inject a sense of intimacy into the afterglow of their lust-filled evening.

He'd wanted to spend the day together and see her off to the airport later, but Livia declined. She needed to be alone—away from both Mitchell's and Quincy's influence. This time, guilt was not the culprit pushing him away; exhaustion and confusion were.

After such a life-slash-morals altering evening, Mitchell could not possibly stay for what was left of her trip because Livia needed silence and solitude in order to think through her situation and hopefully find clarity.

It had been a long and exhausting night of partying. Waking up, Livi was still pooped after hours of drugs, drink, dancing and debauchery. But more than tired, she was confused about sharing a kiss and a highly sexual moment with another woman. Confused about what that might mean about her, and of course, how it recolored her harsh reaction to Jasi and her bathroom tryst. She was also unsure about Mitchell. He was an intimate stranger about whom she knew little, except that he made her feel alive, adventurous and youthful in a way she'd never felt, even when she was young. He'd also made her feel safe and cared for. They had bonded so quickly and naturally, that even though Livia was fully aware, and at peace with the idea that Mitchell was nothing more than a delicious secret memory to take into her old age, there was something about their coupling that still confounded her.

"You're not regretting last night, are you?" Mitchell had asked, true concern etched across his face.

"No, I'm not regretting anything that happened on this vacation. Not even the jellyfish sting," she said, giving him a playful wink.

"Good, because, baby, there is no shame to your game," he said, standing at the door of her hotel room, gently brushing the curls away from her eyes. "I have never known a woman like you—one who is as innocent as she is wickedly nasty. You are truly the first woman I've met who makes that saying, 'a lady on the street and a freak between the sheets' real."

"Thank you, but it takes a special man to bring out the freak in a woman. So, trust me, you will not be forgotten anytime soon."

"And you will forever be my fantasy, Quincy Charles. If the spirit ever moves you, please give me a call," he requested, grabbing the postcard from the desk and quickly jotting down his number and pushing it into her hand. "And I hope it does, because I'd love to see you again and help you finish your list."

"You knew?" she'd asked, feeling both embarrassed and slightly duped.

The gotcha smile on his face answered her query.

"That's why you took me on the boat?"

"And in the bathroom, though the phone sex was all about just wanting to talk dirty to you," he admitted with a mischievous smile.

"And the woman," Livia whispered under her breath.

"I didn't get to see it all," Mitchell continued, not hearing her comment. "I only got as far as having sex in public."

"How? When?"

"I saw it when I was putting things back into your purse on the beach."

"Omigod," she'd said, raising her hands to cover her humiliation.

"Don't," he demanded while gently peeling her palms from her face. "I told you on the phone the other night, I love bold, sensual, fun-loving women. When I saw that list, I thought then, and still do now, that you are one sexy-as-hell woman."

"Why didn't you tell me you'd seen it?"

"Because if I had, you'd have been too embarrassed to do with me what you had obviously come here to do," Mitchell explained.

He'd been absolutely correct. Jellyfish sting and all, Livia would have run to the opposite end of the island if she'd known that he'd seen her list. Once again, Mitchell had read her accurately, and done her a great favor in keeping his discovery secret.

The urge to hear his voice in her ear again was overwhelming. Deciding to return to the bold woman Mitchell knew, she dialed the number, rehearsing what she would say as she waited to be connected. She'd settled on an invitation for a sunset drink when a voice came through the phone.

"We're sorry, you have reached a number that has been disconnected or is no longer in service. Please check the number and try again."

Surprised, Livia inspected Mitchell's handwriting. Was that a three or a five? And what she thought was a seven could actually be a one.

Liv exhaled deeply, shaking Mitchell and the recollections of their time together from her head so she could concentrate on the big picture for a moment.

This fuck-it list adventure, though initially forced on her by her friends, had started with the goal of rebooting and changing her life around for the better. It was to be a bold exercise in self-discovery, pushing away her fears and getting to know, and eventually own her sexual desires. The trip, with its comforting anonymity, had allowed her to pull things off, and had been an enlightening and productive vacation. Mitchell had helped to lift her out of her rigid and conservative ways, and change her views on passion and physical pleasure. But the truth remained: she'd scratched her itch and instead of making it go away, she'd broken out in an acute romantic rash.

It was becoming increasingly clear to Livia that one sad side effect of this escapade into Lustville was the spotlight it left shining on her extreme loneliness. Yes, she'd wanted to continue to stretch her sexual wings, but it was now glaringly apparent that she wanted to do so with someone she loved, not simply lusted after. Someone like Mitchell, but who wasn't Mitchell. And yes, it had all been about sex, but he'd never made her feel used in anyway. In fact, whether he'd intended to or not, Mitchell had made her feel like part of a couple. And feeling that way had made her realize how much she missed being one of a loving pair.

Mitchell had really shown himself to be a kind, intelligent and compassionate man. He was nurturing and supportive, didn't judge her and seemed to naturally exude an intimacy and honesty that was both refreshing and ultimately magnetic. He was also handsome and studly, but oh so damn young! A bit of a slut puppy, for sure, he was the perfect vacation boy toy, and would be the ultimate catch for some young woman.

But fast approaching fifty, Livia was no longer young, and didn't want a boy. She wanted a man whom she could call her own for the rest of her life, not just the week. A man closer to her age, one with similar life experiences, whose soundtrack to his life included songs (not just hip-hop beats) by Earth, Wind & Fire, the Isley Brothers, and Prince in his absolute prime. A grown man who didn't need to go out of the country to pick up women, one who had sown his wild oats and was ready to settle down with a fellow quinquagenarian and do some seriously energetic, albeit slightly less thrill-seeking, fucking into the sunset.

What was she thinking to even try and call? Mitchell's poor penmanship had saved her from making a huge mistake. Livia slowly tore Mitchell's number into several pieces and sprinkled it into the garbage can, picked up her pencil and got back to work on Naomi Maddox's cake. He was perfect for what ailed Quincy, but could not satisfy what Livia was craving. The decision was made: What happened in St. Bart's, how it happened, and with whom it happened, would forever stay there.

"It was the craziest thing," Livia explained to her cousin and friend between bites of spinach, artichoke dip and sips of chardonnay. Finally, they'd all been able to clear their schedules to allow for this all important debriefing. Conspicuous in her absence was

Jasi, but Livia was actually grateful she wasn't there as she was more befuddled than ever when it came to how she was feeling about Jas. "He just picked up my naked behind and carried me over to my chair."

"So exactly at what point did his dick accidently fall inside you?" Aleesa teased, setting the three of them off in gales of laughter.

"That didn't happen until a couple of days later. I needed a few days to get that damn jellyfish sting under control. But trust me when I tell you, it was no accident." Livia took a long sip of her wine before confessing more. "There is definitely something very positive to be said about vacation sex."

"Do tell," her cousin prompted.

"Let's just say, you should be very proud of me. Quincy and I were very productive while I was away."

"Enough back-patting! I want all the gory, or should I say, glory details," Lena demanded.

"We did it in the bathroom at the restaurant," she told them, smiling slyly into her glass.

"Omigod! Livia Charles had sex in a bathroom?"

"A public bathroom, no less," Aleesa chimed in.

"With a stranger! Fantasies five and six, check!" Livia stated with a laugh.

"Sounds like a Quincy move to me," Lena stated.

"Totally. And later, after he left, Mitchell called and we had phone sex. That was a bonus write-in on the list."

"Do I even know you?" Lena laughed.

"Girl, I don't even know myself anymore! And that was just night one."

"How many times did you two hook up?" Aleesa asked.

"Just two. The next night, on Saturday, he took me to a VIP yacht party. Now *that* was pretty crazy," Livia admitted.

"Crazy how?"

"Well, at first it was just a regular party, but then most people disembarked and it turned into a kind of sex cruise for the VIP guests."

"Damn, girl, you went from no-fucking on the fuck-it list to a VIP sex party? Now, that's some kind of progress."

"You didn't put that in your text. What kind of sex cruise? Like an orgy?" Aleesa asked, alarmed by what she was hearing. Yes, she wanted her cousin to find and live her passionate side, but not to become an indiscriminate whore. Had their straight-laced Livia gone too far?

"Not exactly. I mean, if you wanted to, I'm sure you could find a willing group somewhere on the boat. The opportunity to do just about anything you wanted was there, but mainly people got it on with whomever they came with," Livia informed them.

"So tell us what happened," Lena requested.

"Well, it all started with the brownies," Livia began. "They looked so appetizing and of course, I couldn't resist. It wasn't until I'd already eaten two that I found out they were space cakes."

"Pot brownies," Lena filled in after seeing the question marks in Aleesa's eyes.

Livia's girlfriends listened intently as she indulged their curiosity with most of what happened on the yacht. From the desserts that turned out to be drug delivery systems to the bikini-clad dancers who turned out to be ladies hired to deliver sex, Livia began to paint for them a picture of her and Mitchell's carnally rambunctious night.

"We were on the dance floor kind of bumping and grinding like a good ol' 'blue lights in the basement' college party."

"Kind of like that homecoming party I had where you and Bobby Jeffries were doing the vertical dry hump," Aleesa remarked with a wink in her voice.

"Yeah," Livia said, missing the devious looks exchanged between her friends. "And just like that party, everybody was drunk or high and the sexual energy was so thick you could put your hand through it. Between the champagne, brownies, and the depravity of it all, I was really getting turned on. At first, I was kind of scared and embarrassed, but then I realized that nobody was watching us; they were too busy getting busy on their own! But can I tell you, I shocked myself with how much I liked the scandalous feeling…"

"Was Mitchell pushing you to do all of this?" Aleesa's protective side interrupted again to find out.

"No, absolutely not. I was doing it because I felt safe *being with* him. Before everything got started, Mitchell made it very clear that this was about my fantasies and my pleasure, and we could stop at any time. He was really considerate and just—well—great."

Amused glances and she's-so-into-him smirks were exchanged between Lena and Aleesa, as Livia continued with her account. She left out the part where she'd given Mitchell a blow job and he'd sucked her tits and finger-fucked her into a standing orgasm right on the dance floor. Some things needed to remain private.

"Well, the brownies kicked in and I was feeling really high, and ready to do the nasty right, so we went to the cabin. I was lying there blindfolded and Mitchell started kissing me, you know, down there, and then all of a sudden someone was kissing the girls."

"Ah, shit. Now, it's getting interesting!" Lena interjected with a chuckle.

"I knew it couldn't be Mitchell, so I peeked and saw this really attractive woman…she was stunning…kinda looked like Zoe Saldana…well, she took my boob out of her mouth and announced that she was here to give me a massage. I surprised even myself by not freaking out. I let it happen. It felt good and, honestly, I guess

I was too messed up at that point to care who was doling out the feel-goods."

With two sets of eyebrows raised, Lena and Aleesa looked at each other with an omigod-can-you-believe-this-shit look on their faces. Apparently, leaving home to do her dirty dealing had freed up all kinds of pent-up wantonness in little Miss Livia.

Undeterred by the shock on their faces, Livia continued to reveal the activities of her once in a lifetime adventure. She revealed to her friends how much she found herself getting into the girl-on-girl massage. It had been so soft and sensual, and nothing like she'd ever experienced before.

"I let her do her thing. But I wasn't messed up enough to actually have sex with her," Livia added, feeling the need to defend and qualify her actions. "For the most part, I let her touch my body, but Mitchell was the only one kissing me or taking care of Quincy."

"For the most part?" Lena, catching her telling remark, stopped Livia to ask.

Liv paused, quickly debating if she should tell the whole truth. Secure in the knowledge that she would not be judged, and hoping for some clarity, she decided to reveal the entire story. She told Lena and Aleesa how Shana had dripped warm oil on her tits and rubbed it into her chest, belly and nether regions. How she had surprised her by slipping her tongue into her mouth and giving her a slow, teasing kiss that matched the stroke of her hand between her legs, and how the whole thing was driving her snatch crazy with want.

"So naturally, I asked them to stop," Liv revealed.

"Why? It sounds like you were enjoying yourself," Lena commented.

"I was, well, my body was, but I felt like I was crossing too many boundaries. It didn't feel…you know…right. I wanted sex the old-fashioned way—dick in coochie. One man, one woman."

"Well, I'm glad you let yourself enjoy the experience," Aleesa told her.

"And learned the lesson that a tongue is a tongue."

"I'd never have done it sober, but it did kind of satisfy a curiosity. I'm like you, Lees, what did you call it? Strictly dickly."

"Like we told you before, curiosity doesn't make you gay. But, hell, even if you found that out that you were, who gives a damn?! We'd still love you anyway," Aleesa reassured her.

"Who you fuck says more about who you are than what body parts you use to fuck them with," Lena added.

Livia took a long sip of wine followed by a mouthful of calamari. She wanted to keep her mouth full so she could think instead of talk. *We'd love you anyway.* Aleesa's words buzzed through her head. If these two could think that about her, shouldn't she be a big enough, loving enough, a loyal enough friend to feel the same about Jasi?

"So speaking of being strictly dickly, this Mitchell, where does he live?" Lena probed with a smile.

"I don't know, but he works for some hedge fund in New York."

"Omigod! Lucky you! Handsome, hot, and local. It's like you ordered him from a catalog," Aleesa added. "He sounds perfect. When are you going to see him again?"

"You are going to see him again, aren't you?" Lena pressed, reading the look on Livia's face.

"No. I never gave him my number, and I threw away his, so that's that." Livia looked at both of their faces, perplexed by their obvious disbelief. "He's too young."

"There you go with that too young crap again," her cousin responded. "What do you have against attractive young men who are obviously attracted to you?"

"It's not like that. Mitchell's only a few years older than Ashri. How would you feel if your son was dating a woman as old as me?"

Aleesa took a minute to think about the situation. "I might have a few misgivings," she was forced admit. When painted on such a personal canvas, the scenario did take on a different look.

"Exactly. Mitchell and I are at different stages in our lives—"

"But I wouldn't try to stop Ashri. It's his journey," Aleesa interrupted Liv to clarify.

"We have nothing in common," Livia continued to insist.

"How would you know that? You only spent a few days together, and most of that did not involve talking," Lena pointed out.

"Uh, I think that the sixteen-year-age gap pretty much says it all. What could I possibly have in common with that boy?"

"Besides some insanely, freaky sexual attraction?"

"Okay, I'll give you that, but that attraction was with a man who doesn't even know my real name. As great as it was, as Mitchell is, I realized that I want more than sex. I want to be in a relationship again. I want what you and Walter have."

"Which is all fine and reasonable, but what are you going to do until then? Let your cupcake get all stale again?" Aleesa countered.

"Exactly," Lena chimed in. "Why can't you continue having fun with Mitchell until Mr. Right Age comes along?"

"Look, I did what I set out to do. I accomplished seven out of ten fantasies on my list, which is five more than I ever thought possible. I'm a little late, I know, but I've finally experienced my wild, crazy teen years. I'm walking into my fifties feeling confident and sexy, and open to what comes next. It's all good. So, give me a break!"

"Okay, okay. You're right. You fulfilled your promise. And we are definitely proud and happy for you. So we will back off on your boy toy. Now, speaking of walking into your fifties, we've made plans," Aleesa said, adroitly changing subjects.

"Two weeks from today, your time belongs to us," Lena added.

"What are you two cooking up?" Livia asked, her eyes moving from one woman to the other looking for clues.

"Nothing big and flashy like your tits out party. You know the reason it was so over the top was because Jasi had a hand in it. This time, it's the exact opposite—a few cocktails, a quiet dinner, and well, let's just say Jasi and Lena did manage to pull off a little somethin, somethin."

At the mention of Jasi's name, discomfort darkened Livia's face like an approaching thunder cloud.

"Okay, I know you don't like surprises, but humor us, will you?"

"It's not that."

"Then what's that look about?" her cousin demanded to know.

"I'm just surprised that Jasi is part of the planning."

"She told us what happened and why you're so upset with her, but it's time for you two to get past this nonsense and talk," Lena filled in.

"She told you everything?"

"Yep, and I can see why you might have been pissed, but if you had let her explain, you would have found out that she knew the bartender. He wasn't a stranger. She's known him for years," Aleesa said. "She always had your back, Liv."

"That's all she said?"

"Yes. And after all these years, you should know Jasi well enough to know that she'd never put you at risk like that."

It was clear to Livia that Jasi had not revealed all. She wanted to let them know that after all of these years, none of them knew Jasi as well as they thought they did. But she said nothing. This was Jasi's story to tell, not hers.

"You two need to get it together. Life is too short to lose a friend-ship over a silly misunderstanding," Aleesa concluded.

"You're right," Livia replied. "Jasi and I need to talk," *and about so much more than you know.*

Shadow Boinking

J asi lay back on the couch and listened with affection to the less than harmonious melody emanating from Belinda's very kissable mouth. With each sweet and sour note, Jasi's heart tightened with a sentimental dread. She'd finally found the one person who made her feel whole and happy to be the flawed and fabulous person she was. After years of living like a sexual gypsy, flitting about and fucking whomever struck her fancy, she'd suddenly, and irrevocably become a one-woman, woman. Since falling in love with Belinda, her wandering eyes now only sought the gaze of her beloved.

Breaking things off with Todd had been hard for everyone, particularly her parents, but it was the most liberating move she'd made since deciding to teach art instead of create it. Jasi no longer felt capable of giving her body to a man she wasn't attracted to or in love with in order to maintain a lie. And the need to secretly whore around with women in order to satisfy the natural lust she couldn't sate with Todd, had disappeared. In such a short and happy time, Belinda had become her friend and lover and the love of her life. When she was with Belinda, she didn't have to play any games, didn't need to the curb her desire for the soft, sexy touch of another woman.

Belinda's tonally challenged serenade ceased as she wandered into the living room from the kitchen. She affectionately ruffled the soft fringe of hair lining Jasi's neck as she passed. Jas responded with a gentle sigh of pleasure. She could never grow tired of this incredible woman's touch.

"Painting today, *Mami?*" Belinda inquired, lifting Jasi's head, sitting down and gently replacing her lover's head in her lap.

"No. I'm going to catch up on some school work this morning and then later, I'm meeting up with a girlfriend for lunch." Until this moment, Jasi had not mentioned Livia's phone call requesting that they meet and finally talk about what had happened between them.

"Humph!" Belinda's look and tone let Jasi know that she had some explaining to do.

"Don't look at me like that. Trust me, she's all the way straight. I've mentioned her. She's the one who had breast cancer." Jasi stopped short of revealing that Livia was also the same friend who'd caught them in the bathroom at Jessebelle's. It was a deliberate omission because she didn't want to talk about the status of her relationship with Livia and the reason it had fallen into such a sad state. And even if she wanted to, she couldn't, because Belinda still didn't know that she was a coward, still living her life in the closet.

"So, when am I going to meet this trio of straight *amiguitas* you're so fond of? I'm starting to feel like you're ashamed of me," Belinda said, only half-teasing.

"Never, Love. Look at you; you're a brilliant doctor, smokin' hot, sexy, and other than your inability to carry a tune even in your frickin' pocket, you're perfect."

"Then why haven't I met any of your friends or family?"

"Because I've been too busy falling in love with you, pretty girl," Jasi said before reaching up to deliver a kiss. It was both a punctuation on the truth and an effort to quell any further questions leading the conversation down that slippery slope.

Jasi lifted her hand to Belinda's face and lovingly caressed her cheek while her tongue explored her mouth. Her kiss was warm and loving, and through it, Jasi tried to convey the feelings and thoughts she wanted her beloved to walk away with. *I love you. Trust me. It's just so damn complicated.*

Belinda pulled away, and looked deeply into Jasi's eyes. *"Te quiero,* Jasi."

"I love you too," Jasi said as she felt her heart melt. No combination of words had ever sounded or felt so good before.

"But I am nobody's secret."

The truth stung, leaving Jasi feeling as if she'd been physically slapped. The guilty look in her eyes caused Belinda's brow to rise in suspicion.

"Of course you aren't. I have been totally selfish and wanting to enjoy having you all to myself," Jas said, lathering on the charm and hoping it worked.

"Then, *Mami,* it's time for me to meet your friends and family and you, mine."

"Soon. I promise."

"Okay. *Este Domingo.* You take me to brunch with your family *this* Sunday."

"I uh…well, it's just that…I'm not sure that this Sunday is… uh…"

"What is this?" Belinda demanded, interrupting Jasi's hemming and hawing. "Tell me *ahora* why you don't want me to meet your *familia?* Because I am Puerto Rican? *Que? Dime ahora! Que?"*

Jasi swallowed hard. She'd come to learn that the more Spanish Belinda peppered into her speech, the more pissed she was. Jas had to make a quick decision. She could either make her parents and friends look like terrible racists, and buy some more time, or reveal herself to be the cowardly lesbian she was. Both choices came riddled with additional problems. Adding a new lie on top of the existing deceit seemed a surefire way to lose this beauty forever. But by telling the truth, Jasi risked Belinda walking away after deciding she'd fallen in love with a woman she didn't really know or couldn't trust. Either way the margin of hurt loomed large.

The sounds of the household were magnified in the silence. Most prevalent was the ticking of the living room clock. With each tick, Jasi's shame and fear expanded, and with each tock the distance between the two lovers seemed to grow. Jasi sat up, reached over, and tightly wove her fingers into Belinda's, desperately needing a physical anchor to keep her close.

"Tell me, *Mami*," Belinda softened her voice to a plea. "Why do you think your family won't like me?"

"They will love you," Jasi assured her, deciding to tell her the truth. "How could they not? It's just—"

"Have you told them about me? Told anybody about us?"

"No. They don't know about you because the truth is, Belinda, they don't know about *me*."

Time stopped as the two women stared each other down, digesting the cold hard fact that Jasi had shared.

Disbelief colored her voice. "You're telling me that nobody in your family, and none of your friends, know that you like girls?" Belinda finally broke the silence to inquire.

"My parents don't know and neither do any of my close friends."

"I don't understand. You're not a teenager, or even in your twenties. How can you be as old as you are, and people still don't know the real you?"

"I don't even know the real me," Jasi sadly confessed.

"How could you? You live a lie."

"It's not something I'm proud of. I never found the right time or way to tell them. It's fucking complicated."

"That's bullshit, Jasi. Life is fucking complicated. And everybody's is, not just yours."

"I know, but I couldn't risk telling my straight friends because word might get out. And I was afraid if people knew I might lose my job. Parents are funny. They may not want a lesbian teaching their daughters."

"Are you ashamed of who you are?" Belinda asked, getting to the heart of the matter with point blank accuracy.

"No. It's not about shame. It's more about not wanting to disappoint my parents. They would never understand."

"So. Whose life is it?"

"You don't understand…"

"I understand because I lived it. I had to be brave and take control. My *papi* didn't speak to me for months when he found out that I was gay, and my mother cried for nearly a year, but they came around. You assume they won't understand. It is easier than being honest."

"Let me explain," Jasi pleaded. The look in Belinda's eyes frightened her. Gone was the endearing love she'd showered her with earlier. It had been pushed aside by a suspicious disappointment. Jasi needed to make Belinda understand the fears, rational or not, that had led her to live such a secretive existence.

"I'm listening."

Jasi went on to explain her mother's belief that children were a direct blessing from God and all her mother had lived an exemplary Christian life, wanting only to be blessed with a large family that would carry on for generations to come. But when Harolyn's wishes didn't coincide with God's plans, she'd had transplanted her dreams to her only child and daughter. The expectation for Jasi to marry and fill her parents' life with the large family they were not able to create themselves had started in high school and loomed large for the majority of Jasi's life.

"When did you know you were gay?"

Jas told her the entire story, starting with her first girl crush on Kimberly Brand in the seventh grade. Three years later, in her freshman year of high school, she had a revelation about her bisexuality, thanks to the nimble hands and kisses of first, Jackie Russell, and then later in the year, Timothy Smith. By her sophomore year in college, she'd realized her strong sexual preference for girls, and began her life as part of the closeted sisterhood. She was a covert lesbian, sleeping around with women while maintaining a heterosexual relationship on the side to assuage her parents. Over the years, Jasi developed a strong sexual appetite, enviable bedroom skills, and a keen knack for getting laid and walking away with no hard feelings.

"I was basically a good time girl. In and out, bodies satisfied, but emotions sanitized. Not pretty but it worked—until I met you.

"And that's continued until now," she said, pausing to try and read the emotions on Belinda's face.

"You have a boyfriend, still?" Belinda asked, refusing to fall under Jasi's spell.

"No, we broke up."

"When? Have you fucked him since you've been fucking me?"

"Yes," she confessed in the lowest possible voice to be heard. "But I promise you, Belinda, it didn't mean anything. Todd was a friend, a front, a man to put in front of my parents and friends and school colleagues to assure them that I was normal. We didn't even screw that much and once I realized that I was in love with you, I broke up with him."

"You *puta!*" Jealous rage shrouded Belinda's face, as her open hand delivered an irate blow across Jasi's cheek. Without warning, she pounced on her girlfriend in a moving fury of lips and limbs. Her hands pulled at the scoop neck of Jasi's tank top until it ripped. With angry lust, Belinda tore it in half, exposing Jasi's naked breasts. Lips, tongue and teeth descended on her tits, anger removing the desire for gentle loving, and mixing punishing pain with hurts so good pleasure. Belinda's teeth captured Jasi's tender flesh leaving marks in their wake before pulling at her nipples. Fingers replaced teeth, squeezing and twisting Jasi's swollen nipples. Jas screamed as the pain of her lover's bite sent shockwaves through her body, waking up her forlorn snatch.

"Pero no voy viven en las sombras," Belinda hissed with a sexy, dominatrix tone as she reached for the hairbrush on the end table. Jasi had no time to wonder what her lovely Latina had uttered, as Belinda expertly pulled the string on her pajamas pants and watched them drop to the floor. "Bend over the couch," she demanded.

Drunk on a cocktail of remorse and lust, Jasi obeyed without comment. Usually she played the alpha role in their lovemaking, and Belinda's unexpected rough and demanding vibe was turning her the fuck on.

She knelt on the seat cushions resting her elbows on the back of the sofa. Seconds later, she felt Belinda's soft, warm palm circling the fleshiest part of her left butt cheek, followed by the quick stinging slap of wood on bare ass.

"Ow!" Jasi groaned.

"Don't you ever lie to me again," Belinda ordered, giving her another slap with her hairbrush.

"I won't, baby. Now please lick me. I need you to eat me."

"No. You make yourself come while I watch," Belinda decided, slapping Jasi's ass one more time for good measure.

Every nerve in Jasi's body was throbbing, but the smarting sensation only made her hornier. She grabbed her own breast, squeezing it hard enough to bruise before tweaking the sore nips. For whatever reason, the pain was making her feel incredibly vibrant and alive. Rather than feeling like a punishment, this mild dawdling into the S & M arena felt more like a prize.

Jasi ran her hand down her torso, caressing her belly before sliding down toward her nearly hairless snatch. Before her hand could delve inside, Belinda slipped her hand between Jasi's legs and forcefully slapped her lower lips. Jasi jumped slightly, enjoying the sensations traveling through her nether regions.

"Turn around so I can watch."

Again, Jasi followed orders, lying back on the couch with her knees up and spread, allowing her easy access into her hole, and Belinda an unobstructed view. She dipped inside to harvest the warm juices of her turned out pussy. Slowly, Jasi smeared her engorged clit and began to rub, feeling it getting longer and harder in anticipation of orgasm. She closed her eyes to better savor the intense pleasure as she pushed, tickled and taunted her nib almost to the point of no return.

Without warning, Belinda sprang on her lover, grabbing and sucking on her titties while shoving three fingers deep into Jasi's twat. Jas pushed her pelvis against her palm wanting to fully partake in Belinda's relentlessly raw and demanding finger-fucking.

"*Pero no voy viven en las sombras,*" Belinda hissed again, after lifting her head from Jasi's breasts.

"What, baby?" Jasi managed to breathlessly squeak out between moans. "I don't understand."

"I will not live in the shadows. Not for *mi familia* or you," Belinda informed her, leaving a trail of angry bites down Jasi's torso as her mouth traded places with her hands. She used her teeth to gently tug at Jasi's labia before slipping her stiff tongue into the ocean of pink and tongue-fucking her.

"It's over, I promise. I love you," was Jasi's breathy response.

The hot and briny scent of sex permeated the living room and raised Jasi's arousal to the point of no return. Jasi tried to relax her body and give into the sensations overtaking her. Just as she'd momentarily settled the tension, Belinda disrupted her calm by reaching up and squeezing her nipples while she rhythmically licked and sucked her big fat clit until it began to contract and pulsate.

Belinda repositioned herself, scissoring her legs between Jasi's so her furry mound kissed Jasi's nearly bald one. She thrust back and forth, rubbing their pussies together and totally enjoying the fantastic friction it was creating. She spread her lips so her clit could rub directly on Jasi's smooth, wet pussy.

"I'm the only one you fuck from now on!" Belinda screamed as she felt herself getting closer to exploding.

"Yes, baby, only you," Jasi responded, feeling her twat getting fired up again. The lovers continued to rub and grind on each other until Belinda screamed, releasing her anger and love and announcing the arrival of her orgasm as her clit throbbed against Jasi's.

Belinda collapsed on top and tried to regulate her breath, while Jasi relaxed into the fading tide of her own emotions and physical pleasure.

"I love you," Jasi said. "I promise. No more shadows. I'm not sure how. I don't have all the answers yet, but I'm going to make this right."

"Good, but first you need to find the answer to one important question," Belinda, back to her soft and gentle self, informed her. "Why do you not trust anyone to love you for you?"

Let Bi-Girls Be Bi-Gones

"You look great," Jasi remarked as she quickly looked up from her coffee mug to observe. "Have you lost weight?"

"Not really. Must be the new jeans. Thank God for spandex," Livia quipped with polite reserve.

"Have you seen the new Billy Dee Williams exhibit at the Loth Gallery?" Jasi asked, hoping their mutual talent and appreciation for art would kick start the discussion.

"No, I always had a kind of a ho-hum feeling about actors turned artists. I guess because it so often feels that it's their celebrity, not true talent, that gets them revered as artists."

"Yeah, I get that joke."

Both women sat nervously at the table making the smallest of talk, neither exactly sure how to begin this most uncomfortable conversation. Other than a few early, and ultimately unsuccessful, outreach attempts by Jasi, the two had not spoken since "the incident."

As the waitress approached and warmed their coffee, an uncomfortable silence descended over their table. If the air was to be cleared between the two of them today, somebody needed to get the conversation moving.

Tired of the silliness, Jasi decided to apply her own brand of air freshener. "I owe you an apology."

"For what, setting me up to have sex with a perfect stranger?" Livia asked. Lena and Aleesa had already explained all of this to her, but it was easier to talk about that than delve into the delicate reason Livi thought she deserved an apology.

"I would never do that to you. There was never any safety threat because Julian was no stranger. I've been going to Jessebelle's for years and he's a good guy. I knew you'd be safe and in good hands.

"Another lie," Livia said under her breath.

"What?" Jasi felt the prickles of anger beginning to surface.

"I said, that's just another lie. You let me think that he was a stranger, just like you let me think…let all of us think…" Livia's accusation died in her throat.

Jasi took a deep breath in an attempt to monitor her anxiety. This conversation had the potential of blowing up in so many ugly ways she really wanted to avoid. The truth of the matter was that she missed Livia, and wanted to put get their friendship back on track, but in a more open and honest place. Belinda was absolutely right; she didn't deserve to live and love in the shadows and neither did Jasi. She really hoped her girlfriends could deal with and accept the truth about her sexuality, but if they couldn't, there was no choice to be made. Now and forever, Belinda would always come first.

"Yes, it's true that I let you believe that your Mr. Fox was a stranger, but I wasn't trying to deceive you. I was trying to help you have some fun and get through your list."

Livia listened to her friend, instinctively believing that she was telling the truth, just like she knew that the bartender had little to do with what she was really upset about.

"I know."

"Then why don't we talk about what's really bothering you?"

Silence once again descended around them as both women took the time to digest the seriousness of what was not being said. Several months' worth of divergent thoughts ran through Livia's mind.

Everything from walking in on Jasi and that woman in the bathroom, to her discussions about the idea of sex with a woman turning them on, to her own quasi bisexual experience on the yacht.

Livia looked across the table at her friend. Jasi sat nervously tapping her fingers against the table while a telling look of distress colored her face. Behind all of her bluster, Livi could tell that she was apprehensive about opening up about this deeply personal subject. Compassion flooded her body as Livia remembered her own reluctance to admit to Lena and Aleesa that she simply liked watching two women making love. She could only imagine how hard it must be for Jasi, after all of this time, to admit to it being her preferred lifestyle.

"Are you a lesbian?" Livia asked, dropping the question on the table as an act of compassion.

"Yes, I'm gay," Jasi admitted and then exhaled sharply. There, she'd said it, and it felt strangely liberating. This was the first time she'd ever spoken those words to anyone other than Belinda. Even the many women she'd messed around with always were told that she was bisexual. Only Belinda had made her realize how she'd been hiding behind the term to keep from admitting who and what she truly was.

"What about Todd?" Livia asked as she tried to process Jasi's confirmation of what she'd already figured out.

"I loved Todd. I still do. He is a kind and decent friend, but basically he was in my life to keep my mother happy," Jasi admitted.

"You mean fooled, like the rest of us."

"Okay, I'll accept that. Yes. I kept Todd in my life to fool the rest of you into believing that I was straight."

"Why? I thought we were friends."

"So did I."

"Well, friends don't lie to friends, especially about something so huge. You've been lying to all of us for years," Livia shot back. "Where's the friendship in that?"

"Yeah, well, friends accept their friends for who they are," Jasi responded with a quiet bite to her tone.

"You never gave me, or anyone else it sounds like, the chance. Clearly, you believed that none of us—neither your friends nor your family—would have accepted you knowing you were a lesbian."

"Did you? Because correct me if I'm wrong, but ever since Jesse-belle's, you've been avoiding me like I've got bird flu or something. Instead of reaching out, you cut me off. You've been upset with me for months just because I had sex with a woman. So where's the friendship in that? Where's the acceptance in that?"

Livia felt the sting of Jasi's accusation. She honestly could not dispute anything she'd just said. Ever since she walked through that restroom door, a myriad of thoughts, opinions and judgments against Jasi had swirled around her head. If she was to be truthful with herself, Livia had to admit that she'd settled on being mad at Jasi for lying to her as a way to avoid her own wrong and unsupportive actions against her friend.

"Honestly, I didn't know what to think," Livia admitted. "All my life I was taught all kinds of things about homosexuality from my family and church. Most, I can see now, were bullshit. I never had to deal with how I felt about gay people in any real way. I never really knew any."

"Well, now you do," Jasi interrupted, feeling stronger and more at ease about opening up. "And I'm the same crazy-ass bitch you knew before you found out that I like sleeping with women. Nothing else has really changed."

"I think I always understood that. But to be honest, what really pissed me off was that there you were at my party and at Tickle Me Pink, making all of these demands that I make this list and go out and screw the world, and that I own it, and make no excuses. I mean I teased you, but I've never told you how much I really did admire you for being so open when it came to sex, and then I come to find out that it was all bull. You couldn't even do those things for yourself."

Jasi covered her face with her hands to hide the shame. Livia spoke the truth. She had pushed and damn near shamed the poor girl into branching out and taking control of her sex life and there she was being a hypocritical chicken shit.

"I'm really sorry, Liv."

"And I'm sorry, too. Despite all of that, I should have given you the opportunity to explain instead of ignoring you. All I can say in my defense was that it was easier for me to be mad at you for betraying me than to face the fact that I was betraying you. "

"Apology accepted. Don't worry about it. In hindsight, it was probably best that you didn't. I doubt that I could have been truthful with you then. I probably would have stayed with that bullshit story about being drunk and trying to satisfy some one-time girl-on-girl curiosity.

"I should have been honest with you and the girls, but the real deal, Livia, is that I've been living a lie all of my life. Nobody knows who I am, not my parents, my friends, Todd, my past lovers…shit, I'm pretty shaky on the subject my damn self. I've been too ashamed of who I really am, and too afraid of disappointing people to be honest with anyone, including myself. I wasn't ready to be real back then, but I am now."

"So what's changed?"

"For one, I'm too fucking old to be worried about what other people think about me, or my lifestyle choices. But it was Belinda who really helped me see that when it came down to it, the only person I was hurting with all of my deceitfulness was me."

"Belinda?"

"Yeah, ahh, actually you've met…kind of."

"The woman at Jessebelle's? In the bathroom?"

"Yes. Dr. Belinda Rodriquez," Jasi said, loving the taste of Belinda's name in her mouth.

The wide grin traipsing across Jasi's face said it all. In the two years that she'd dated Todd, Jasi had never looked or sounded so happy.

"Jasi Westfield, I'll be damned. You're in love."

Like the teenager she felt like, Jasi burst out into giggles. Her joyful laughter was contagious, beseeching Livia to join in. The sounds of their combined mirth melted away any residual angst and anger, finally bringing the two back together.

"I'm genuinely happy for you, Jas. I've never seen you like this."

"I've never felt like this. I am officially a one-woman, woman!"

"To love," Livia said, raising her coffee mug for a toast. She touched the side of Jasi's mug while pushing down the twinges of jealousy threatening to rear its ugly head. She was genuinely thrilled for Jasi, but couldn't help wishing that she had a love in her life to giggle over and feel gushy about. Envy was quickly swallowed by an aching sense of lonesomeness. For the first time since her divorce, Livia felt ready, willing and truly wanting to be in love. Mitchell immediately came to mind. Their vacation affair had turned the spigot on those emotions. Livi quickly shut down that thought, wistfully reminding herself that theirs had been a lustful relationship, not a loving one.

"Now, I've got to figure out how to tell Lena and Aleesa." Jasi looked over at Livia, trying to read her face.

"They won't be a problem, and no, I didn't say anything to them. I figured it was your story to tell, not mine."

"Thank you, I think."

"So, when do we get to meet Belinda?"

"Soon," Jasi promised. "She's dying to meet you all and my parents. Though I don't know how that's going to go down."

"The same way it went down with me. Tell them…without shame or embarrassment or looking for approval. Tell them about her. When they see how much you love this girl written all over your face, like I did just now, they won't be able to deny your happiness."

"Let's hope."

"It's like you told me at my party, 'take no prisoners and make no excuses.'"

"I am one sage bitch, ain't I?" Jasi said with a giggle.

"So you keep telling us! Now, speaking of parties, why don't you bring Belinda to my birthday dinner? It will be a perfect time for us to all meet her."

"She'll love that. Thank you for asking."

Livia held out her little finger. "Pinky swear."

"On what?"

"Pinky swear that you won't let your stupid fears or what you think people will think mess this up for you. That you'll love this girl openly and honestly and let her love you."

Jasi wrapped her little finger around Livia's. "I am going to try my damnedest; because, Livi, I do love this girl and don't want to fuck it up."

"Good, speaking of fucking, promise to keep that wandering dick…well, girl dick in your pants."

"Gladly. I don't want to be with anyone else. So, back to your birthday, I have to ask, how's that list of yours coming?"

"I think you'll be surprised and very proud of me," Livia mentioned with a coy twist to her mouth.

"What's that about?"

"Well, let's just say that while I'm definitely not Lebanese, I better understand your attraction to women."

"WHAT! You and your no having sex self got down and dirty with a girl?" Jasi asked, her mouth wide open with genuine surprise.

Again the giggles began, and both knew that they were back to being BFFs. "Not exactly; see what had happened was…"

Master That Piece Theater

"Happy Birthday!" her friends shouted as they led her to the front doors of the Broadway Theatre.

"*Sister Act!* Really? Thank you; thank you. I've been so wanting to see this."

"We know," Jasi said, "which is why we're all here."

"And we've arranged for a little surprise after the performance," Lena chimed in.

"Backstage passes? This gift just keeps getting better."

"We're not saying. You'll have to wait to find out," her cousin teased.

"Okay, but if Whoopi Goldberg shows up with a cake, I'm warning you now, I'm going to embarrass all of us."

"Why should tonight be any different?" Jasi laughed. "Belinda and I are going to head to our seats. We'll see you later. Enjoy the show, birthday girl."

"We're not all sitting together?"

"Sorry, we couldn't get all the seats together," Aleesa informed her. "So you and I are sitting together and Lena is sitting with Jasi and her girlfriend."

"No worries. I really appreciate all the effort you put into this. Cocktails together at Nobu. I don't know how you wrangled those reservations, and now *Sister Act*. It's been a great birthday so far. Thank you."

"Hey, you're only fifty once," Jasi remarked.

"Unless you're my mother," Lena quipped.

"Enjoy the show, Livia," Belinda said before she and Jasi walked, hand in hand, into the theater to find their seats.

Livia's eyes followed the couple. "So before we go in, what do you all think?" she queried the remaining two.

"I don't know why, but I'm not shocked," Lena commented.

"Me either. It's not like I ever suspected it, but Jasi is so damn wild, anything is possible. Belinda seems cool."

"And I've never seen Jasi so happy," Liv added.

"Belinda might be the one to settle her ass down."

"Poor Todd, though. I wonder if he even had a clue," Lena questioned.

"Forget Todd; it's her mother who's going to have a conniption," Aleesa added. "We should all be there for support when Jasi finally tells them."

"If she wants us there, we will, but my hunch is that Jasi will want this to be a private family moment. We can discuss all of this later. We'd better get to our seats," Lena suggested, giving Aleesa a knowing look. "I'll see you later. Enjoy the show!"

As Lena walked off, Livia and her cousin followed the usher down to their seats. Just as they got to their row, Aleesa stopped and announced she had to visit the ladies' room.

"You go sit. I'll be right back."

Livia entered the row and found her seat. She sat quietly, studying the program and basking in the pre-performance energy buzzing around the auditorium. The people around her included couples and families eagerly awaiting the curtain rising. *Sister Act* had been advertised as a feel-good show, and clearly the audience had arrived with the same preset attitude. Her roving eyes were drawn to a couple nuzzling together in their seats. The haunting sense of envy and lonesomeness returned. As lovely as it was to have her girlfriends' loving thoughtfulness and support, Liv would rather be celebrating this milestone birthday with a man—her man. The quest to complete that damn list before this day had oiled up her rusty libido and left her feeling hot and horny and wanting sex like never before in her life. But even more than great sex, she wanted to be in love.

The lights flickered, signaling the imminent start of the play, and prompting Livia to stand and survey the room looking for her cousin. There was no sign of Aleesa, prompting Livia to decide that there must already be a line in the ladies' room. She craned her neck toward the other side of the aisle and the corner of her eye caught a profile that stole her breath and violently threw her heart against her chest.

Could it be? No? Maybe. Was that Mitchell? A cocktail of hopefulness and trepidation stirred in her belly, while a myriad of questions burned through her brain. Was fate bringing them together again? Should she go over? What if he was on a date? Should she let him make the first move?

His face was temporarily blocked by the bodies of theater-goers hurrying to their seats. As the aisle cleared, Livia's anxiety was quieted when the face in question turned in her direction, turning her dashed hope into disappointment.

Omigod, you actually miss that man!

It's not Mitchell I miss, it's the sex. No, it's the companionship, not the companion, Livia argued in her head, needing the clarity. What she'd really like on this milestone evening was a love to share it with. *Livia Charles, get that young boy out of your head*, she commanded herself.

Feeling uncomfortably discombobulated, Livi picked up her purse and rummaged inside looking for breath mints. She didn't want to think about Mitchell or her lonely existence. She simply wanted to get lost in this show and enjoy her evening.

The lights flickered again while the row began to undulate as those seated rose in a wave to accommodate a latecomer. *Finally,* Livia thought, looking over and expecting to see Aleesa, but instead of her cousin, she found herself looking into the waist of a very tall, well-dressed gentleman about to sit down beside her.

"I'm sorry, but this seat is taken," Livia barely looked up to inform him.

"This is Row T, seat 110, isn't it?"

"Uh, yes."

"Then it's my seat."

"Well, then, there's obviously some mistake."

Before she could call the usher over, the lights went out and the man sat. As the curtain came up, Livia ignored the opening action and craned her neck around from left to right trying to find her cousin. Aleesa was nowhere to be found.

The confused look on Livia's face was too unsettling to ignore.

"Happy Birthday, Livi Girl," the man leaned close to her ear to say.

Livia's eyes went wide. Could it be? Nobody had called her Livi Girl in over thirty years. In fact, only one person had nicknamed her that, the first love of her life.

"Bobby?"

"The one and only."

"What are you doing here? I mean, how did you…what are you…who…"

"Your cousin. Aleesa and your girls planned all of this, and flew me here to surprise you."

"Shhhh," the woman next to them insisted.

"We'll talk after the show."

Livia smiled and turned her attention back to the performance. Shocked by the unexpected appearance of her first true love, Liv fought to keep her thoughts focused on the energetic musical performance before her. Once the singing stopped, however, Liv couldn't help but to sneak a sideways peek at her apparent birthday gift. Bobby had the same idea, and their smiling eyes met in the dark. They shared a grin before returning their attention back to center stage. Livia felt her heart once again jump and slam into her ribcage.

He looks good! she thought as her mind quickly compared Bobby to the boy she'd last seen over thirty years ago. Even in this dim light, she could tell that the years had obviously been kind. Time had brought changes, but underneath the additional pounds and salt-and-pepper hair, was the body and soul of the gangly kid she'd once known and loved.

They were just kids back then, both crazy in love with each other. Bobby, a senior and star basketball player, had showed up one day at Livia's cheerleading competition. He'd sat in the seats, watching her every move and eating her up with his eyes the entire time. His lavish attention definitely added to her nerves, but in a pleasing and awesome way that bolstered her confidence. After the competition, the rest of the squad had been disappointed by their third-place showing, but when the awesome and oh so popular Bobby Jeffries met her outside and asked her out, Livia felt like she was walking away with the grand prize.

As the weeks progressed, his good-humored audaciousness and ability to make her feel adored and protected, turned a schoolgirl crush into full-fledged love. She and Bobby became a well-known, and happily clichéd entity—the high school superstar athlete and his cheerleader girlfriend. They were together his entire senior year, and during that time, Bobby Jeffries proved himself to be a

loving and thoughtful young man. He was high-spirited and adventurous, and in so many ways made a relatively shy Livia blossom.

By the summer after his graduation, Bobby's yeoman patience
with his girlfriend had reached its limits. As time marched on, and
kissing and heavy petting with Livia became more painful than
pleasurable, he, as young men have a tendency to do, began to
pressure her to go all the way.

Livia's body was more than willing, but the powerful convictions her parents and pastor had planted within her won out over
temptation. For 16-year-old Livia Charles, living in the early 1970s
in a strict Catholic household, sex before marriage was not an option.
Bobby had been as understanding as a teenager with raging hor-
mones could be, but eventually, his tolerance for celibacy wore
thin. He did have the decency to break up with her before he took
up with the much more amenable Sandra Middleton.

Livi had been crushed at the time, but looking back, she couldn't
blame him. Her memories of their time together had always been
fond and full of happiness. Over the years, wondering what she
might have missed and given up had haunted her, which is exactly why she'd added him to her list of fuckable wishes.

Your cousin planned all of this. Bobby's words interrupted her
reverie. Those sneaky bitches! So this is what they must have
meant by a surprise after the show. She'd assumed that they'd
secured backstage passes for her to meet the cast. In reality, they'd
set her up for the night with the one item from her list that she'd
never expected to fulfill. She didn't know whether to be grateful
or spiteful. Livia couldn't worry about that now because the overwhelming emotion overtaking her at the moment was curiosity.

The first act ended to the sound of thunderous applause. No
doubt, *Sister Act* was a hit. As the crowd filed out for intermission,
Livia was unsure about what to do. Part of her wanted to run and

find her friends, first to beat them down for setting her up like this, and then to ask their advice on how to proceed. She hadn't seen this man in over thirty years. And it wasn't like they'd just bumped into each other. Whether Bobby knew it or not, this meeting had been prearranged for the sole purpose of having sex. They might as well have hired a male escort. It would have made all of this much easier. Without intending to, her cousin and friends had placed her in the exact same place Bobby had left her years ago, wondering if she should or shouldn't have sex with him.

Does he know why he's here? That disconcerting thought shot its way to the forefront of Livia's frazzled mind. She wouldn't put it past Jasi or Lena to have fully explained the situation to Bobby. Jeezus. How desperate must she seem? Livia felt the armor of shy reserve fall around her.

"Excuse us," the woman on the other side of her requested. Livia stood to let them pass, causing her to drop her forgotten purse from her lap, spilling its contents under the seats. Once the couple exited the row, Bobby retrieved all of her scattered belongings and returned them to their embarrassed owner.

"Thank you," she said, accepting her things with a wrinkle of her nose.

"I guess some things never change," he commented with a grin.

"What? Me being a clumsy doofus?"

"No, the way you do that bunny thing with your nose when you're embarrassed. Like you're trying to erase it off your face. I used to think it was really cute back in the day. And like I said, some things never change."

"So then you still must dance like you're doing the Charleston," Livia said, her face breaking out in a huge smile.

"Oh, that was cold. It's wrong to talk about a black man's ability to dance."

"Or lack thereof…"

The two broke out into companionable laughter. Their good-natured teasing felt wonderful, like it had when they were kids.

"Well, it's true, I still can't dance, but I can still pick out the finest sister in the place when I see her. You look amazing, Livi Girl."

The way his eyes traveled her body and drank her in reminded Livia of the way Mitchell had looked at her on the beach. It was the same polite, albeit hungry, ogle that was a true turn on. Liv could feel her shy reserve began to melt, slowly revealing the grown and sexy woman Mitchell had brought out in her. Quincy was in the house.

"Thank you. As do you. So, how have you been, Bobby?"

"All in all, I can't complain. After college, I had a few hard looks but wasn't able to crack the NBA, so I played ball over in Europe for ten years. Got married and had a couple of kids, but once we got back to the States, the marriage started to unravel. Rita and I limped along for more years than we should have, and finally, after twenty-one years, we divorced."

"Sorry to hear that, but I understand completely. I married my college sweetheart and we lasted twenty-three years."

"So you're divorced as well? Just how does a beautiful single lady like you spend her time?" Bobby flirted.

"Oh, mostly working hard. I own a bakery, Havin' Your Cake, in New Jersey. We specialize in wedding and other special occasion cakes. I was even featured on the *Today Show*," Livia bragged.

"No wonder you smell like sugar."

Livia lifted her eyes to his and let them do the thanking.

"But I remember you being an artist. I always thought I'd find your sculptures in a gallery somewhere."

"I like to think that my work is edible art. I use frosting instead of clay to make it."

"So what do you do to play?"

"I love to travel when I get the chance. I most recently visited St. Bart's," she told him with an *"I've got a secret"* twist to her voice.

"Love St. Bart's."

"Yeah, me too. And what about you? What did you fall into after basketball?"

"I'm in the Coke business." Bobby watched with amusement as Livia's eyes grew wide, drawing her mouth open with them. "I see you still have absolutely no poker face whatsoever. Your thoughts have always been broadcast right across that beautiful mug of yours. I'm a Coca-Cola distributor. In fact, I own the largest bottling company in California," he revealed, doing a little boasting of his own.

"That's where you live?"

"Yes, down South in Del Mar, San Diego."

"Success becomes you, Bobby."

"Just like that dress becomes you," he flirted, smiling while he surveyed her simply sexy, David Meister little black dress. His appreciative look stopped at her eyes.

Bobby's smile remained steady as the house lights flickered. Livia broke their gaze to take a quick look around the theater, hoping to catch the attention of at least one of her traitorous friends. There they were, across the aisle and several rows ahead, smiling and waving like the lovable fools they were. Even Belinda, the new girl to their party, was grinning ear to ear. Livia laughed. She fit right into this motley crew!

Darkness once again fell upon the crowd. Grateful to be alone with her thoughts, Liv quickly analyzed the evening thus far. While it was unclear to her whether Bobby knew why he'd been summoned here tonight, a spark definitely remained between them. They were both still attracted to each other, even after all these years. And the idea of finishing something between them that never got started was as much of an aphrodisiac as the citrusy-smelling cologne Bobby was wearing. But the reality remained that they were basically strangers—familiar and friendly, yes—but all of the time that had passed between them rendered them mere acquaintances.

Lately, intimacy with comfortable strangers seemed to be the running theme of her fledgling love life. First, with Mitchell and now, Bobby. What the hell was the universe trying to teach her through these guest lovers that she hadn't been able to learn from nearly a quarter of a century with her ex-husband?

As the curtain rose and the cast broke out into gleeful song, their attention got caught up in the thrill of the second act. Livia smiled into the darkness. As much as she adored them, she was happy not to have to spend her fiftieth birthday in the company of her girlfriends. Whether she spent it in the arms of her former love, and this evening turned into a cheery check on her fuck-it list, still remained to be seen.

A Fantasy Real

Bobby and Livia stood outside the theater waiting for the rest of the group. The crowd had thinned considerably and there was still no sign of the girls. Knowing her friends, especially the delightfully devious Jasi Westfield, something was cooking besides dinner after the show.

"Maybe they went backstage?" Bobby suggested.

"Without me? That's not right. I'm the birthday girl!" Livia kidded as her pocket began to vibrate. "Excuse me." She pulled her phone from her pocket and saw Aleesa's text message screaming across the screen.

We're out. Enjoy yourself. Happy Birthday 2 U!

"Well, it looks like we've been abandoned. I'm sorry. I have no idea what my cousin was thinking to put you in such an awkward position."

"I always liked that Aleesa. And as far as awkward positions go, it's a matter of practice," Bobby remarked with a crooked smile.

Okay, what's up with all of these sexy comments? Does he know, Livia thought to herself, *or is he just flirting with me?*

And so what if he is, Quincy popped up to argue. *I thought the whole idea was for us to get some tonight.*

What if he decides he doesn't want to? Livia argued with the voice in her head.

Trust me, curiosity fucks the cat every time, Quincy shot back.

"So, Livi Girl, shall we go somewhere and get better reacquainted?"

This time it was Bobby's phone that interrupted them. He looked at his cell and burst out laughing. "Aleesa's timing is impeccable," he told her. "She's texted me our instructions for the evening. Apparently, dinner is awaiting us at the Mandarin Oriental Hotel on Columbus Circle. I'm supposed to check with the concierge for instructions."

Livia had to chuckle. Lees had arranged for them to have dinner at the exact spot that Walter had booked for her as his anniversary gift—the gift that gave Aleesa permission to hook up with that sexy photographer. The gift that, thanks to both her cousin and her husband coming to their senses, never got redeemed.

"Good memories?" Bobby asked, noticing her amusement.

"Not quite. It's kind of a family joke."

"Well, let's grab a cab and you can make me laugh on the way."

Less than ten minutes later, Livia and Bobby were navigating Columbus Circle and arrived at the Mandarin Oriental Hotel. They walked through the front doors and into a posh entry where they were directed through another etched glass door to a bank of elevators. The two traveled in companionable silence up thirty-five floors, each enjoying the quiet buzz of anticipation. As she'd done in the theater, Livia snuck a few sideways glances at her old flame, marveling at his well-preserved physique. Dressed in a gray suit with a thin pinstripe, Bobby had the commanding presence of a successful CEO. The man beside her exuded power, a power that was both compelling as well as intimidating. Her eye caught their reflection in the rose-patterned swirls of brass embedded in the gleaming dark woods of the elevator doors. There they were again, the basketball star and his cheerleader—still a golden couple at the onset of their golden years.

A soft chime informed them that they'd reached their destination. The elevator doors parted and Livia and Bobby stepped out of the lift and into the soothing, Asian-inspired design of the hotel lobby. Bobby followed Aleesa's instructions and went directly to the concierge to find out what was coming next in what was turning out to be an evening full of surprises. First, at the theater, not only had Livia been surprised, but he also had been pleasantly shocked to learn that the girl he'd loved so long ago was as sweet and beautiful as ever. Ultimately, curiosity had been the impetus behind Bobby's acceptance of Aleesa's invitation. Over the years, he'd often thought about Livia, sorry for any pain he'd caused her, and wondering what had become of her, as well as what might have been. His Livi Girl was as sweet as before. Was she still as innocent as well? They'd broken up over unfinished business. Now he was in New York City ready, if she was willing, to complete what they'd begun over thirty years ago.

"It's for you," Bobby told her, handing her a lovely handmade gift card.

Livia opened the envelope and read silently to herself, unsure if what had been written was appropriate to share with her date.

When one reaches a milestone like fifty, one can't help but look back and ask: What if? But fifty is also the age when one should either find out the answer or forget the question. Happy Birthday, Livia. Enjoy your special evening with a special friend. Whether you decide to cross Bobby off the list, or keep the fantasy alive, is up to you. All we've given you is the opportunity. Dinner is on us at Asiate. For dessert, we've booked you a suite here for the night. Do with it what you will, share it with Bobby or treat yourself. Just promise you'll go wherever the evening takes you.

Much love, Jasi and Belinda, Lena and Me.

PS. Walter and I had big fun at this hotel; hope you do too!

Enclosed were two condoms and a hotel key. Livia quickly tucked them it into her coat pocket. Her friends had set her up right and given her sage advice that immediately cleared her head and soothed her anxiety—"just go wherever the evening takes you."

"We're having dinner here at the Asiate. I hope you like Asian," she said as she turned to fill Bobby in.

"I live in California, need I say more?" His words did not reveal his thoughts. With all of the great restaurants to choose from in New York City, why were they sent to a magnificent hotel for dinner? True, the Asiate had a world-class reputation, but he had to wonder, were the beds surrounding this splendid eatery included in her birthday surprise? Staring at a beautiful piece of a mostly happy past, Bobby's imagination whet appetites that had nothing to do with what was on the menu.

They walked past the huge glass floral display and into the bright, stark and airy aesthetic of the award-winning restaurant. Livia was immediately struck by the giant, silvery white tree branch sculpture that adorned the ceiling. It was like standing under a snowy branch in Central Park. Looking around, it was clear that the simple décor was a decision to let the city and park views from the floor-to-ceiling windows speak for themselves. The view's only competition was the wall display of what looked to be thousands of bottles of wine.

Bobby gave the *maître d'* their names and Bobby placed his hand lightly on the small of Livia's back as they followed him to one of the private booths lining the sides of the room. Livia noticed heads turn as foreign tourists and well-heeled New Yorkers looked up and wondered who they were. Few faces of color populated the dining room, and the question marks swirling around the room seemed to punctuate the same ignorant thoughts—they must be *somebody* if they can afford to dine here. Because of Bobby's height, most, she was sure, took him for some famous, albeit retired, athlete. Livia noticed several complimentary gazes directed at her as well. She smiled. They recognized what she herself had in the elevator. She and Bobby still made a stunning couple.

The two slid into the booth on opposite sides of the table. They sat across the table, alternating their gazes between each other and the gorgeous city vista outside their private window. Silence between them was the perfect soundtrack for the moment. This was all so beautiful and perfect. It was impossible not to feel the romance surrounding them.

"May I take your drink order?" the waiter inquired.

"Champagne?" Bobby asked her.

"Sure."

While Bobby and the sommelier discussed the wine selection, Livia stared down on Columbus Circle and made the decision to turn back time. This setting was too incredibly romantic, and she wanted to be part of a pair way too much to pass up the opportunity. Tonight, she was back to being Livia Draper, young and in love with her man, Bobby Jeffries. But instead of a nervous, untested vagina in her pants, she had Quincy, a horny hot box who was ready to pull out all of the tricks in her newly acquired sex bag, and give Bobby a taste of what he'd been wondering about all of these years.

What makes you think he's been wondering about it? the pesky naysayer within queried.

One, because I've been thinking about it, and two, it's pretty clear by the way he's looking at me.

In her heart, Livia knew that Bobby hadn't missed much way back when. Hell, if this evening had happened a few short months ago, he probably wouldn't have missed anything then either. But thanks to her accelerated tutorial at the very capable hands of one island boy toy, the newly liberated, grown-ass, "bringing sexy back" Livi Charles was about get Mr. Bobby's belated homecoming party started.

"Why are you smiling?"

"Because it's really nice to see you again," she said, giving him a flirtatious grin, followed by the Mitchell-approved lip bite.

"It is, isn't it? I'll admit, uh, that when Aleesa contacted me, I wasn't sure if this was a good idea. I mean, it's been a long time and I didn't know what had become of you or your life."

"Completely understandable, but I'm glad you decided to come, and hope..." Livia paused to lower her eyelids for two seconds and then lifted them and looked directly into Bobby's eyes, "that you aren't disappointed."

A slash of white spread across his face. Any forthcoming comment was waylaid by the appearance of their wine. A delicious tension began to percolate in the silence while the waiter uncorked the bottle and poured their flutes.

"To be honest, I am slightly disappointed," he teased, "but only in myself for not having the guts to contact you years ago. You, my Livi Girl, are a sight for very sore eyes."

This time it was Livia's turn to smile. "Let's toast to new light through old windows," she offered, raising her champagne glass.

"Beautiful words, almost as beautiful as the woman who spoke them," Bobby commented, raising his glass and touching hers.

"It's hard to believe how fast time has gone by," Bobby commented.

"It seems like yesterday that I was on the sidelines cheering at your basketball games."

"I used to love watching those long, sexy legs of yours. Made me proud, knowing you were mine."

"So did either of your kids follow in your footsteps? Were they sports' stars in college as well?"

"No. Neither of my sons had the discipline necessary to excel at sports, or business for that matter," Bobby admitted. The disappointment in his voice was real.

"Oh, so what do they do now?"

"Honestly, Livia, I don't know. We had a business disagreement. The boys and their mother seemed to think that because it was a family-owned company that they should be able to walk into the executive offices on day one, following a very lackluster college career. I thought otherwise. They sided with her and we haven't spoken in over three years." His tone was lackluster and confusing. Was he upset or indifferent?

"I'm sorry to hear that," Livia remarked without revealing her surprise. True, she didn't have any children of her own, but she couldn't imagine Aleesa or any of her other friends letting an argument—over business no less—keep them from being in touch with their own flesh and blood.

"What about you? No children?"

"No." The tone of her voice and shortness of her reply made it crystal clear that Livia did not intend to discuss the subject any further.

The appearance of a tray-laden waiter changed the conversation from children to food. Livia watched as he placed before them several Asian-inspired appetizers. Some she recognized, some she didn't, but none she'd ordered. She hadn't even put an eyeball on the menu yet.

"I'm sorry, but we haven't ordered anything yet," she told the waiter.

"The gentleman…"

"I took the liberty of ordering for both of us," Bobby interrupted the server to tell her. "I hope you don't mind me taking care of my Livi Girl. Old habits die hard." He punctuated his statement with a disarming smile.

His gallantry erased any initial thoughts Livia had about Bobby being somewhat presumptuous. When it came down to it, he was simply being thoughtful. Had she been away from those two desirable qualities for so long that she didn't even recognize them anymore?

Livia smiled into her glass as she drained its contents and began to enjoy the buzz. She refused to allow reality to interject its practical self into the evening. Livia wanted more than anything to celebrate her fiftieth year with an evening full of fantasy, romance and lust. *And love*, she declared to herself as Bobby refilled her glass. *Even if it is thirty years late.*

They took their time nibbling through the appetizers, and catching up on the events that had populated their individual lives over the past three decades. Bobby talked while Livia sipped, and soon she could no longer hear the words he spoke. Her mind was busy weaving past memories with present fantasies, while her eyes remained focused on his lips.

As a young woman, those lips had been the first ever to kiss her until her panties got wet. They'd been the first to tease her breasts and taste her skin from her face to her feet. Most importantly, those manly lips had been the first, other than her father's, to say the words "I love you." And right now, at this moment, grown up Livia wanted to feel those lips in all those same places, and in a few more they'd yet to discover.

"May I?" the waiter asked, bringing Livia out of her head and back to the table.

"Yes," she said, not bothering to look up. Instead, her eyes dipped to the table before rising to look into those of her dinner companion's. Livia ran her finger seductively around the rim of her wineglass.

Bobby returned her grin with a "message received" one of his own. Clearly, after all of this time, he and Livia were finally on the same page.

Like a Virgin, Touched for the Very First Time

"You were beautiful back in the day," he told her, "but you are positively sexy as hell now."

"Thank you, though I think you deserve some credit for me feeling this way," she flirted.

"I'm glad you feel that way."

"Bobby?" she said, adding a touch of dreamy to her tone.

"Yes?"

"I'm suddenly feeling a little light-headed…and warm," Livia said as she smiled across the table.

"Are you ill?"

"I wouldn't exactly call it an ill feeling. More like an ache." Liv reached in her pocket, perplexed by Bobby's apparent confusion.

"I don't quite understand."

"I'd like to go upstairs and celebrate my birthday." Livia slid the key card across the table, making her intentions crystal clear.

Her frank comment sent Bobby's eyes in search of hers for clarification. They were met with a wide grin that tiptoed the tightrope between shyness and seduction.

"Now?"

Pffffft. Livia felt a miniscule pinprick to her lust.

"Yeah, there's no time like the present, wouldn't you agree?"

"But I've already ordered dinner."

Pfffft…pfffft. Her lustiness continued to leak. Bobby's initial reaction to put food over fucking shocked her. Mitchell would have jumped at the chance. Wouldn't most men?

"So, we'll ask them to send it up to room 4221," she suggested, refusing to be waylaid. "I'm sure it won't be a problem. Please? I am hungry for those lips of yours….I can't wait."

"Well, when you put it that way…" he finally acquiesced. As Livia gathered her belongings, Bobby called the waiter over to make the arrangements to turn dinner out on the town into room service.

Livia called for the elevator the moment she saw Bobby head in her direction. As they stepped inside, Liv had a sudden inspiration. *Mitchell would be so proud*, she thought as she pushed the button for the thirty-sixth floor and turned to plant an *I'm about to rock your world* kiss on her old flame before he could notice.

Just as his toes began to curl, the elevator stopped, and the two stepped out onto a quiet floor face to with face several plaques hung on the dark wood wall, directing them to various ballrooms.

"You're on forty-two. We got off on the wrong floor," Bobby said, stating what he believed to be the obvious.

"No, we didn't." Livia grabbed his large, meaty hand and led him over to another sign.

"What are you looking for?"

"The restroom."

"You couldn't wait until we got upstairs?" he asked, still not catching on.

"Nope," she informed him, as she cracked open the door to the ladies' room. "Wait right here." Livi took a quick reconnaissance tour inside and determined two encouraging things: first, the bathroom was empty, and second, the doors on the stalls went from floor to ceiling, so if they were joined in mid-boink, no one had to be the wiser.

Feeling a similar, but markedly different rush of sexy adrenaline than she'd felt in St. Bart's, Livia checked her image in the mirror before heading out to retrieve her lover. In the islands, she'd allowed herself to be led into one sexy scenario after another. Tonight, she was the tour guide. Livia smiled at her reflection as she unbuttoned her blouse to reveal her up and at 'em breasts showcased in her favorite fuchsia-colored bra. The lessons she'd learned from Mitchell had taken hold. And what a joy it was to truly love her body enough to actually desire sex—when and how she wanted it—as opposed to simply going along when someone else did.

"Care to join me?" She invited Bobby in, opening the door wide enough to reveal her awesome breasts and naked intentions.

"Oh, well..."

Livia refused to hear the sad hissing sound of escaping lust. She quickly analyzed his reaction, noting the admiration in his eyes as they quickly scanned her body, as well as his confusion and dis-comfort.

"I don't know about you, but for years I've thought about what I was missing for the past thirty years. I can't wait another mo-ment to find out," Livi told him as she led him to the handicapped stall in the back. She latched the door before turning and latching her lips on his.

Her hands slipped inside his jacket, easing the garment from his shoulders while sneaking a feel. Despite being in his mid-fifties, Bobby had held onto his muscular body. As his jacket slipped onto the floor, Mr. Jeffries slipped from her grasp.

He hurriedly picked up his jacket and took two steps toward the door. "Let's go to the room."

"I told you, I don't want to wait that long," she informed him.

"I'd really rather go to the room, Livia. What if someone walks in? Plus, it's the bathroom. I mean, it's not really sanitary."

Livia paused before answering as what was left of her lust flew across the room before fully deflating and landing in a big pile of *what the hell?* This was the bathroom at the five-star Mandarin Oriental Hotel, not some grubby gas station. There were orchids and goddamn cloth hand towels on the sink, for Christ's sake. If you're going to fuck in the bathroom, this would be *the* goddamn bathroom to do it in!

You're missing the point, Quincy broke in to adroitly clue her in. *There will be no fucking in the bathroom for us tonight.*

"Come on, my beautiful Livi Girl," Bobby said, taking over as tour guide as he reached over to button her blouse. "Let's go to the room and find out what we've both been dying to know."

Livia allowed her lips to give him a quick, toothless grin. She was disappointed and his refusal had rocked her confidence. She'd approached him feeling seriously sexy and adventurous. Now she was back to feeling unsure and confused. After her unsuccessful come on, did he think that she was a desperate, old slut? Had she turned him off by throwing herself at him? Mitchell had told her that he loved women who were bold and went for what they wanted. Was Bobby the polar opposite?

Livia, back to being the *go along to get along* girl, followed Bobby out of the bathroom and back onto the elevator. They traveled to the forty-second floor in silence, but it had a totally different feel than their earlier ride. When they'd first arrived, it was companionable silence that provided the soundtrack. Now it was a discomfiting lull of an unbearable duration.

"Here we are," Bobby said with a forced cheeriness as he opened the door. He stepped aside to allow her to enter a sumptuously sensual bedroom suite designed for nothing but some major lovemaking. The city lights flickering through the wall of floor-to-ceiling windows set the tone and eliminated the need or desire for any further light. The bed was covered in a textural masterpiece of silky Egyptian cotton and nubby raw silk pillows and accents, strongly suggesting that the best way to enjoy it would be through a bare skin experience.

Livia, feeling a whisper of lust skimming her body, walked into the bathroom and stood wide mouthed. Cool marble floor and walls, a double sink stretching across the back wall. A glass enclosed shower and separate toilet stall stood on the opposite side of the room's piece de resistance—a sunken marble tub with an amazing city view.

Wonder if he'd have sex in this bathroom, Livia found herself thinking. She tried to beat back the sarcasm, not wanting to spoil the rest of her birthday evening.

"Okay, this was worth waiting for," she said, stepping back into the room. "Now, where were we?" For the protection of her ego, Livia didn't move, letting Bobby come on to her.

"Come here," he said, patting the bed beside him. Bobby waited for her to sit down before taking Livi's face in his hands and giving her a perfected kiss, one that let her know that they were back in sync. They sat on the bed smooching, as they'd done so many times years ago. Only this time, in both their minds, they were going all the way.

Feeling more timid than before, Livia once again pushed off his jacket and continued undoing buttons and removing items of clothing until he was sitting on the bed with his muscular chest exposed. Looking at him, it was clear that the things her hands had revealed were true. Bobby was still a hot and handsome hunk of man. The sight of his bare pecs and broad, toned shoulders made Quincy hiccup. Livia wanted to see more and reached for Bobby's belt buckle.

"Let me go hop in the shower first," he told her, once again stopping all forward progress.

"It's okay. You're fine."

"It's been a long day. You know…all the traveling and everything."

Apparently, Bobby had turned into a clean freak since they'd last met.

"Okay. I'll come wash your back," Livia offered, trying desperately to get back to feeling grown and sexy.

"Uh, I'll be quick and then you can jump in and then…baby, I'm going to seriously make up for lost time."

Okay, two for two. Livia tried to quickly think of something else to keep the sting of another rejection show up on her face. Mitchell's face pressed up against hers as he fucked her in the bathroom immediately did the trick. It definitely made her feel better knowing how much she'd turned that handsome stranger on.

Bobby was true to his word about being quick. In less than fifteen minutes, they were both freshly showered, and between the sheets.

"My God, you're beautiful," he said, paying homage to her ears, neck and shoulders with his tongue. His mouth traveled across the pillowy tops of her breasts and down toward her nipples. He gave both a squeeze and pushed them together to take a long look. His curious attention to her manmade mammaries brought back the self-conscious feelings Livia thought she'd left in the Caribbean.

"These are beautiful…"

"But?"

"…but I would have never taken you for the fake boobs type."

"I'm not, but sometimes life has a way of making decisions for you," Livia explained while avoiding the "C" word.

A look of concern overtook Bobby's face as the reality of what Livia hadn't said penetrated his brain. "Livi, I'm so sorry."

"No need to be. The hard times are over. Just rainbows ahead of me. So let's forget about all that and get back to the subject at hand," she said, taking his palm and placing it over her breasts to emphasis her point. Livia was trying hard to stay in the mood, but every little thing seemed to distract Bobby and pull him out of the moment.

"You always were an amazing kisser," she told him.

"I had the best student in the world. I'm looking forward to seeing what lessons tonight will bring."

Okay, so you're still in student/teacher mode, Livia talked to him through her eyes. *Well, I might school you on a few things my damned self.*

"What's going on in that head of yours, pretty girl?"

"Not much. I was thinking about how much I'm going to enjoy doing what I wished I'd done when we were in your bedroom the night your parents were at the O'Jays concert."

"And exactly what was that?"

"Having your rock-hard dick, balls deep in pink," Livia announced, channeling her inner nasty girl, and placing her hand on his dick. It jumped with glee while his face registered the shock of his little Livi Girl's potty mouth. Livia wanted to take them back as soon as the words left her mouth. Clearly, Bobby was not into smut talk.

"Shhh," was his only reply as he pounced on her body with full force. He may not have wanted to hear her intentions but they obviously matched his own. In one swoop, Livia was on her back, looking up at the man to whom she had given her heart but not her virginity.

"Wait," Livia said, pushing him away.

"What? I thought this is what you wanted."

"I do, but we need to use a condom."

"Livi Girl, it's me. We don't need a rubber. I want to feel you all the way, like I never got to way back then."

Livia was so tempted not to insist that he sheath his shaft, but rational thought won out. She may have known and loved him years ago, but she had no idea where this dick had been between then and now. "Sorry. No cover, no lover," she repeated Aleesa's words to him. Livia was not trying to become a sad statistic.

She quickly got up and retrieved the condoms from her coat pocket. On the way back to bed she tore open the wrapper and quickly rolled it onto his dick. With safety behind her, she laid her head on the pillow. She smiled up at him, ready to receive her lover.

"Spread your legs more," he said, his tone getting gruffer as the tip of his dick kissed the slit between her legs.

Livia, back in the subservient seat, did as she was told. Without any pomp or damn circumstance Bobby pushed his dick into her. As his rod rubbed up against the nooks and crannies of her coochie, she waited for the pangs of pleasure to appear. Bobby kept pumping and with every few strokes he hit the right spot and Livia tried to encourage him by verbally enunciating her pleasure.

"Oh that feels so good," she said, though what she really craved was a good pussy licking.

Again, Bobby's response was to shush her as he went about the business of laying his pipe. "Come up more," he demanded, scooping her butt into his hands and pushing it toward his driving cock.

As Livia was trying to adjust and get into the moment, Quincy was enjoying the hell out of their session. She started to perspire, letting her sultry sweat drip down his member and between Livia's legs. Excitedly, Quincy pumped against him, wanting to feel the full force of his primitive fucking.

"Yeah, faster!" he shouted. "Go faster."

While Quincy dutifully picked up the pace, Livia excused herself from the moment to assess the situation. As much as she tried not to, she couldn't help comparing and contrasting this moment with the last time she'd had sex. Her mind took her back to Mitchell's arms where she'd felt sexy and alive and unfettered by another person's judgments or her own self-conscious feelings. With Mitchell and his anything-goes attitude, having sex became her delicious right. In stark contrast, Bobby's negative reaction to her spontaneous come-on had clipped her wings and left her once again feeling like having sex was her duty, not her delight.

Bobby continued his aggressive fucking, complete with escalating grunts and position-altering directions. His lovemaking style was rough and aggressive, but not in a good way. Even in their brief affair, Mitchell had showed her the magic of combining intensity with nuance. Clearly, Bobby had yet to learn that sometimes hard fucking was just fucking hard.

"Close your legs some," he told her. Livia looked up, trying to make eye contact, but his eyes were closed. In her detached state, Livia felt like she was having an out-of-body experience of sorts, observing and mentally commenting on the action at hand. Mitchell had certainly been forceful in expressing his wants and needs, and yet his demands, unlike Bobby's, were wrapped in an irresistible request.

Let it go, Livia demanded of her memory. She had thought of Mitchell at least a thousand times since their island romp together, but this was the first time she'd had sex since then. Not only was bringing Mitchell into the bed with her and Bobby, rude and inappropriate, it was proving to be surprisingly painful too.

"Oh shit, baby, I'm about to give you some cum. You want this cum, baby?" Bobby grunted, clearly not caring if she wanted it or not.

Livia gave him a moaning "oooh and aaah," happy for it to be over, but still wanting to be polite. Bobby's body went rigid on top of her as he ejaculated. Immediately after he came, without so much as a kiss or a thank you, he pulled himself out of her and headed into the bathroom.

Liv lay in bed and listened to the toilet flush and water running in the sink. Fantasy, she decided, was often better left unfilled.

"Here, so you can clean yourself up," Bobby proclaimed as he handed her a box of tissues.

Livia didn't know how to react. She'd come to like the wet, sticky part after sex. It was now part of her sexual afterglow, because as Mitchell had pointed out, it was the sign of a job well done. Bobby seemed to be waiting for her to tidy up, so she slipped out of the other side of the bed and into the bathroom with her thoughts.

Talk about your douches.

"God, I needed that," he called out from the other side of the wall.

Once again this evening, Livia found herself unsure how to react. Should she be insulted?

"Really?"

"Yes, now I can stop wondering what it would have been like between us," Bobby revealed through his yawn.

That makes two of us.

"Me too," Livi concurred, stopping her comments there. There was no reason to hurt his feelings by informing him that the fantasy of fucking him was exponentially better than the reality.

"If you don't mind me saying, you've learned a lot over the years, Livi Girl."

If you only knew the half of it, she thought as she came back into the room to find Bobby asleep in her bed.

Feeling disappointed and bored, she climbed into bed, careful to stay on her side. Funny, after sex with Mitchell, he couldn't get enough cuddling. Here with Bobby, she might as well be in bed by herself. That aching feeling of loneliness seeped back into her body. Only this time it was worse because she wasn't alone.

As Bobby quietly snored beside her, Livia mentally scratched number eight, finding and fucking Bobby Jeffries, off the list. Lying there in the dark, with the city lights twinkling around her, she also came to recognize two telling and exceptionally pertinent things. One, past memories have an unfortunate way of growing into bigger and better recollections than the present realities; and two, whether she wanted to or not, erasing her memories of Mitchell was proving to be an impossible task.

Hot Cross Bun
(in the Oven)

Surrounded by seventy-four anatomically perfect, fondant lilies, Livia sat sculpting the last flower needed to top Naomi Maddox's three-tier wedding/anniversary cake. She and her husband were renewing their vows tomorrow, and as she did for all of Naomi's big celebrations, Livia was creating the confectionary centerpiece.

The phone rang, and Livi continued working as Jasi's excited voice traveled through the Bluetooth and blitzed her ear.

"Hey, doll."

"Where have you been? I haven't talked to you since after the Bobby debriefing, and that was three weeks ago."

"I have been mega busy, which is why I need to talk to you."

"What do you need?"

"A cake."

"Well, this must be something. Isn't ShopRite your usual baker?"

"It is something, something big. I need a really special one."

"Damn it, girl, *all* my cakes are special…oh wait…I know…you want me to make some nasty, erotic, *Lebanese* cake, don't you?" Liv joked.

"Oh shit, now that you mention it, we're going to need one of those, too—for the bachelorette party."

"Jasi, what are you talking about?"

"I need you to bake one of those nasty, *Lebanese*, as you so stupidly put it, cakes *and* a wedding cake."

"Wedding cake?" Livi repeated, putting down her tools so Jasi had her full attention.

"Yep, a *lesbian* wedding cake. Belinda and I are getting married!"

"Oh shit, oh shit, oh shit, oh shit! Jasi, you're getting married!! I love Belinda. She is so damn cool, and perfect for you. When did this all happen?"

"At Sunday brunch."

"WHAT! Not home with the folks, Sunday brunch."

"The one and only."

"So how did it go down? Tell me everything."

"Well, I followed your advice. Well, actually *my* advice that you were wise enough to remember and give back at me. I took Belinda to brunch, and immediately without apology or looking for approval, introduced her as my girlfriend."

"What did they say?"

"Well, at first they didn't get it, but I made it pretty clear when I announced that I was in love with her and I wanted to get married. That's when it got a little crazy."

"Oh shit. I'm sure Ms. Harolyn lost her ever-loving mind."

"This is where it gets crazy," Jasi agreed. "But not the way you think. Mom said she always had a feeling that maybe I was 'that way,' which is why she decided that I hadn't got married. She said she didn't want to say anything because maybe I didn't know myself."

"So Mom knew all along, which makes her far more astute than the rest of us."

"Apparently. I'm going back next weekend alone so we can talk about everything. I want to make sure everyone is all good."

"Good idea, but back to brunch. What did your dad say?"

"My dad was really quiet throughout most of the meal. After we ate, he asked me to come upstairs for a minute, gave me a hug and said that if Belinda is who I wanted, and she made me happy, then he was happy. He gave me my grandmother's ring and I went downstairs and immediately popped the question. Of course, she said yes—"

"Of course; she'd be a fool not to."

"And my baby is no fool, which, of course, is another thing my mother loves. Her daughter is marrying a doctor! And here's the kicker, once Belinda told her that we were planning to have lots of babies, there was no way Harolyn couldn't fall in love, too!

"So, immediately, we had to sit down and plan the wedding. All she wanted me to promise was that I would wear a dress."

"Are you?"

"Of course! If me wearing a dress is all my mother wants and needs to be happy about me marrying the love of my life, I'll wear a fucking hoop skirt!"

"So you need a cake."

"That's what I said."

"One with you in a big ole hoop skirt on top."

"Funny. Nope, just flowers—purple irises—they're Belinda's favorite."

"When's the wedding?"

"In two weeks at Sunday brunch. I know you usually have a waiting list for your cakes, but Liv, you've gotta hook us up. It will be a small affair at the house. Of course, all of you are invited, and you can bring a date," Jasi said, the implication clear that she expected to see Bobby on Livia's arm.

"Don't go there. I told you it was a one-time, cross-it-off-the-list affair."

"So you're not going to see each other again? Really? Sex only gets better once you know what you're working with."

"Nope. That chapter is closed. Trust me, the reality paled in comparison."

"And who were you comparing him to?"

"Shut up. Don't go there either."

"Why are you being such a hard ass about this? If you like him and he likes you, does age really matter? Or race? Or gender, for that damn matter? Liv, when it comes to love, the packaging isn't what matters."

"Whatever, but the reality of the situation is I don't know his last name, nor how to get in touch with him. It's done, so let it go. I have."

"Sure, you have."

Livia heard the front door to the shop open, giving her a plausible excuse for ending this uncomfortable inquiry about a man she was never going to see again.

"Got to go. Somebody just came into the bakery and Karen is out. I'll sketch out some ideas for the wedding cake. I promise, you will have the most beautiful cake for your special day."

"Okay. Livi, I am so happy. I never thought I would feel like this."

"Jas, I'm really happy for you," Livia said, the sincerity obvious in her tone.

"I know you are, and that makes everything perfect."

Livia hung up the phone, honestly jazzed for her friend. Clearly, Jasi, a woman who they all thought would never marry, was in love and finally ready to make a commitment. Funny, all of her close friends seemed to be settled and happy. Aleesa and Walter were going stronger than ever, Lena was truly content being single at the moment. Perhaps there was hope for her to find a sweet, companionable, sexy love to spend the next fifty years with.

She quickly washed her hands and stepped out into the front of the bakery where she and her staff usually met clients. With a smile left over from hearing her best friend's news, Livia came face to face with a very attractive, vaguely familiar face.

"Hi, I'm here to drop off a check from my mother, Naomi Maddox, which I apparently have left in the car. I'm sorry. I'll be right back." She turned and revealed her pregnant belly.

Livia's eyes followed Naomi's daughter through the door and outside to her car. Her mouth dropped open as a handsome man, his companionable laughter only making his features all the more compelling, met her midway to hand her the forgotten check. It was Mitchell. What the fuck? She and Jasi were just talking about him. Had they somehow managed to conjure him up? Because now, after all of the nights of thinking and fantasizing and reliving their Caribbean boink fest, Mitchell was outside her door, running errands. With his fucking girlfriend. His pregnant girlfriend.

Livia felt the breath being sucked out of her body. To assure that Mitchell would not see her, she quickly stepped away from the windows and out of sight, as she tried to corral all of the inexplicable pain and jealousy into one corner of her heart, so she could deal with her customer.

A disturbing thought grabbed her heart and squeezed. Had Mitchell purposely given her a bogus number so she couldn't get in contact? She'd built him up and put him on a pedestal, making him out to be some kind of sexy demigod. Was he really a horny dog dressed in nice-guy clothing?

"I am so sorry about that. This baby is sucking up all of my brain cells. I swear, I can't remember a thing these days!"

"Congratulations," Livia managed to squeak out.

Her fear was now confirmed. *A motherfucking horny dog.*

"Thank you. We're really excited. Anyway, I'm here to bring you this," she said handing Liv the retrieved check, "and to confirm the delivery time for five tomorrow."

"Thank you, and yes, uh…tell your mom that I uh…will be by at…um…five to assemble the cake." Livia stopped talking for a moment to try to hold back the tears that were threatening to fall. "It should take no longer than…uh twenty minutes. The party is at six, yes?"

"The ceremony begins at six; the party will follow."

"I know it will be beautiful," Liv said, ready for Naomi's daughter and Mitchell's baby mama to leave, so she could finally break down. "Thank you for bringing this by, and good luck…with the…baby."

As the woman walked through the door, Livia scurried to the back. She could not believe how devastated she felt. Nor could she understand why. Mitchell had been a vacation fling. Her partner in a holiday ho-down, as Jasi had so humorously put it. But it didn't feel funny anymore. Nor like a fling for that matter. Seeing Mitchell with someone else had finally cleared the fog and let the sunshine on what was the truth. For all of his gentlemanly qualities, he was only another dick trying to get laid. That said, she had fallen for that young boy, and fallen hard.

The phone continued to ring as Livia sank deeper into the hot, sudsy water. She didn't feel like talking to anyone. Didn't want to analyze her feelings with Aleesa, discuss the merits of single life with Lena, or make wedding plans with Jasi. All she wanted to do was drown her sorrows in a bubble bath, and wallow in her ridiculous emotions of feeling betrayed and abandoned.

The fact of the matter was that Livia had absolutely no legitimate right to feel hurt in any way, shape or form. Mitchell had done nothing to hurt her. Theirs had been a mutually pleasurable tryst that, while tempting and fulfilling, had been built on a foundation of temporary access. There had been no promises made, no covenants reached, no pacts put in place between them. Hell, they hadn't even traded complete names.

You were so stupid to throw away his phone number, Quincy scolded.

She had torn it up, deciding that it was best thing for everyone if they didn't stay in touch. Had she made a huge mistake? If she had stayed in contact after their return, would Mitchell be with her instead of Naomi's daughter? Would he still be her lover instead of a doting father-to-be?

"It wasn't even the right number," she said into thin air. "And even if it was, it was the right thing to do."

You don't know if it was bogus, Quincy reminded her.

We're really excited. The woman's words raced through her mind, causing Livia to sit up. The sting of cool air on her exposed shoulders seemed to provide a new jolt of clarity. Just as Livi understood that she was in love with Mitchell, she was now convinced that her initial reaction of staying away had been correct. He was young, but now his youth played a very different role in her decision to let this go once and for all. Before it had been about her discomfort, but now it had to do with Mitchell's right to be with a woman capable of giving him what it was now obvious he wanted—a family. It was physically impossible for Liv to do that for him, even if she wanted to. Not only was she too old for children at this stage of her life, she'd never been able to have babies, not even when she had been married. Livia had made peace with her barren lot in life decades ago.

She sunk back down into the warm tub, recalling that this was the place it had all begun. The fuck-it list that had started the journey that had ultimately brought her to Mitchell. Looking back at it all—from the party to the toys to St. Bart's to her night with Bobby—she was happy the girls had forced her into this erotic experiment. Livia had learned a lot, specifically that sex is what you make it and the attitude you bring to it, that there was nothing wrong in selfish pleasure because that meant you were really enjoying it, not just doing it. She now understood that women had every right to claim their desires and act on them, and doing so didn't make them some kind of whore. But perhaps the most telling lesson she'd learned from this experience was that truly great sex was not a function of the body alone, but an encounter of the heart, mind and soul. She hadn't had that with her husband or her first love. Ironically, the only man she'd experienced such emotional and physical rapture with was a thirty-something stranger who had literally picked her up at the beach.

Life really is a mother-fucking riddle.

Havin' Your Cake (Redux)

L ivia drove her car along the long, prestigious driveway leading to the kitchen door of Naomi Maddox's plush suburban estate. She turned off the car and looked at the time. It was two minutes to five, though Livi didn't need the clock to tell her so, as the ever tightening knots in her stomach were counting down the minutes for her.

According to her plan, she'd arrived right on time. Livia's goal was to get in, quickly assemble the cake and get out before any guests arrived. The last people she wanted to see were Mitchell and his gorgeous baby mama.

Which is why you've been getting ready since three o'clock, are made up like you're going to a black-tie event, and made a special trip to the dry cleaners to pick up your most figure-flattering chef's coat, and wore a dress instead of your usual pants, her annoying ego pointed out.

Livia tried to ignore the voices in her head as she swung her bag of pastry tools over her shoulder. Just as she was about to pick up the two-tier cake base, a deep male voice called out from the back door.

"Need help with that?"

Livia's mind, body and heart froze. Her face squinted in nervous frustration and she felt the threatening breaths of hyperventilation looming. *Please don't let it be him; please don't let it be him,* she furiously prayed.

"Let me get those for you."

Livia looked up and felt relief immediately wash over her. The offer came from one of the catering staff, and a grateful Livia was happy to accept. One less trip to the car meant less time in the enemy's kitchen.

"Thank you." Livia turned back to the payload to retrieve the boxes containing the last tier and the fondant lilies. She followed in the waiter's path toward the door and watched helplessly as his foot missed the step and he and her cake went lunging forward.

"NO!" she heard herself shout.

Thank God the kid had balance. He was able to juggle and keep himself and the cake from falling to the ground, but when the sous chef came out to see about the screams, the edge of the door went right into the top tier of the cake.

Livia rushed to the door to check out the damage. At first glance, the gash in the fondant appeared ugly but not catastrophic. Hopefully, there was no damage to the actual cake. She had enough of what she needed to make repairs; it was just going to take time. Time she desperately did not want to spend in Naomi Maddox's house.

"I am so sorry," the waiter muttered through embarrassed lips.

"Let's get inside so I can fix it. I'm going to need some work space here," she informed the staff as she stepped through the door. Her eyes immediately went to the clock glowing from the microwave. Seven minutes after five.

As the caterer cleared space on the kitchen table for her to work, Livia more closely inspected the damage. The gash ran nearly the length of the two tiers. Additionally, the top layer had been nicked down to the cake, which meant she'd have to remove a section of fondant, reapply a base coat of icing to keep crumbs at bay, and then reapply and smooth the fondant. All that before she could apply the lilies. What she'd estimated to be a twenty minute assembly job, had now turned into at least a one-hour repair and rebuild.

The knots in her belly continued to tick down the precious moments between her finishing the job and getting the hell out of there before the guests arrived. The ceremony was being held in the living room area on the other side of the house. She could only pray that none of the family, or those who were like family, would have any reason to venture to the back.

Livia laid out her tools and got to work. Her mind momentarily wandered back to the last time she was in this house, causing Quincy to giggle and twitch. Talk about your muscle memory. Liv smiled before shutting down the recollections so she could fully concentrate on the task before her. The destroyed section of fondant was gone, the crumbs brushed away and the cake re-iced. Now she had to let the base frosting set so the fondant would stick. Livi's eyes turned up to the clock. Five forty-three.

Her attention no longer consumed by the repairs, Livia could hear the hustle and bustle of guests arriving and being shuttled to their proper places for the ceremony. She breathed a sigh of relief. In the forty-five minutes since she'd arrived, nobody other than the catering staff and Naomi's event planner had entered the kitchen. It looked like she was going to be able to get in and out before the ceremony was over.

Fifteen minutes later, Livia was back at work, smoothing out the frosting and re-icing the pearlized borders. The harpist played the first notes of the wedding processional as she began to apply the lilies, strategically placing them over the patched area. Six-ten. Done.

With the help of the sous chef, Livia rolled the cake to its proper place of honor. It looked beautiful. Rather than sugar, the flowers looked spun by Mother Nature and thanks to Livia's impeccable eye and considerable skill, nobody would ever know that this all-important cake had recently gone through such trauma.

The sounds of cheerful laughter and applause filled the house, letting Livia know it was definitely time to head back to the kitchen, pack up her tools and make a quick escape. The kitchen was nearly empty as the wait staff exited in order to serve the hors d'oeuvres and signature cocktails. Liv headed over to the table area and began gathering her belongings and cleaning up the mess.

She was wiping up the table when she heard a voice that made her heart stand still. It was low and buttery, exactly as she'd heard it in her head a million times since last he'd spoken.

"Excuse me, could I get a few crackers and a glass of water?" His urgent request for saltines was delivered in his signature fashion—wrapping a demand in a request, and it was filled with the same compassion she'd heard when he'd come to her rescue a world away.

Livia kept her back to him as she continued to wipe the table, hoping that he'd get his crackers and get the hell out of the kitchen without laying eyes on her. Her ears were pounding and she felt the heat of embarrassment creep through her body.

"Excuse me, miss. She needs something to eat now. Please. She's feeling nauseous. I'd get it myself but it's kind of crazy in here and I don't want to mess anything up."

It was now clear that Mitchell was speaking to her. Short of acting like a deaf mute, there was nothing she could do but turn around and help them out.

"I'll see what I can find," Livia mumbled, walking over to the counter without looking up or into his face. She located a box of crackers, put several on a plate, poured a glass of water from the Poland Spring cooler, and walked them over to Naomi's daughter, maneuvering her body so her back stayed toward Mitchell.

"Here you go."

"Thank you. After six months, I thought I'd be done with this morning sickness."

"I hope you feel better," she said and attempted to walk away.

"'S'cuse me," the woman blurted out, covering her mouth, as she bolted toward the bathroom off the kitchen, leaving them alone.

"Hello, Quincy."

Hearing her name exiting his mouth again forced her head up and her eyes to his face. She tried hard not to notice how fine he looked in his tuxedo. "Mitchell."

"You didn't think I'd recognize you or your voice?"

"It's been a while."

"Too long. How are you?"

"Good. Looks like you're doing well," she commented with a touch of sarcasm.

Surprise at her tone registered across his face. "I must be doing something right to run into you like this," Mitchell said, writing her coolness off as a cover for some kind of misplaced embarrassment. "I was hoping I'd hear from you when we got back."

"I figured what was the point? It was a fling that got flung. That's it."

"Well, that might work for you, but I can't stop thinking about you."

Mitchell closed the distance between them and took her hand in his. His touch felt like a torch on her skin. What she really wanted to do was to lean in and press her body against his so she could once again feel the arms she fantasized about each night. But what she actually did was remember the situation for what it was, and stepped away. Livia felt the heat of desire morphing into hot ire. How dare Mitchell come on to her while his pregnant girlfriend was throwing up in the next room? Class act. But what did she expect from a man who trolls the beach looking for strange women to pick up and screw?

Do you really believe that?

Livia felt a tear threatening to escape from the corner of her eye. She wasn't sure if she really believed those things about Mitchell, but angry thoughts and over emotional accusations at this moment seemed to be the perfect inoculation against his proven charm and persuasive powers. He'd so obviously moved on. Why was he pressing her like this?

"I have to go," she said, picking up her bag.

"Well, hopefully that's the last of that for today," Naomi's daughter said, stepping out of the bathroom looking recovered and ready to go back and join the party. "Mitchell, we've got to get back out there. You've got to do the toast."

Livia took the opportunity to nod her good-byes and head for the door.

"You're Livia, the cake artist," she stopped her to say. "The cake looks amazing, by the way."

"Thank you."

"Livia?" Mitchell said with a huge question mark in his voice, as he stepped in front of her.

"You two know each other?"

"No, apparently not," Mitchell said, wearing a quizzical look on his face.

"Congratulations, you two," Livia said, looking him in the eye before she walked out of the house, leaving Mitchell and her heart behind.

She climbed into her car, threw everything into the back seat, and did a three-point turn so she could quickly get out of Dodge. Livi drove around the back of the house only to stop suddenly. The bride and groom's limo was parked at the other end of the driveway, effectively blocking her escape.

"FUCK! FUCK! FUCK!" she screamed into the air as she pounded the steering wheel in frustration. She exited the Lexus and walked over to the limousine, hoping like hell to find the driver sitting in the back. Her frantic taps on the window were answered with silence. Other than driving up on the lawn, Livia had few options. She could either wait for the chauffeur to return, which may not be until after the reception was over, or she could go back inside and look for him.

Livia decided to be proactive. She grabbed her keys from the ignition and trooped back up the driveway to the kitchen door. This time, however, the anxiety she'd arrived with had been blown up a hundred fold.

She returned to the kitchen, which now with the reception in full swing, was a flurry of activity. Livia immediately checked the breakfast nook, but was met with disappointment. "Have you seen the limo driver?" she asked the caterer.

"You're back." Mitchell stepped in to answer before the caterer could speak.

Livia could hear a mixture of surprise and gratitude in his voice. It thrilled and at the same time irritated her that Mitchell seemed almost relieved to see her again.

"Are you looking for me?"

"I'm looking for the limo driver. His car is blocking the drive-way." Her tone was much more clipped and curt than Livia intended, but being rude seemed the only way to defend herself against that damned sexy smile of his.

"I'm thinking that this can't be a coincidence. That somebody upstairs is doing me a huge solid, and yet you seemed pissed off to see me. I don't understand why all this attitude."

"Look, Mitchell, we had a great time in St. Bart's but let's leave it there."

Confused disbelief traipsed across his face before morphing into an inexplicable anger. There was no true basis for his feelings. Livia spoke the facts when she described, in the broadest of strokes, their time together in the islands. But the truth was hidden in the fine lines. Something had happened between them. Something big. Something powerful. Something definitely worth investigating further. This woman—Quincy, Livia—whatever her real name was, had gripped his imagination with a force unlike anything he'd ever experienced before. Mitchell had begun to lose hope when Livia had not contacted him in the months since their return, but they'd somehow been brought together again. And instead of feeling the same excitement he did, she was giving him attitude and dismissing him like a pesky fly. The entire thing was totally pissing him off.

"Oh, now I get it. Like the phony name, the rest of your story was bull, too. What? Are you married with a couple of kids? Went on vacation with your freak list and a fake name, got busy with some sucker, and then came home to resume being a proper wife."

"Are you kidding me? I'm not the one who is being totally dishonest here."

"What are you talking about? I was never dishonest with you."

"You don't think it's dishonest to pick up a woman, seduce and sex her up for four days, give her your phone number—"

"A phone number you never used, and perhaps if you did—"

"I did use it. And you know what I got? A wrong number. You come off like such the good guy and it was all part of your make 'em feel safe, get 'em into bed and tell her you'd like to see her again so she doesn't feel like a slut or a whore for doing all those things with you, plan. You pulled the oldest trick in the book and gave me a wrong number."

"I didn't do that. I wouldn't have done that because I really wanted to see you again."

"Why? So you could fuck me when your pregnant girlfriend doesn't feel like it?"

Mitchell's brow frowned with confusion before his cheeks were lifted in laughter. "Woman, you are so off base that it isn't even funny. Nora is not my girlfriend; she's my sister."

Relief washed over Livia in a tide that felt strong enough to knock her down. She was unable to control the look of joy that his clarification had put on her face. "Your sister? Really?"

"Yes, really. Now can I give you a proper kiss?" Mitchell moved close enough for her to smell the mint on his breath. The close proximity of his body to hers was kicking Quincy into hyper drive. Knowing Livia had tried to call him, that she wanted to see him again, had his heart doing happy backflips.

"Come with me," Mitchell said, grabbing her hand and letting her know he was not taking no for an answer.

Well aware that there was a houseful of important guests and clients nearby, Livia allowed Mitchell to lead her down the hall to the opposite side of the house. She didn't know whether to laugh or cry as he took her past the same spot where she had stopped to pleasure herself and into the den.

He closed the door, locked it, and then pushed Livia against it, before devouring her lips with a series of hot and hungry kisses. Kisses he'd been wanting and waiting to deliver for months.

"You have no idea how many times I have dreamed of kissing you again," Mitchell admitted while playing with the curls around her face.

Livia smiled, feeling strangely like she was home. She wanted nothing more than to lock lips, hips and private parts with Mitchell again. And though her body was ready to submit, Liv's heart was reluctant to commit, realizing that she still knew very little about this sexy man.

"And you will, in a minute. I have a few questions."

"Okay, but hurry up and ask. My lips are impatient."

"Nora is your sister?"

"Yes. Half-sister to be exact, but we don't play the fractions."

"Naomi is your mother?"

"Yep."

"Are you married?"

"Not anymore."

"Engaged?"

"Nope."

"Girlfriend?"

"It certainly is beginning to look that way," he admitted with a devilish tilt to his lips. "At least I'm holding out hope."

Livia's face broke out into a huge, happy smile. It still felt surreal that she was here, that she and Mitchell were together again, and if things kept going in the direction Quincy was pushing, she was about to make love in Naomi Maddox's house!

"In that case, there are a few things you should know about me."

"Besides the fact that you smell like sugar and vanilla?"

"Yes, like my real name is Livia Charles. Quincy, is, well, my vagina's nickname."

"Oh, I'm definitely in love with the right woman," Mitchell said, laughing.

In love? Did he just say in love? His words delighted and disturbed her.

"And I'm fifty years old." Livia bit her lip out of nervousness, not seduction.

"And getting finer by the day," he said, nibbling on her neck.

"You don't care that I'm sixteen years older than you?"

"No, not now, and I doubt I will ten years from now. But we're at the beginning of our journey. Let's see where it goes. Who knows, you may decide you don't like babysitting."

"True," she said, smiling broadly, her anxiety beginning to abate.

"Which brings up the fact that there are some things I need to know about you, Mitchell Maddox."

"That's not my last name."

"See, a girlfriend should know her boy toy's name."

"Point taken. It's Jenson. Maddox is my stepfather's name. Any more questions?" he asked while snacking on her earlobe. "God, you even taste like cake."

"Do you have a pen?"

"Yes, and I also have a rock hard dick that's been wanting to be inside you since I got back from St. Bart's. Which do you want first?"

"Is this a test?" Livia asked.

"More like an offer." Mitchell pulled back in order to get a full-on view of her face.

"In that case, have a seat," Livi said, pushing Mitchell into the yellow chair before straddling his lap. Quincy could feel his hard dick through his tuxedo pants, and giggled in response.

"It's a shame that you didn't get to see the rest of my list," she told him as she cradled his face in her hands and brought her lips to his ears.

"Did you finish it?"

"Thanks to you, I got through all but two: having a nine-and-a-half-week food fuck, and well, it looks like I'm about to take care of number ten right now."

"Tell me about it."

"Well, number ten is all about this very chair."

"This chair?" Mitchell, queried, confused by her comment.

"Yep." Livia went on to explain how the yellow leather chair had made its way on her fuck-it list. "Eww, I think I saw your stepfather getting his porn on watching a nice little girl-on-girl fantasy."

"Guess again, baby. I think I might be the one you caught with his pants down. You said it was a party for my grandmother's birthday? I was staying here then," Mitchell revealed, once again turned the fuck on by this incredible woman's sexual boldness.

"I don't know who it was. All I saw was a thigh. I'd like to think it was you," she flirted. "How crazy is it that we ended up together in St. Bart's."

"Fate knows what the fuck he's doing."

"*She's* doing," Liv teased as she undid the buttons on his shirt.

"I'll go with that." Mitchell ran his fingers up her bare leg, dipping in close to tickle her pink box. He could feel Livi's body tingle in response.

"Mmmm. You have no idea how many times I have had my way with you in this chair," Livia confessed.

"Well, there's no time like the present to make your fantasy come true."

"I can definitely go with that," she concurred, unbuckling his belt and pulling the zipper down on his pants. "Do you have a condom?"

"In my wallet."

"How convenient." She laughed as she waited for him to retrieve it.

"Just call me Seven-Eleven."

"I'll take care of that, she said, taking the condom and leaning back in order to have access to Mitchell's belt. "So about that pen…"

"I also have a pen."

"Good, because we need to make a list," she said, pulling his dick through the fly of his pants, encasing it and then deftly lifting herself up and pushing her panties to the side. She took his rod into her hands and guided it into her waiting Quincy.

"Now?"

Mitchell's question went unanswered as time stopped and the two took this exquisite moment to let their bodies reconnect. Livia gently bounced in his lap, drenching his dick with her vaginal waterfall. She enjoyed the fireflies flitting around her pelvis for a bit before settling down on his cock, and picking up an envelope from the desk. "This will do nicely," Livi said, her voice gruff with passion.

"For what?" Mitchell asked, taking the opportunity to unbutton her chef's coat and unleash her naked breasts.

"A new fuck-it list…"

"For two."

"For us."

"Quincy, Livia Charles…"

"Yes, boy toy."

"I think I love you."

THE END

EDEN'S TICKET TO PARADISE:
How To Create Your Fuck-It List

You've heard of a bucket list—a list of things you want to do before you kick the proverbial bucket—well, a sexy girl like you needs an addendum to her b-list...a fuck-it list. You've witnessed how much fun Livia had fulfilling hers. Now it's your turn to make a list of those deliciously naughty fantasies rolling around in your head and turn them into real life adventures.

What You Need:

Invest in a journal or special notepad for this sole purpose. Sure, you hot, techie types can keep your ideas on your smartphone, but there is something highly satisfying about being able to physically cross off each carnal accomplishment. And to experience this bit of after the afterglow, you'll definitely need a hard copy of your F-list.

What You Do:

Collect ideas. Gather them from everywhere—from the pages of the Eden Davis Series, movies, TV shows, conversations between friends—look for ideas that capture your curiosity and hold your attention. These are the ones you'll mostly likely succeed in accomplishing.

Write your first draft. Brainstorm. Now's the time to go with the flow. Let your Quincy be your guide. Write down what comes to mind without judgment. Don't edit yourself. Free your imagination and see where it takes you.

Refine your list. Now that you've got some pretty sexy ideas on the table, it's time to weed out the more impossible and improbable tasks. Don't keep anything on your Fuck-it List that would force you to cross the line of your personal safety, welfare or self-respect. This is meant to be a fun blueprint for you take control of your sexy life. Don't set yourself up for failure. Carefully eliminate anything that you know you won't have the courage or willpower to accomplish. Keep these fantasies hot and happening on your mental playground.

Start small with things you are certain that you can accomplish and build to those things that will take more preparation and planning. Accomplishing the easy goals will build your confidence and allow you to take on the more adventurous ones.

Find meaning in both selecting and accomplishing your Fuck-it List goals. Yes, you want to have some erotic fun as you dare to be bold and tempted, but you also want to grow from each experience and ultimately become the sexy, confident woman you're meant to be. Remember: no item on your Fuck-it List is too small if it helps your feminine confidence grow. The intent behind your list is not about *losing* control, but rather *taking* control of your sexual self. You are not trying to prove anything to anybody.

Eden's Advice:

Your sensual To-Do List has no time limit or expectations attached. This means that it is a fluid document that can, and should, change as inspiration hits you. Recognize that this F-list is *your* personal guideline to sexual self-awareness and fulfillment.

Don't let it become filled with someone else's fantasies. Let *your* desires guide you. So be as adventurous you want to be, always remembering that SAFE is SEXY.

About the Author

Eden Davis is the erotic alter ego of one grown and sexy *Essence* best-selling author. An accomplished writer of both fiction and nonfiction, she created the Eden Davis Series featuring women of a certain age, to be enjoyed by lusty women of all ages. Eden lives in the New York area and is currently working on her next series.

IF YOU ENJOYED "DARE TO BE WILD,"

BE SURE TO READ

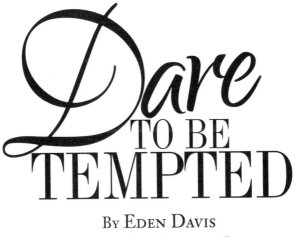

Dare TO BE TEMPTED

BY EDEN DAVIS

AVAILABLE FROM STREBOR BOOKS

Chapter One

Aleesa took her time climbing the eight steps that led to the front door of Josiah Newman's studio. Her breaths came in short puffs, not from overexertion, as her regular workouts at the gym left her lungs plenty strong enough to take on this minor physical effort. No, it was the jangle of nerves eating through her stomach lining that was taking her breath away.

"You *need* to look hot, Lees," she coached herself. "Smokin' hot. Halle hot. Angelina hot. Tina frickin' Turner hot!"

"What am I doing?" she turned to query the cat sprawled on the stoop next door. "On what planet am I, Aleesa Raquel Davis, a fifty-two-year-old married woman, mother of two grown boys, going to get naked in front of a perfect stranger?"

The thought paralyzed her, stopping her legs two steps from the door. Continued forward motion was not an option. At least not without some serious coaxing. She reached into her pocket, pulled out her cell phone and dialed her advice guru.

"I don't think I can do this...what the hell was I thinking...that is, what were you thinking when you suggested this...how did I ever let you talk me into doing something that is so...so...so not me?" she said, as soon as she heard the tepid hello.

"Lees? Slow down," Lena Macy's groggy voice suggested, both out of concern and confusion. It was nearly 11:30 p.m. in London and she'd just drifted off into a heavy, jetlagged slumber. "Where are you? What's going on?"

"In Brooklyn. It's almost six-thirty. Six minutes before I'm supposed to strip down to my birthday suit in front of some guy whom I've never laid eyes on. Aside from my husband, my gynecologist and that freak at the pool in Puerto Rico when Walt and I thought we were alone and decided to go skinny dipping, no man has seen me naked in ten years."

"Look, you're beautiful. For a woman two years into fifty, your body is rocking. Hell, for a woman of any age it's a killer. Now did you prepare like I told you to?"

"Yes. I'm waxed, exfoliated, and shined up like a new penny."

"Good, but I'm referring to the other..."

"Yes, I've been masturbating damn near nonstop for the past two days. I've rubbed, lubricated, vibrated, and worn my poor clit practically down to a nub. And frankly, I'm not any less nervous. I'm horny as hell and so on edge that I'm hoping with everything I've got that this photographer is Jimmy '*Good Times*' Walker ugly because if he's even the least bit sexy, I'm likely to burst out in spontaneous orgasms!"

"You are certifiable. Look, getting yourself off wasn't about calming your nerves. The idea was to make you feel sexy as hell, which you now do. Remember who you're doing this for. And why," Lena reminded her best friend.

"For Walter and the cover of his welcome home gift."

"Yes, your nasty ass journal that you've been keeping this past year. God knows, you've recorded every impure thought…" Lena paused to yawn, "and fantasy you've had since the good doctor's been in Afghanistan."

"I want him to know how much I love and missed him."

"Oh, he's going to know all right. One quick read and he's going to know that absence has not only made his woman's heart grow fonder, it's turned her into a big ole freak!

"Seriously, Lees, it's a sweet and loving idea and deserves a great cover. I can't think of a better model, can you?"

"Maybe Sofia Vergara."

"That Colombian chick from *Modern Family?*" Lena asked, not bothering to stifle her yawn.

"Yeah, she's Walter's fantasy lover—the only woman he has my permission to have sex with. My free pass is that fine as hell French actor, Gilles something, the one who was naked in the first *Sex and the City* movie and almost won *Dancing with the Stars.*"

"Oh, please, like that would ever happen. Not because some other guy, actor or not, wouldn't think you're smokin' hot, but because you and Walter are so in love and up each other's behinds, that you two don't even look at anyone else, which is pretty remarkable in this day and age."

"Oh trust me, I look, and God knows, think about it, *a lot*. I can't help it, especially since I started writing all these hot and horny fantasies. But it stops there."

"I believe you, but, Aleesa you're stalling, and I'm falling. Look, Josiah is the best in the business. He is fast becoming known in the photography world as the black and male Annie Leibovitz, for his trademark techniques with light and unusual poses.

"So between your boudoir photos and that nasty book of yours, Walter is going to be blown away by his hot-to-trot wife."

"Well, fantasy and reality are two different animals. Just because I write about all that stuff, doesn't mean I'm bold enough to actually do any of it," Aleesa reminded her friend.

"Yeah, well rest assured, you got a bit of the exhibitionist in you and a whole lot of freak! If you didn't, you wouldn't have been so eager to get your sexy on with hubby in the massage room down in Puerto Rico."

"Nobody was in the room watching us."

"That you know of! Now, I gotta get back to sleep and you have a nasty, nudie cutie photo shoot to do."

"Not nasty nude. Sexy…nice sexy," Aleesa corrected while smiling broadly at the San Juan memory.

"Yeah, well take it from me, nice can turn nasty real quick like. Now, push the doorbell, already."

"Okay, okay. Tell me I can do this, Lena."

"You. Can. Do. This. Think sexy. Be sexy. Now, I leave you with my final two words—Veuve Cliquot."

"So when in doubt, turn to alcohol?"

"Liquid courage, baby. Now ring the damn bell. Nightie-night."

"Ringing!" Aleesa said in place of goodbye, grateful that her friend, despite being a rich, powerful businesswoman, and an ocean away, was there to hold her hand. She hung up her phone and immediately pushed the doorbell.

"Think sexy. Be sexy," she muttered under her breath, repeating Lena's words. Waiting for the door to open, Aleesa closed her eyes and tried to settle her nerves by thinking sexy thoughts. Immediately, the last time she'd seen her husband's handsome, chocolate brown face came to mind. She had no problem conjuring up the memories of his surprise visit to San Juan. Their lovemaking at the spa had been mind blowing, largely because it was so unexpected and following such a long drought.

Standing there, her breasts began to tingle, as they'd done when Walt's mouth had begun its happy pilgrimage down her neck, across her shoulders and toward the large chocolate nipples he told her he'd gone to bed dreaming about. He'd given each a warm tongue massage before latching on to the left breast and sucking hard. Aleesa's hips had bucked. Walter's lips had smiled. The nipples were still Clitina's wake-up call.

"Hmm, I got it good," she informed the cat as she opened her eyes. "My man is a great step-father, an amazing friend and one kitty to another, a fanfuckingtastic husband and lover!"

The cat replied with a bored yawn and lazy stretch. "Yeah, well, you wouldn't say that if he'd licked you the way he licks me!" Aleesa sighed as her vajayjay gently clutched at the thought. After dreaming and fantasizing for so long, Walter had shown up and given her the real thing, reawakening her vagina and making her cravings stronger and more difficult to ignore. Damn, waiting for his homecoming was going to be the longest thirty-seven days of her life.

She intended to make the time go fast by staying busy. In addition to her demanding job as the Vice President of Marketing for the Sports Fan Network, she had big plans in store for the Colonel's return. If his Caribbean visit had been sexually spectacular, his welcome home was going to be downright epic. And today's errand was the first step toward making it so.

The sound of shuffling of feet approaching the door halted the conversation between her and the pussy next door. And as the door cracked open, she took a deep breath, knowing that there was no turning back.

"You must be Aleesa." His buttery words floated between perfect white teeth framed in dimples deep enough to lose your inhibitions in. "I'm Josiah. Welcome. I'm all ready for you." He opened the door wide to reveal the unlawfully good looking face and body that matched his "smooth as twelve-year-old Scotch" voice.

Aleesa swallowed a big gulp of "oh no" as her eyes went renegade and, against her wishes, thoroughly checked out the fine specimen before her. He looked to be in his early to mid-thirties and stood over six feet. He had the slim, lean musculature of a track star, and the way his jeans and untucked navy blue T-shirt clung to his body with an unspoken dare to reach out and touch, was borderline criminal. His long, thin locks were flowing free across his shoulder, giving a nonchalant sexiness to the man that left Aleesa's nerve endings perked up and on edge.

OH FUCK! OH FUCK! OH FUCK! WHY DO YOU HAVE TO BE SO FINE?!! Aleesa screamed at him in her head, all the while wishing she'd changed her clothes. Why hadn't she worn the form-fitting blue dress instead of the boho chic get-up she'd thrown on at the last minute? *Because if you'd worn the other, he'd know that you don't have any bra or panties on.*

But he knows that anyway, it occurred to her. He was the one who'd told her not to wear any so she wouldn't have elastic lines on her skin.

"You okay? Here, let me take that for you," he said, reaching for the tote bag containing her cosmetic and hair products.

"I'm fine. Thank you," Aleesa replied, embarrassed to be caught arguing with herself. She felt the butterflies in her stomach stir. Josiah was not only good looking, but apparently a gentleman as well.

"That shade of blue looks great on you," he complimented her as she stepped inside, noticing immediately how the turquoise color complemented her chestnut brown skin. Her ensemble was attractive and while fashion forward, completely covered up the body underneath. Josiah smiled to himself. His clients always seemed to fall into two camps—the wannabe *Playboy* pin-ups that arrived practically naked on his doorstep, and couldn't wait to get started; and the quiet, reserved types who required his special brand of coaching to coax the femme fatale out of them. Aleesa Davis *appeared* to fall in the latter category, but only time would tell which camp she truly belonged in.

She held the chuckle in her mouth, wondering if he could really read the thoughts running through her head. She hoped not because a few of them were totally inappropriate for a married woman, especially one who was truly in love with her husband, to be having about a man *nearly* young enough to be her son.

"Thank you." Nerves caused her voice to spike, giving her words a Minnie Mouse quality. She was even more aflutter now. Getting nude in front of a stranger was one thing, but getting nude in front of a *fine-ass* stranger whom she obviously found attractive, when she was already horny as hell, was a completely different level of intimidation.

Josiah led her down the short hallway and into a studio space that looked like it was once a living room or parlor. She followed his well-formed butt wondering if, no frantically *wishing*, that he was gay, but knowing instinctively that he was not.

"So based on the questionnaire you filled out online, I've set up three scenarios for you today," he informed her. "And as you can see, per your request, no 'cheesy red velour or whorehouse set-ups.'"

Aleesa looked around the room, checking out the white, claw-footed bathtub filled nearly to the rim with popcorn standing against a white background in one corner, and in the other, a beautiful mahogany chair with heart-shaped back, placed on a white fur carpet in front of sheer drapes. The chair's back reminded her of a woman's torso—a full bosom, tapering down to a tiny waist. Until this moment, it never occurred to her that furniture could be so sexy.

"There are only two," she said, choosing to share her observation rather than her thoughts.

"There is a small bedroom down the hall that I use for shoots as well."

"A tub of popcorn?"

"You said it was your husband's favorite snack food, so I thought we'd do something fun. Trust me; it's all going to be great. Now before we get you undressed and in front of the camera, let's talk for a minute." Josiah extended his arm, inviting her to sit on a chaise on the opposite side of the room. "Tell me a little about yourself, Ms. Davis."

"Aleesa. Well, I'm married. The mother of two grown sons— Aden and Ashri, 25 and 23. I live in Montclair, New Jersey, and work in Manhattan as the Sports Fan Network..."

"Very impressive, but tell me about you—the woman. What gets the charming and lovely Aleesa Davis's heart racing? What kind of music do you listen to? What do you like to eat? Where's the sexiest place in the whole wide world? "Josiah asked, leaning in close like he couldn't wait to hear her voice.

Damn this boy was good! Aleesa knew that he was just doing his job—trying to get a feel for her so he could bring it out in the photographs, but damn if it didn't feel like she was on a date. The alarming thing was she didn't mind as much as she probably should.

"Well, let's see. I love the full moon, the sound of the ocean. Champagne. My favorite food isn't actually a food. It's a dessert. I absolutely love ice cream. Plain old vanilla bean ice cream. Simple, satisfying and yummy."

"Oh, I get that joke. I'm a coffee ice cream man," he added.

"But I agree. I don't need any extra cookies or candy mixed in and getting in the way."

"Exactly," she concurred, feeling herself relax a bit. Josiah was a charming conversationalist.

"And let's see, musically I have pretty eclectic tastes. I'm still a lover of old school funk and R & B—Earth, Wind and Fire, The Commodores, Prince…"

"Teddy Pendergrass?"

"Absolutely. Now that boy could sing. I love me some Teddy P."

"Before or after Harold Melvin and the Blue Notes?"

Aleesa looked at Josiah with surprised eyes. Baby that he was, what could he possibly know about these old school musicians? "I'm definitely in the solo, 'Close the Door' and 'Turn Off The Lights' Teddy fan club. But like I said, I also enjoy tango music, Latin salsa, Sade. I even like some of these new kids like Usher and Ne-Yo, and especially Maxwell. He has that same kind of smooth, sexy edge that Teddy had. Somehow, they both always manage to make me feel like they're only singing to me."

"Only a true master can make a woman feel like she's the only one in the room. And hey, if you like Maxwell and Usher you should check out this British artist named Omar. I think you'd really get into him, too."

"I will," Aleesa replied. She quickly swallowed the millions of questions she was dying to ask. Ones that would clue her into his likes and dislikes, and give her more insight into him as a man. She hadn't realized until now how much she'd missed having a quiet, personal conversation with an interesting companion. But any further queries about Josiah would be unnecessary and border-line inappropriate. Besides, he wasn't interested in her. He was simply doing his job.

"And the sexiest place in the world?"

Aleesa thought for a moment, conjuring up past places she'd visited around the world. The thought that kept coming to the forefront of her memories were the rather unremarkable places she'd been when she either was inspired or was composing Walter's stories. "Hmm... that would have to be wherever I am."

Josiah's eyes registered amused surprise. "I have asked that question over a thousand times, and you're the first to say that," Josiah informed her. Her reply impressed and intrigued him. "So what brings you into my world, Aleesa?"

"Well, I wanted to do this as a, uh...you know...gift for my husband."

"Lucky man," he replied with a tone and admiring look that made her think he was speaking the truth. "Anniversary? Birthday?"

"A welcome home, actually. He's been in Afghanistan, running a dental clinic for the soldiers for the past couple of years and he'll be stateside again at the end of May, in about a month."

"Nice. So you're thinking a standard, bedroom portrait?"

"Well, no. More like a book cover."

Josiah's eyebrows lifted, the corners of his mouth registering surprise before quickly falling back into place.

"I've been keeping a book...well...more like a journal...of well, you know...thoughts..." Embarrassment blushed her cheeks and kept her from continuing.

"What kind of thoughts? Fantasies?" he queried, his interest piqued. *Still waters run deep.*

"Uh...well...yes. You know...that I've had since he's been gone. It was a way of keeping him close to me and I thought it would be a nice welcome-home surprise."

"Like I said, he's a lucky man."

"Thank you, but I'm the lucky one," she told him, truly believing her words despite being fascinated by Josiah's full and luscious upper lip. "Anyway, my friend suggested that I do a cover shot, and recommended you. So that's why I'm here...in your world."

"Welcome. I'm happy to have you," he replied, flashing his dimples at her. "So, Aleesa, tell me how far you're willing go."

"How far?"

"Robe? Lingerie? Full-on nude? Each is sexy and provocative in its own way. What's most important is your comfort level. Though, if you don't mind me asking, how risqué are your...uh...thoughts in this book?"

Aleesa could feel the flush of embarrassment mixed with arousal invade her body as she thought about the sexy and sometimes outrageous scenarios she'd written over these past months. All of her fantasies had Walter either actively participating or watching. Like the butler going down on her in the hotel in Phoenix; tying Walt up while she fucked herself on the hood of his car; masturbating in the window of the hotel directly across from Walt's Manhattan dental office; being titty and finger fucked by the guest of honor on her apartment balcony during a birthday party; having her feet licked by her favorite salesman at the Jimmy Choo store.

Aleesa felt the tingle of her clitoris back on high alert. Even recalling the fantasies turned her on. Risqué? Maybe not for the kink and fetish crowd, but for her married and maternal self, Walt's freak book was as blue as the sea, and hellishly racy.

"Your face says it all," Josiah interrupted, with a flirtatious twist to his lips. "Oh, the camera is going to love you! So, since it's for his eyes only, do we match the cover shot to the contents or give him a sexy, beauty shot to admire? Completely your call."

Aleesa said nothing. She simply bit her bottom lip as she pondered the options. Writing about sex was so freeing, even though most of the stuff she'd scribed she'd never dare try. Still the experience of opening up her sexual imagination this year had definitely made her more curious and adventurous. She now felt that both risqué *and* sexy beauty were part of her sexual personality.

"Aleesa. Don't be frightened or nervous or feel like you're being judged," Josiah said as he brought his head close to tell her. She knew he intended his voice to sound soothing, but the smooth timbre and tone of it only managed to further ruffle her feathers.

"This boudoir session is totally based on your desires. Every woman has her own idea of what sexy is, as well as what she is comfortable with. Don't worry; today will be part cute, part fun, part flirty and all sexy.

"You're safe here. I am going to take good care of you. I promise. So like you did when you wrote your book, you can drop your inhibitions and be free here as well."

Aleesa continued to chew on her bottom lip as she looked into Josiah's brown, almond-shaped eyes. As gorgeous and sexy as he was, and as horny but married as she felt, dropping her inhibitions and being free was definitely not an option.

"Let's play it by ear, and see where the evening takes us."